B. E. Jones is a former journalist and police press officer, now a novelist and book obsessive. She was born in a small village in the valleys of South Wales, north of Cardiff and started her journalism career with Trinity Mirror newspapers before becoming a broadcast journalist with *BBC Wales Today*.

She has worked on all aspects of crime reporting (as well as community news and features), producing stories and content for newspapers and live TV. Most recently she worked as a press officer for South Wales Police, dealing with the media and participating in criminal investigations, security operations and emergency planning. Perhaps unsurprisingly she channels these experiences of true crime, and her insight into the murkier side of human nature, into her dark, psychological thrillers set in and around South Wales.

Also by B. E. Jones
Where She Went

Halfway

B. E. Jones

CONSTABLE

CONSTABLE

First published in Great Britain in 2018 by Constable

This paperback edition published in 2018 by Constable

1 3 5 7 9 10 8 6 4 2

Copyright © B. E. Jones, 2018

The moral right of the author has been asserted.

*All characters and events in this publication, other than
those clearly in the public domain, are fictitious
and any resemblance to real persons,
living or dead, is purely coincidental.*

All rights reserved.
No part of this publication may be reproduced, stored in a retrieval system,
or transmitted, in any form, or by any means, without the prior permission in
writing of the publisher, nor be otherwise circulated in any form of binding or
cover other than that in which it is published and without a similar condition
including this condition being imposed on the subsequent purchaser.

A CIP catalogue record for this book
is available from the British Library.

ISBN: 978-1-4721-2791-4

Typeset in Sabon by SX Composing DTP, Rayleigh, Essex
Printed and bound in Great Britain by Clays Ltd, Elcograf S.p.A.

Papers used by Constable are from well-managed forests
and other responsible sources.

Constable
An imprint of
Little, Brown Book Group
Carmelite House
50 Victoria Embankment
London EC4Y 0DZ

An Hachette UK Company
www.hachette.co.uk

www.littlebrown.co.uk

A Literature Wales Writer's Bursary, supported by the National Lottery
through the Arts Council of Wales, was received to develop this novel.

For my mother and father, with love, always

Prologue
Halfway – 22 December 2007, 5 p.m.

When she sees the hatchet in his hand she knows it's going to happen, right here, right now. It's been coming for hours, longer probably, since before the storm howling and keening around the eaves began its slow creep across the countryside, before the car was abandoned at the side of the snowbound road.

This moment was waiting even before she raised her hand and knocked on the door of this godforsaken place, squatting below its slipping slates and bowing brickwork, beneath the low iron sky, under the weight of winter.

So here they are.

She's glad now that she'd had the foresight to arm herself, downstairs, when the unpleasant ticking started in her chest, when she'd finally realised the answers to the questions plaguing her since her arrival: Who are these people? And why are they lying?

She'd been sure that something was very wrong for hours. She just hadn't been able to gather the quiet nudges in the back of her brain into a single, clearly defined thought until now, now it's punching itself to the fore, bullying her into the realisation she'd have been safer out in the storm.

But it's too late to leave, now that there are only three of them left alive, assembled under the twinkly Christmas star: a hitchhiker, a nurse, a landlord, everyone, everything, bending itself into this moment, before the weight of what has been and what is to come. How could she have imagined for even one moment that she was the only one with anything to hide?

She knows it's her own fault for allowing herself to be caught off guard, first back on the road and then over and over again until she stepped into this room. It happened so easily because this is the sort of place that's supposed to be safe and steady, a quiet, nothing-ever-happens kind of village where people look out for each other, still leave their doors unlocked and never, *ever* try to kill you.

Trouble is, you should never read only the surface signs and signals of anywhere or anyone, she knows that. There's a lesson here, never assume you're the biggest, baddest thing in the woods unless you're prepared to prove it.

So this is it.

That bloody balding donkey understands, his red and white trimmed Santa hat at a jaunty angle as he gives her that look again, as if he's thinking what she's thinking, knows what she knows – not all of them will leave this room alive. He may be happy to wait passively for the outcome but she isn't, so she readies herself, plants her feet firmly apart on the floorboards, aware of every inch of her body, every twitch of muscle fibre and sinew, careful not to show that her hands are waiting and ready to move.

The ticking in her chest tells her it's too late to stop the countdown, there's no way back, the explosion is overdue. There will be noise and fury. There will be damage. There will be casualties.

So here they go!

The Hitchhiker – 22 December 2007, 9.30 a.m.

I don't mind the cold. It's a relief today, the clean, cutting feel of it, like cool water on hot skin in the summer heat. I like the quiet too, or as close to quiet as you can get in any place on earth. Here there's almost no wind to stir the absence of traffic and the snow has white-felted every sharp surface into soundproofed silence. Thank God for silence.

I walk. I breathe in. I exhale.

Sometimes I think I've spent my whole life waiting to fully breathe out, to cough up that cluster of something spiky, stuck in the bottom of my chest, held by the last inch of muscle refusing to relax. When that trapped breath is finally freed I hope the next one will be the most wonderful I've ever tasted, air coursing through me, clean and sharp like the world's best non-chemical rush.

Today is not that day, but the bitter sting on my face foretelling another snow flurry; the empty corridor of patient trees alongside the road; the high, heavy sky, all make a nice change from the crush of bodies I endure every day, in close quarters, back to back, toe to toe, hand to mouth – shared space, shared air. I've never really got used to it. I just wish I were here under better circumstances.

I'm relieved to see there's no one waiting at the bus stop on what's optimistically signposted the 'village green'. I'm in no mood for small talk, glad to pull up my hood and enter my quiet zone for bit. Almost immediately, though, before I can begin my breathing exercises, the old coach arrives, full of human heat and breath.

As I squeeze up the steps, handing my exact change to the driver so chat can be kept to a minimum, everyone on board is muttering about the weather. It seems the beleaguered passengers were forced to get out of the bus they were originally travelling in, as it struggled on the icy gradient back in the valley, to walk to the top of the slippery hill, joining this replacement bus for the journey down again. Quite an adventure apparently, judging by the driver's enthusiastic explanation of why the shuttle is so crammed today.

'We'll take you as far as we can now, love,' he says, grinning under his bobble hat. 'Off we go.'

The passengers applaud as we judder into motion, the mood jovial with the air of a good teatime story in progress. People who live in the country are used to this travel chaos every few winters. They'd almost miss it if no snow fell, bringing with it a welcome injection of drama. What would they talk about otherwise? The weather? The price of sheep feed? The cost of heating? Death, taxes and each other's affairs?

I find a spare seat, keep my hood up, slide in against the window and settle down for the long haul; it's yet another opportunity to practise my patience. It's a living thing inside me these days, my patience, with its own moods and colours, known for tantrums and sulks. It needs constant tending and training. It has hooks and thorns that catch at me unexpectedly. If I'm not careful they can draw blood, especially in moments like this, enclosed in my own personal idea of hell, a hot, oblong box full of other people.

I've endured worse, of course, more immediate discomforts than the worrying of old ladies with cigarette-slit mouths, bundled in a fog of wet woollen coats; worse than the over-ripening of sweaty bodies and the tinny drone of earphones burrowing under my skin from the teenagers seated in front of me. This is pleasant by comparison.

A slight holiday feeling pervades as we descend the ribbon lanes. It's three days to Christmas and the women's feet and laps are already insulated with bags of supplies, boxes containing presents to be dropped off at friends and neighbours, stocks of mince pies and tins of chocolates for the church collection. At least if we stall again we won't starve.

One of the teenage girls carries a tinsel wreath on her lap. Another is wearing a bobble hat with a knitted reindeer on it, without any apparent embarrassment. While the oldies are bundled up like tardy Bonfire Night guys, each youngster is scantily dressed for this -2 degree day in the heart of Western Wales. The teen ensemble is cheap trainers all round; two thin hoodies and one leather jacket – a careless uniform, too cool for school, and there's no school today anyway.

They're probably just too young to feel the gnawing cold. It's not until you've slept on the stone-hard ground or in a piss-smelling corner of an empty building, dampened and stiff, that you really appreciate creature comforts, like the value of a good coat, preferably with a hood, sturdy boots and woolly socks.

I keep my own coat and gloves on, hood still up, even though the bus is super-heated, the steamed windows melting the darkening morning into a soup of snow and condensation. Behind the glass the country looks as if it's been frozen under the whim of a wizard's wish – a single wave of a wand, a fizzle of icy fire granting it stiff immortality, unchanging for eternity. It's actually a soothing thought but it's an illusion. Something is happening out there somewhere, something is always happening.

In the gloom the frosted fields show hunkered-down gangs of houses, waiting, perhaps pretending, to sleep, watching the passage of anyone foolish enough to be away from their fireplace on a bleak midwinter day, under-dressed, unarmed. Wisps of smoke from the chimneys speak of huddled locals, guarded against the winter and I find myself humming along to that Christmas song on the bus radio, the one that's been floating in and out of my head for hours now: 'earth stood hard as iron, water like a stone' and 'snow on snow on snow'.

It had been playing on the kitchen radio last night, while I'd waited for my mind to click into action mode, trying not to think of what is behind me and what might be ahead, fearing a knock on the door, the sound of a siren.

I don't think people will understand. It wasn't part of any plan. It just got out of control, not that that's a legal defence.

The occasional empty chapel slides by as we slow-crawl

through the treacherous hollows. In the homes of my fellow travellers tea is probably on the boil, dogs ready to lick a welcome, hugs waiting to be handed out as in all good homecomings, but this is not my homecoming. This is not the Christmas reunion with soaring violin music, a cheerily popping log fire and mistletoe kisses. This is the opposite – the running away, the flight into the darkness, the escape.

The old ladies fuss and cluck as the bus winds onwards, a gaggle of hens well past laying, looking for something to coddle or squawk at.

'We'll get stuck for sure. We'll have to walk all the way back to the depot.'

'Walk? We can't walk in this – we'll be stuck in the bus all day and night.'

'What if we get stranded and have to eat each other?' asks a teenage lad with flares of acne on his cheeks and a bumfluff top lip.

'You'd keep us going for weeks, you fat twat!' grins his raw-faced chunk of a mate.

Like the pioneer Donner party, I think, famously caught in a wagon train in the Sierra Nevadas in California in the 1840s. Snowbound in the winter white of the high passes they'd eaten their horses first, then each other, to survive, until the thaw came and those left behind passed into infamy because their instinct to survive overrode everything else. Well, survival is brutal.

'Eat me!' the mate shoots back, sticking up his middle finger to his friend, making me wince. I hate it when people 'flip the bird'. I hate it even more when people say, 'What's up bro?' like they're trying to be American and funny and 'gangsta' when they're just being dicks. I hate a lot of things these days.

'Jesus, we might not make it home tonight at this rate,' says the acne kid. 'My mam will go nuts.'

But what's the worst that could happen on a bus somewhere south-east of Aberystwyth in twenty-first-century Britain? This isn't some Middle Eastern warzone or African civil war shithole. It's not as if hordes of guerrillas are about to leap from the hedges and order everyone off to wait in a sleety line on their knees, AK-47s pointed at the backs of quivering necks.

'Fuck you, man,' laughs the skinny friend on the receiving end of the fat twat's American bird gesture – I try not to hate him as he laughs like a drain, or to think about punching him in the throat to shut him up.

'It's not good for your karma, mate,' says Lilli-Anne's voice in my ear, ever on my shoulder like a wise and annoying parrot; 'It's toxic,' says Pam in the other. 'Toxic' is one of Pam's favourite words, as is 'positivity', which I'm not sure is actually a word. If Lilli's a parrot, brash and insistent, Pam is a dove, soft, quiet, cooing: 'Thoughts become things,' says Pam. 'You must foster a positive mental attitude.'

I really hate my fucking counsellor when she says things like that. It reminds me of the simple fact that so much of what comes out of people's mouths is redundant. Dead air. All those wasted words, circling around, make me tired. And when I'm tired I sometimes do things I regret, like yesterday, a perfect example of a classic overreaction.

At times, despite Pam's advice and endless mantra practice, my patience still extends beyond its limits, has been known to break. A cheese wire, stretched tightly, can slice and slash when it snaps; it's best to stand well back, but the counselling is mandatory, so I nod in all the right places during our endless forty-five-minute sessions to the 'Soothing Sounds of the Sea' CD, making the right noises to avoid saying, Please shut the fuck up!

As we trundle onwards I stick my headphones in and crank up the volume to drown out the teenage inanities. The music was Pam's idea, to help me not think about the cries that loop around in my head when I get like this, the pleading voices in the past that I just can't help hearing in stereo over the lines of the base beat.

A face crashes into my memory, one creased with lines, sweat and fear – a voice saying, 'Please . . . Please . . .'

Please what?

'Please don't? Please help me? Please don't hurt me?' All of the above?

As we pass a farm in the foot of the valley I'm almost grateful for the different memory it triggers, older, frayed by time. With the tug of a loose thread I'm back in the old hay barn at night, lamplight in the eaves beating back the blackness, the lowing of the best cow, that look on the vet's face, Dad sweating and stern. But the old woman's face returns soon enough, it always does, and she's not alone. The faces are never alone.

It's started now, the dark rush beyond my control, behind my screwed-up eyes and tight fists. My heart rattles around the cage of my ribs, heat spreading out under my jacket and into my face. The invisible handle turns, my chest crushes and I try to flick the switch the other way, to turn it off.

'Choose your reaction. Choose to breathe.' That's what Pam says, that silly bitch with her bun-hair, bleached teeth and pink sweaters. Sometimes it works; sometimes not. It's a work in progress. Like life.

So I practise, repeating the prescribed words in my head, willing them to work: My story is my own. I can change it. I am calm, I am not afraid. I can let the thoughts pass. I am a passenger on a train and they slide by, just like the darkening morning slides along the bus windows, separating me from the world beyond.

Not a moment too soon the hell-bus gives a lurch and we come to a halt. When I open my eyes we're at the single shelter on the next brown grass village green – all change for going south. I remember this place; I used to change buses here all the time. I can't get off fast enough now, almost falling down the steps under the weight of my rucksack on my suddenly weakened legs. There isn't enough air in the world to stop the hitching of my lungs. There's no chance of my speaking a word.

For a moment I can't comprehend it all, how I'm standing here now when just two days ago I was in another world on the edge of another life. That was before, of course, before the sight of the kitchen, the living room, the bedroom, before the phone call, before the words, before the world fell to pieces in paper and ash.

The idea of the blood and newly broken bones is still strong in my mind's eye. It had all blown up in two atomic seconds, even though I'd said, 'Flick the switch,' over and over again. Something inside me had taken control, shouted me down – the old enemy. It said, 'This is not my story. I cannot change it. I am afraid.'

What's that Chinese proverb Lilli-Anne always trots out when the unexpected shits on us from a great height? 'The best laugh you can give the universe is to make plans.' The best laugh of all being my big idea, of something solid, something safe at last – everything that had dispersed at the sight of a single green metal canister, a pile of papers.

My jaw throbs. I'm grinding my teeth and make an effort to stop as the bus driver gets off and announces, 'OK, folks, I'm really sorry but there're no more buses today. They're closing the B249.'

By the time he's got to the end of this sentence I'm already striding away into the morning gloom. I'm not sure where to exactly, I just know I can't sit there another moment in the communal clutch of this village. I can't go to the community centre across the grass with its ancient paper garlands and artificial flammable tree, the inevitable tea in an urn, camaraderie and complaints and plastic-packed sandwiches. Someone will see me for sure.

First things first, move and don't think, let a plan come. I know roughly where I am now that I'm walking out of the village, along the road, into the woods. It's only eight or nine miles to the mainline train station where the bus would have dropped me eventually. There are a good few hours of daylight left, even on the shortest day of the year. I have no reason to fear the dark. Most of the bad things that have happened to me have happened in broad daylight. Terrible things are done then, too. I have done them.

Even if the train isn't running down to Carmarthen, then on to Swansea and Cardiff tonight, there'll be a waiting room to kip down in, a vending machine and quiet, wonderful loneliness. For now I need to move, walk, march off the panic. Breathe.

The winter day pulls me into its cold embrace as I set my feet on the whitening road.

The Old Man – 9.30 a.m.

Inside he waits, lying in his bed under the silver-foil star, swirling slowly on its string from the beam of the sagging roof. Within the walled space that has become his world he hears the sound of a held breath, somewhere between the constant click of the clock on the wall a hundred miles away. Tick tock, tick tock. Wait. Listen. Watch.

The side of the bed is a cliff face now, unassailable, the sheets snow white, for-show white, cold and clean. Time has stretched and distorted his small attic domain into a vast untravellable landscape. If he could raise his head far enough from the pillow he'd look down across the wooden wastes of the floorboards towards the bedroom door. If he could raise his voice he would call out, but who is listening, just now, at this hour?

If he could waken the dead with a howl he would; he'd call them from the other country of the past where things are done differently if not necessarily better. He will try to soon, when the knock comes on the door to welcome a traveller of miles and years. His voice may be thick and

14

dulled but his hearing is still close enough to knife-edged to torment him – if only he had a knife! He might use a knife. A blade of any kind could mean more than one sort of freedom now.

Without one he strains for the sound of a car on the gravel, for a footfall approaching the front step. Here is the day and almost the hour, halfway through the long drifts of weeks and winter, of the relentless march of luke-warm, gravy-softened ready-meals and the burr of quizzes on the flickering TV screen.

How long has it been since his last journey along the icy landing, down the glacier slope of the stairs to where the letter had shone, white and wondrous beneath the bolted front door? Such an epic effort of conquest and discovery, painful, sweating, shuffling, sliding; all to answer the thump-thump knock and 'hello' voice that had moved away too quickly, before he could answer with the words, 'Please don't go, help me!'

The letter is tucked in darkness now, well-hidden, but he can still hear it holding its breath. He waits for the hands to climb around the clock face, willing the old ghosts that whisper behind his back in the other rooms to be silent, to not give the game away that a visitor is expected at last.

The room is cold. The electric heater is on full blast but pushes out only a thin orange glow. He can see the occasional puff of his breath, raspy and floury in the air. He hasn't heard any sounds from below since the front door slammed shut earlier. He's not sure if it was someone coming in or going out. He thought he'd heard a car engine too, but that could have been the wind. It's almost time for a hot tea and soft-dunked biscuit.

He's pretty sure the twitchy oaf is still down there, doing God knows what since he turned up out of the blue, smelling of dog and diesel. Not boiling the bloody kettle, obviously. Seems like a dodgy one that, though he does as he's told by the looks of it, by *her*. Not that he's much better himself, obedient, a helpless prisoner in his own bed and, even worse, trapped deep inside a body that's under siege, locked down, dug in.

Everyone knows this moment will come to them eventually, but they still like to think they'll end their days tended by loving children and a plump, soft-handed wife or husband. Look where such optimism has got him. Rose used to laugh at him for that, among other things; she always said, 'Optimism is the triumph of hope over experience.' She got that much right, if bugger all else.

How ridiculous they seem now, the dreams he'd had when he was young, the worst kind of naivety, of arrogance. Lying here in this tomb, shackled by the tightly tucked sheets, he hears Rose sometimes, snickering in the other bedrooms along the hall, scorn in the sound of her slippered feet swishing along the landing at night.

Staring at the spider twitching its web into elaborate artwork among the rafters above, it's hard not to remember how different it had been once, to recall that swallowing rush of love that had surged up in him on the day Brian was born. The reality of something so warm and desperately alive had almost suffocated him. There was an appeal in those outstretched hands, the cry of that tiny, wet-headed bundle, craving acknowledgement, ready to be shaped by and imprinted with love.

He'd been certain he wouldn't get there in time for the

birth, while he'd been haring, breathless, in his fishing sweater and boots, up through the high grass of the lower field to the cottage hospital. The fathers waited in a little curtained-off anteroom then, with hard plastic chairs and a black and white TV. The only other expectant dad there on that sweating, heat-heavy August afternoon, had been that prick, Russell Bradach, expecting his second son, the very picture of an important councilman, well-pleased with himself.

Odd really, considering how his fancy banker and businessman father had fared, how people still whispered about it. He'd looked at him like he was shit on his shoe and he'd known why. He'd known what people had already started to say about him. They'd been saying it under their breath for years.

'Congratulations.' Bradach had grinned. 'I hear you're a *married man* now.'

And he'd smiled back until he'd thought his cheeks would crack, until the ward sister appeared, leading him through to Rose in her pink hospital nightie, open at her breast, fat with milk. It was a state of undress he'd barely seen her in since the night of Brian's conception, or in the weeks afterwards, when she'd feared the worst, waiting with increasing panic for the slightest smudge of blood in her knickers.

He'd wanted to look after her though, Rose and his boy, *his boy*. They could make it work somehow, even though he'd never loved her, not even at the beginning. He still blushes a little bit to think how he hadn't made the first move, but it was something normal, wasn't it? Something that was supposed to happen if you are a red-blooded man and a woman lies back, whisky on her breath, unbuttoning her cardigan, smiling?

There'd been the hurried wedding later, his new mother-in-law's tight lips, their violet-lipsticked 'O' pursed with their little secret, because it was still just before her twenty-two-year-old-daughter had started to show. She didn't know that Rose wasn't a virgin.

'You're not my first,' Rose had said to him, no subterfuge, 'just so you know.'

'You're not mine,' he'd lied.

Brian was officially a 'honeymoon' baby, a stupid, sticky word but apt. They were stuck together all right, snared in a story so banal it hurt. With resentment seething around Rose like silk filaments, twisting, trapping, how could Brian have grown anything else but tight and tense? Such a nervous boy, awkward and clenched in his bony body, painfully eager to please.

All *too* eager to see the worst in him, even before *that* day, that single sunlit hour in the late summer – the image of a bronzed leg, stretching out, a shadow in the cleft of the groin where skin met fabric and slipped . . .

The smell of those years is still the smell of heat to him. Even lying in this attic room he catches the scent of coconut oil and weak lemonade, sparking a slideshow of frying chips, cheap cider on eager breath, parted lips. There's that slightly sour smell too, the one that never really leaves the wooden skin of any bar, or the hands that pour the pints, flush the lines, tap the barrels. The froth on the top . . . licking lips . . .

He's thirsty now, thinking of a pale, cool pint. The water jug on the table is almost empty. He knows why it's never more than half full. He can just about manage to reach across and grip the glass, take a few sips but they don't want him filling up like a 10-gallon barrel when he can't lift himself onto the bedpan to piss any more.

He's already pissed himself a couple of times. When it first happened it was pretty much the most humiliating thing ever, sitting in his own urine as it turned cold, watching the clock, wondering when someone would turn up, knowing the hands that eventually gripped him, rolled him over and stripped the sheets would be as angry and rough as the cheese-grater voice accompanying them.

How long has he lain here now? Since the bowl of instant porridge was spooned into his mouth? Since he was given tea in a child's sippy cup, half a slice of toast, bibbed like a baby? He gets a clean pair of pyjamas every week. The bed's changed every two. This is how he counts the sections of the weeks and days – the sound of the door, the kettle boiling, the TV sputtering bright inanities. Sometimes he can't even make his fingers press the buttons on the remote control to turn that racket off. The radio's worse, the voices he troubles to understand sometimes, talking, talking.

He thinks he hears other voices too, in the night, spooling out through the hours that have no ending. But no, he mustn't forget the letter – though he's not sure when it came exactly. So many things are foggy now. The near-to-hand things, the recent things are harder to recall than those of years past that unspool in his head as if they're on a projector – films about ghosts and wishes. But the letter *is* real, the letter has stopped time or put a finite cap on it. He's coming! All this will finally have an expiry date.

There will be time now, to say the words somehow, out of his throat, his sagging lips, the words that bloat and stretch and dribble. He will say them with his eyes if necessary – he will be understood. I'm sorry!

He will leave this place once and finally and he won't be alone at the end. He will make his peace. He will be forgiven.

The Law – 9.30 a.m.

It's a shock when all the radios start buzzing at once, crackling the early-morning silence into twenty-four-hour urgency. I'm not ready, not up to anything more than tea and a biscuit yet. I've only just arrived at our little out-station on the eastern edge of town, half an hour late, winter-sleepy and grudging the short move from bed to office.

I usually need at least two cups of tea to get my head in gear, though my sergeant, Jim Price, has already been here since 8 a.m., early bird, every day, despite being just a few months shy of retirement. The lamp is on in his tiny, cupboard-like nook as he scans the morning reports and I boil the kettle, not even close to pretending to do the paperwork that's been sitting on my desk for three days straight.

It's colder than frozen hell out, I have a prime, toasty spot by the radiator and I'm not planning on moving for several hours. That is, until the frequencies start buzzing and a voice reels off a sequence of crime codes and collar numbers that can only mean cars and response officers being mobilised.

While I'm still staring at the speakers in goldfish-like surprise, Jim emerges from his cubbyhole with startling speed, grabbing his helmet, cuffs and belt kit, already fastening his woollen cape, the one that's hung on a hook behind his chair since the 1970s. No one has ever seen him wear this museum piece until now, as he emerges ready for action, buttoning the collar, and I almost laugh at the archaic vision of 1950s policing before me. Pont may be stuck in its own time warp but we usually try to at least pretend we're in the twenty-first century. I'm about to make some sarky remark when the serious look on his face stops me.

'Yeah, yeah,' he says. 'You won't be laughing when you're freezing your bum off on a cordon, love. Get your stuff. Something big's going down, up at Ridgeback Farm, right now. Chop, chop, then! Time for the blue-light show to hit the road. You waiting for a personal invitation or what? Nine nine nine means now, not when you're good and ready.'

He barks at Carron our desk clerk to get on the blower to Central and check the rota for who'll be coming on for the late shift. He's already thinking of the hours ahead and the night to come – obviously this is Jim in 'efficiency mode', much rumoured but rarely observed in the last decade. I know straight away that it's something serious, thank God! At last! It's what I've been waiting aeons and ages for, some action.

Except now that it's here and 'action' has been called, I have no idea what to do. So I duckling along behind Jim, keeping my eyes and ears open, trying not to get in the way; the best thing a PC just six months out of probation can do, according to my inspector, who is full of unsolicited advice, not to mention being a world-class prick.

As we scramble through the cold and frosty morning to the patrol car I'm thankful that Jim has already taken the time to clear the windscreen and de-ice the locks. He doesn't remind me that it was my responsibility to put the car in the single garage last night or that I forgot, which I'm grateful for. As we trundle through the barely daylight morning as fast as the pricking snow will allow, blue light but no sirens, the ambulance crews are already clogging up the radio channels with high-pitched instructions.

'What do you reckon?' says Jim. 'Suicide? Neighbour dispute gone wrong? Burglar shotgunned? Think of the options, arrive prepared. What legislation might you need to use? What scene protocols will you need to invoke if there are five dead bodies in the lounge?'

We're not really expecting five dead bodies in the lounge of course, or anywhere else for that matter, not even one, come to that. That would top the yearly body count for Pont by quite a few, and no one's muttered the all-important words 'code blue' on the radio yet, meaning someone is deceased. Jim is just being a good mentor, trying to make me 'think strategically', marking off the items of the seldom-used emergency tick list.

Still, I disguise a prickle of excitement fired up by the sparking delight of the unknown and the possible. Something is actually happening for a change, in our stupefyingly dull, slow-time, permanent hangover-like village, where sheep probably outnumber people three to one if anyone could be bothered to count.

I've been in training and on probation for three years and, until now, the most exciting thing I've been part of was a scene where Jim talked a thirty-seven-year-old drunk down from the bridge over the river because his missus had left him. I'm not saying that's not a valuable civic service, or that it doesn't take a certain type of skill, but it's hardly what I signed up for. I know I have a lot more to offer if I can just get the chance to show it. Opportunity might be knocking for me at last and Christ, it's been long enough coming.

Finally the game's afoot, the heat is on. The show is on the road. As we drive I'm smiling out of the window at the bleak morning.

When we get to the farmhouse at the top of the hill an ambulance is already parked at the edge of the higgledy flagstone path, doors yawning wide. Its blue light casts spectral shadows on the violet misting of early morning snow but the siren is off, the urgency passed – I realise it's no longer a race between life and death. One of them has won.

Three other police cars have turned up, not a bad turnout since this is more than half the available workforce in peak flu and Christmas holiday time, and most of them are probably hung over. Half a dozen uniformed officers I recognise, all of them men, are rubbing their hands together and milling around on the front path, looking for someone to tell them what to do.

The strangest thing of all is the silence. It hits us as we wind down our windows; it's as if someone has turned the volume off on a TV show. None of the usual off-colour banter is taking place, no joshing, joking, chit-chat is being exchanged. The only sound is the occasional crackle and mutter of radios and the cackle of alarmed crows in the close-knit trees rising all around us.

Light blazes from the windows of the farmhouse, illuminating it like a film set at the point when the actors are about to take their places before someone calls action. Determined to get closer, we crawl our squad car past the unhinged front gate, taking care to avoid the banked snow, pulling up around the back and slipping unchallenged along the brambly path towards the open back door.

That's when I see it, the dog.

It's strung up in the kitchen window, electrical wire looped from its neck to the curtain rail above. In the full light of the kitchen, through the panes of glass between us, we can see it's a small collie, black and white, dangling full length, its legs limp, empty eyes half open.

'What. The. Fuck?' says Jim, half to me and half towards the two young officers already flanking the door. Jim is part of that generation that never curses in front of a lady, and it's a mark of his shock that he doesn't automatically apologise. Not that I care, not when I'm horribly fascinated by the string of pinkish drool stretching itself from the dog's mouth. After a moment I realise my own mouth has fallen open and snap it shut, swallowing heavily.

Neither of us speaks.

'That's . . . interesting,' says Jim, finding his voice first, pulling off his helmet and running his hand over his cropped grey hair in a gesture I've come to recognise as shorthand for, 'I can tell you, love, the world is becoming a strange and unfamiliar place and I'll be glad to get out of this game.'

'Hey, Sarge,' says the youngest officer guarding the door. 'Fucked up or what?'

What is there to do but edge closer, along the path towards the door, though right now every piece of crime-scene protocol, not always my strong suit anyway, has left my brain. Through the gap in the officers' shoulders I can see an old man inside, sitting on a kitchen chair in the hall, eyes glassy-wide, face bruised, right arm hanging limply in his lap. His breath heaves in and out, high and thin, a papery crackle. A paramedic is trying to put an oxygen mask on him but he keeps pushing it off, mumbling, 'My wife, my wife . . . please . . .'

A stretcher is held at the ready by another paramedic, standing in stunned silence while two uniformed officers whisper behind their hands by the door to the living room, which looks like it's been hit by a force ten gale. Drawers are strewn open, furniture kicked over – one officer is holding a broken lamp, seemingly unsure what to do next.

Part of me knows this isn't the best ever observance of crime-scene protocol. I've never dealt with a serious incident but, even just from the TV, I know that forensics need to have a scene like this sealed up tight as a drum in the first few minutes. But it's fairly new to us, the ones who've turned up, those daft enough not to have booked our Christmas leave last February, and we don't usually need to do this stuff, it never happens, and if it does, we leave it to the senior officers.

What's taken place this morning is already very different from the occasional domestic fights, pub tiffs and farm-machinery thefts that are our daily bread and butter. I know everyone who's arrived in the last fifteen minutes is more or less winging it, remembering stuff from training manuals until someone can come up from HQ and start the show properly.

I also know that when the on-call CID shows up, the inspector's going to pop a fuse. It's obvious half the county has tramped through the house already, so we might as well have a sneaky peek and get 'eyes on'.

'Give us a shuftie, lads,' says Jim, reading my mind and trying to politely shoulder his way inside. 'Is the old man all right? It's not another Bedford Row then?'

He's referring to the second biggest incident to hit Pont in its quiet history, a notorious murder-suicide ten years ago (following the armed robbery thirty years earlier), when a perfectly respectable accountant shot his wife to death before turning the gun on himself. I suspect that, very soon, this will blow both of those incidents off the infamy league table for good.

'Sorry, Jim, not this time,' says the pimply PC with a wannabe beard who I know is called Jackson. 'No one goes in or out without the inspector's say-so.'

Jim always calls this particular PC Jackson Bollocks, because of the supposedly artistic mess he once made throwing up after finding his first dead body riddled with maggots (not that most of the shift get this as they're not exactly art enthusiasts and probably think Pollock is just a fish). The story may or may not be one of Jim's exaggerations but I feel a bit sorry for Bollocks. Things like that stick with you, nicknames you earn in your first year can dog you to hell and back. I should know, I already have a nickname and spend a large part of each day trying not to think about it.

'Jesus, Bollocks!' moans Jim, trying to pull rank and push past the PC's raised arm. 'Take the stick out of your arse for five seconds, boy. Budge over so I can take a look. I won't touch nothing! What's happened? Bit of a neighbour dispute thing? Or some junkies?'

To be fair, the kid holds his ground.

'Can't, Sarge, sorry. The DI said so, on the radio. Strict instructions. No one else in, no one out. It's a fucking mess in there.'

Suddenly I'm the tiniest bit relieved. From the way he says it there must be blood and I'm not all that great with blood. But, not to disappoint Jim who will be signing my evaluation forms in the near future, and as the only woman at the crime scene flying the flag for equal guts and grit, I play bravado, sticking my head in between Jackson and his partner's shoulders to grab a look in through the kitchen door.

That's when I see the old girl. At least, I think that's what it is. At first I'm not sure.

'Don't take the piss, love, back up,' says Bollocks, putting out a barrier arm again, copper style – nothing to see here, move along – but it's already too late. I can't unsee it.

'Poor old dear,' he whispers, confirming that the twisted thing on the floor by the cooker, with the red pulp for a face, is the old man's wife. I catch my breath as the stench of shit surges towards me, gaggingly close, thick and warm. I close my newly reopened mouth, but not quickly enough to stop my stomach heaving.

The guys have told me it happens, that people defecate when they die violently, sometimes when they die otherwise. 'You wait till you get your first one.' They laugh. 'Make sure you've got your pot of Vicks ready, lovely, you know, for up the old nose or' – miming a retch – 'watch out for your shoes.'

Useless advice now as I've just got a lungful. I know I've gone the colour of cottage cheese, a parody of the rookie who's wet behind the ears and the last thing I want to appear in this company of men. You only have to show a crack and they'll stick a crowbar in and start prying out chunks of you. I've had plenty of practice at hiding my fault lines so no one will realise I pretty much feel like an imposter all the time, but I'm not ready for this and I hate the fact that it's shown so quickly.

'Jesus, take a breath, love,' says Jim, patting my arm, the smell reaching him a few seconds later. 'Who dropped their load? Bet it was you, Jackson,' he snipes, grinning, 'Overdone it on the canteen Christmas stuffing?'

No one laughs as Bollocks inclines his head to the old man, making a 'shut up' face as Jim ducks his head under Jackson's arm and drops his grin at once.

'Jesus,' he says, his hand moving back over his hair again. 'What the fuck?'

'Yeah, just confirmed, code blue,' says Bollocks. 'I mean, not officially till the on-call doc does his thing but . . .'

We know what he means. No one has ever looked quite as dead as that, not here anyway, not in real life. Swallowing the retch in my throat I try not to think of the mashed eye socket, the pulped jaw beneath the tumble of grey hair, above the pink dressing gown with lace at the cuff. The victim, the deceased, the body.

Until this moment I've never seen real violence, not anything other than a split lip or a bruised face after a pub bust-up, the usual hazard-of-the-job scrapes and cuts. I always told myself I could handle it when it came to the real stuff – I've practised the scenarios enough times in my head to be prepared. Yet, what's on the kitchen floor is something entirely new. To stop myself vomiting, I use my little focusing trick to regain control, explaining silently to myself what's happening around me like a narrator in a book or film would, until I'm ready to speak.

Confronted by the horror of the farmhouse kitchen our heroine exhibits her usual cool courage and tenacity. She holds her breath and waits for the moment to pass, a picture of stoic compassion.

It's a habit I picked up as a child, imagining myself in a movie. Even from a young age reality never really lived up to my expectations and I'd escape the boredom of my parents' farm by slipping into my own adventures where wonderful things could happen and I wasn't scared or self-conscious any more. I spent hours imagining myself as Freddie, or one of the Scooby Doo gang, pulling back the mask of the struggling theme-park owner in triumph, catching the culprit, everyone applauding my bravery.

Later, the scenarios simply became grittier and I was Clarice Starling in *The Silence of the Lambs,* firing the fatal bullet into the serial killer's heart, or Inspector Jane Tennison cuffing the *Prime Suspect.* That's when I realised what I wanted to do for a living, what I wanted to be, who I wanted to be, instead of myself.

My little trick starts to work right away and I feel my stomach settling, my breathing slowing: *Our heroine is shocked. She feels sympathy and horror, but knows there is work to be done. There's a villain to catch, of the worst kind.*

She steels herself as the officers survey the carnage. She is calm and her face betrays no emotion, though she realises that no one has the faintest idea what to do next. (She does not throw up. She absolutely does not throw up.)

I'm almost glad to see the incident commander arrive, his navy unmarked saloon bumping onto the garden verge in a flurry of unnecessary sirens. It's clearly my inspector who's drawn the short straw and answered his phone this morning. As he and I aren't on the best of terms at the moment I'd like to sidle into the background and stay invisible, but the only place to go is into the kitchen.

So we stand where we are as a sense of renewed urgency stirs across the garden and everyone straightens up, pretending efficiency before the glare of his CID uniform of dark grey suit and garish purple tie. We are officers of the law, we are disciplined and at the ready.

'OK. Everybody not given something to do by DS Matthews in the next ten seconds fuck off out of my crime scene,' says Detective Inspector Morris, marching up the path.

Given his cue, DS Matthews begins barking orders left and right as Morris strides up to the back door, pulls his broad, rugby-fed bulk up to its full six foot six height, breathes old coffee and bacon sandwich breath into our upturned faces and sneers, 'That means you two, Batman and Robin.'

This is mainly addressed to Jim's woollen cape, of course, as he surveys our little gaggle, ordering, 'Bollocks and friend, stay on this door until I tell you otherwise. Oi, ambulance guy, get the injured party out of there now, please. Everyone else serving no obvious purpose clear the hell away from here before you contaminate the scene even more than you already have. That means you, darling. We've had enough fuck-ups here for one day.'

He aims this last one specifically at me and the bolt of the insult hits me dead between the eyes. Everyone knows why. My name has preceded me here today and everywhere else in the division at this point in my short career. I've spent a month pretending not to hear the whispers: 'That's the girl, the one from Bryn Mill. You heard what happened up there? You heard about Biggsy? Poor bugger.'

Once the DI is safely occupied inside, Jim whispers, 'Any word on this? Any lead?' to Jackson. 'What're the scores on the doors? I'm guessing we've ruled out a domestic this time, and it sure ain't the old man who's public enemy number one?'

'Fuck knows,' whispers Bollocks. 'No one knows a fucking thing, Sarge. Thinking possibly a burglary gone wrong? Don't look like a suicide-pact thing, not with . . .'

Everyone knows what he means. It wouldn't be that uncommon for an old man to off his wife then turn the gun on himself. The number of suicides is surprisingly high in the farming community. Though we've never had one here, other forces have; it all gets too much, the scraping by on the land, the subsidies that are never enough or in time, the bad harvests, the milk prices dropping, the stain of the soil that works its way inside, dark, wet, corrosive.

But none of us can imagine the old man, still wheezing and wobbling on the chair, doing that to his wife and not finishing himself off as well, and the dog – well, no farmer does that to their dog.

'Come on, love,' says Jim. 'We know when we're not wanted. Let's get our arses back in the warm.'

Except, now that things are starting to move, Jim's suggestion that we leave is an unwelcome anti-climax. The initial shock is wearing off, adrenaline is taking over and my blood begins to buzz with a fascination that almost trumps my revulsion. It starts to buffer me against the horror a few feet away as I realise, in a flash, the potential of the story that's unfolding in front of me, and how, with luck, I could have a potentially noteworthy role in it. Someone has done this. Someone who has fled the scene. Someone we have to catch.

Of course, I'm not so keen that I want to go into the kitchen and carefully document the injuries, not with that stench. Nor do I love the idea of having to bag and tag, photograph, question and console – the mundane details have never really interested me. I just want to cut to the chase, to somehow be part of this, one of the closed circle that's rapidly forming at the heart of Ridgeback Farm. I want to be one of the select few who will chat it all through later, and in the years to come, when everything from this frozen morning will start acquiring the status of myth.

Like the Bedford Row incident decades before – his brains were all over the wall; she was naked in the shower – a hundred-year storm has hit the farmhouse and its occupants and is already drawing the select few along in its wake. I want to be able to answer the question, 'Where were you that day?' with the words, I was right there, in the middle of it all.

Seeing the inspector pulling on his plastic gloves I have a clean and beguiling vision of myself at the heart of this investigation, a crucial player, only a few inspired inquiries away from coming up with a vital piece of evidence that will break this case wide open.

Our heroine follows her nose and a lightning-bolt hunch. She confronts the guilty party with guile and bravado. Our heroine bursts into the parade room with her prisoner, victorious, 'Hah! I, Melissa Lloyd, have got you! Bang to rights.' Cue applause and pats on the back for the maverick thief-taker.

It's what I've been waiting years for – a chance – and, most importantly, if I can make a difference today then everyone will be forced to accept they've been wrong about me. Despite what the DI insinuated moments earlier, despite my false start and the one bad decision I made in someone's front hall at Bryn Mill farm in the heat of the moment. It does not define me. I am not a fuck-up.

I imagine how sweet it will be when the media gather later, eager to interview me, saying, Tell us in your own words. Tell us what happened. What did you do? How did you feel? How did you catch him? And I can tell them how I was bold and brave from inspired hunch to final showdown, like in all good cop movies. Then all this, until now, all this waiting and hoping and dreaming, will finally be worth it.

As we head back to our car I'm not put off at being dismissed from the scene by Inspector Prick. I know the day is young. They'll need reinforcements soon, when they dish out the inquiry tasks, and I'll be ready and waiting. I've been ready my whole life.

The Hitchhiker – 10.30 a.m.

It's bloody cold out here. Though it's not even lunchtime I can feel the air stiffening around me as the road winds on for ever between the deep wedges of trees. Occasionally the pines pull back from their military stance, but only to show the backs of identical brown and white fields littered with crows.

It'll be full dark early today, well before five o'clock on the shortest day of the year, the winter solstice. Technically, it's on the day of the autumn equinox, when day and night are of equal length, that everything is balanced halfway between the seasons. But today is exactly midway through the winter and I find that cheering. From here on out it gets a little lighter every day, the margins of the world tipping towards spring – halfway there, keep going.

Things can only get better, as Mum used to say, on the blunt-ended days of winter, those shivery mornings waking in the dark, rising in the cold, catching at the edges of every hour before and after school to tend the cows and chickens, and help with the endless housework before nightfall.

This is a little like one of those days; there's a sense of hibernation about it, though occasionally, in the unkempt undergrowth of the woodland floor, there's a dart of activity. A rabbit perhaps, a blackbird. Then, when I stop to take a drink from my water bottle, a fox walks into the road ahead, brazen and uncurious. He stands there staring, so I stare back on principle, motionless, my eyes looking into the yellow eyes of the animal looking at me.

We look at each other. We know what we are.

Here, I am the interloper, the trespasser in its winter world, the outsider. I'm used to that. I inhabit my role as the fox inhabits his, from cocked nose to claw tip, but I won't look away first. You should never break eye contact with a wild thing. It shows weakness. After a few moments the animal sniffs, nose high, twitching, then loses interest, wandering across the road into the opposite ranks of trees. Satisfied I've won the battle of wills I walk on.

I like foxes. When I was seven years old one kept getting into the chicken shed, snatching hens, feathers and blood speckles the only evidence of its arrival and departure. Dad got it with the shotgun eventually and I'd felt sorry for the fox – it was only doing what was in its nature, surviving. I never really felt sorry for the chickens. There are predators in the world and there are prey – everyone has to decide which they want to be, if they can.

As I come to a crossroads I pass a boarded-up petrol station with that post-apocalyptic feel that only winter abandonment can bring. A deserted calm has claimed the main cabin, the rusted pumps and cracked forecourt, while off to the side stands a low row of eight 1950s-style motel chalets. They're each a single storey high, wooden, with wide windows and a half-paned door. A sign lying in the snow declares, 'Holiday fun for everyone!' and it's hard to think of anything that could look more out of place here in the dark world of a western winter.

In a former life the chalet rooms had clearly been garishly painted green, blue and red – gay carnival colours, their holiday best – someone's sunshine folly, their idea of the exotic, of a novelty vacation spot. Now the paint is crackled and blown, two of the doors are kicked in, but there's a flicker somewhere, deep in my memory, a vision of sweet lemonade in a paper cup, my fat, sweaty legs dangling from a high stool.

I must have been driven this way as a child, on a rare trip to the coast maybe, one of those epic, bouncing journeys in Dad's Land Rover on broken springs and good faith.

'What's a motel, Dad?' I'd asked him once, watching TV.

'Like a hotel,' he said, 'but you just stop off for a night, on your way to somewhere else. You don't go there for an actual holiday. If you're the sort that has time and money for holidays, that is.'

My father had not been that sort.

The motel looks like the kind of place teenagers hang out, knees pulled up to their chests, sitting on damp mattresses, smoking weed and sharing cans of lager. I know places like this well – the adult equivalent of childhood dens, beer-can littered, scarred by attempted fires. There's a natural camaraderie around a fire or an oil drum, snickering its glow on shadowed faces, though that can change in a crackle. The warmth of the circle, its safety, is always an illusion, but that's true of everywhere.

I don't bother to take a look inside. I've slept in worse places, but it's too soon to settle down for the night, to go to ground, and it's better to put some distance between me and the farm, and Pont, just in case they've started looking for me. If the worst comes to the worst I'll find somewhere to bed down later.

It might come to that. I'm starting to think I must have taken a wrong turn in the last hour. If this is the place I remember I'm more than a bit off track; I must be going east instead of south.

'Preparing for the invasion,' Dad used to say about the lack of road signs. Even then it had seemed true, a subtle plan to thwart the progress of strangers into these lands, like the crumbling and moss-salted pill boxes out on the coast that I climbed as a kid, a reminder of the war, that there are always people who'll try to come in from outside and take what you have, even if that's bugger all.

As I walk I spot an ancient milestone in the white-topped verge, but scuffed smooth by 200 years of wind and rain it's no help. Bending down, I run my gloved hands over the ghost of the carving – a one and a two perhaps? Twelve miles? The etching vanishes beneath my fingers, under the lichen and moss.

Things change over the years, are erased. Here at least.

Not up there, though, in the farmhouse leaning a little more into the valley with each year. When I'd arrived last night I wasn't surprised to see my old bedroom left untouched – not loved and tended, you understand, not a shrine to an absent daughter, just closed up, left to its own devices. It had never waited with clean sheets, promising fabric-softener slumber, for a last-minute phone call heralding a visit home – I'm on way. Can I stay the night? Two nights? A year? Can I come home for Christmas?

How could I have asked that, even if I'd wanted to? After the way I left? When she'd appeared on the doorstep last night Mum had looked at me as calmly as ever and said, 'Come in then,' no older really, no more weathered than I remember, probably because she'd always looked so old to me. Being on your own, ground against the rough edges of a large, disappointed man who brooks no argument and suffers no rebuke will do that.

She'd barely shown surprise at the sight of her daughter out of the wide blue yonder, calm in her old blue cardigan and leather boots, arms folded against the cold, against the moral outrage of who might be calling on such an unholy silent night. Then she'd stepped back with the words, 'Your father's not here. He's up at Blackwater with the vet – staying the night to keep an eye on the calving. What's up?'

She'd meant, what sort of trouble are you in?

I could ask you the same question, I'd wanted to say, startled by the disarray that met me in the kitchen. I should have expected it, from the unkempt path, the broken gate. They'd been a proud pair once, my parents, held their heads high, Dad pontificating endlessly about the importance of honouring your birthright, honouring tradition. But that was before the drinking started and he'd let the place descend into something else entirely.

The sense of decay and disappointment was painful, only the silence was more agonising as no bark had warned of my arrival. Flap the sheepdog was missing from his old rug by the fire, apparently gone home to the place under the tree in the lower field . . . Sorry love . . . by the way . . . it happened last winter . . .

Instead, there was a new dog by the fire, a small sheepdog, soft and lazy, eating chocolate dog treats out of Mum's hand, and hate stirred in me for that dog, for taking such a liberty, for being so at home when I am not any more.

Flap's erasure from the kitchen was worse than the absence of my father, worse than it will feel when his absence is eventually permanent. Is that so wrong? I don't think it's true that all parents love their children and vice versa, though *his* photo was still there, of course, smiling at me from the mantelpiece, the golden child, the original son and heir, the only thing not covered in dust and mildew in that tatty kitchen.

People do have favourites, they just never admit it. Mostly it's just a comforting illusion, the idea of family, the rituals that tie people together, births, marriages, deaths. In a way, that's what brought me back here yesterday, and it's already sending me away again. Make sense of that, if you have the time, Pam. Fashion a story from it. Observe it clinically, see it passing you by. Remember it cannot hurt you.

Up ahead I see a right turn in the road, forking off. It slides on into the trees and disappears, no sign to tell me where it goes, but my ears prick up of their own accord as the quality of the stillness begins to change. After a moment a dull rumble approaches and headlights appear at the edge of the road.

Well, that's no bad thing. I could do with a lift, or at least some directions, but I don't want to get hit by the car, dressed in my dark clothes on a gloomy day. So I step to the side and pull out the little torch from my trouser leg pocket, flashing it a couple of times to warn the car of my presence. It's too dark to tell who's inside but I'm hoping for a good-natured bloke on his way home to his wife – no youngsters who want to chat, or worse, a guy who puts his hand on your leg, then pulls over unexpectedly with the offer to 'work off your fare darling'.

The driver should spot my flashing beam now, left then right. I make myself prominent without standing in the car's path, which is just as well as it doesn't slow down. It pulls level but swishes on by, making no attempt to stop.

'Cheers, fucker!' I yell at the back of the disappearing car, flicking a proper British two-finger V sign as a spray of slushy snow hits my legs. Isn't there some unwritten law in these parts about stopping for a fellow traveller, or a damsel in distress? Except I'm not in distress. Or a damsel.

I lower the torch and walk on, trying to enjoy the rare opportunity of being a free agent for a little while longer. It beats the hell out of constantly living to other people's whims and rules, by their sirens and bells, whistles and commands, with one eye on the clock – enduring the hours of sitting and waiting, always watching. Watching for the signs that something is about to happen, for someone to object to someone's look, smile, lack of smile, clothes, smell, for questions, fists and close-quarter arguments.

It always happens when a group of women are pressed and packed together, with all that time to slice and dice into sections to pass the days. Time to eat, time to exercise. Time to wake, time to sleep. Time for all hell to break loose. Time has to be tamed and packaged and kept on a tight lead, even though it's hard right now with this bloody road going on for ever, unchanging, unending.

As I walk, I try to take Lilli-Anne's advice, to be in the moment, to make friends with the monotony. She says the natural state of the universe is inertia, but then also that the natural state of the universe is change. She sees no contradiction in this.

I can see Lilli-Anne now, probably perched on her bunk, a Regal smouldering between her blunt fingers, bright blue eyes flicking around like a snake's tongue, looking for trouble. Whenever I'd complain about the repetitive march of our days, aching for something to happen, Lil would always say, 'Be careful what you wish for, doll,' reminding me of the old Chinese curse: 'May you live in interesting times,' with a sage nod befitting a fag-end philosopher.

Things got too interesting too quickly yesterday. If Lil had been there, seen me with the hammer raised, she'd have talked me out of it for sure. If she were here now she'd explain to the police for me. But it is what it is, no hiding that, not if I'm still here hours from now, not if anyone mentions my name.

I pick up my pace and have done at least twenty minutes' fast walking before I spot another car, parked this time, pulled in at the side of the verge, almost in the tree line. The headlights are off but there's no movement inside and the windows aren't steamed up, which is good because I don't want to interrupt a furtive teenage fumble. Satisfied there're no surprises awaiting me, I edge closer and try the door handle but it's locked.

There's no path into the trees nearby. This isn't even a

layby as such. The woods are silent. Perhaps the owner's nipped into the woods for a quick pee? Or maybe they've decided to abandon their car in the snow, which is getting worse by the minute.

I place my hand on the bonnet, checking for a trace of warmth. I can barely feel it through my leather gloves and I'm guessing the engine has been off for a while. Peering inside, my hand pressed up against the window, I can see the back seat is littered with taped-up boxes and bags. There's also a creepy-looking clutch of chipped garden gnomes that look destined for the rubbish tip. The crap some people collect. I can fit pretty much everything I own in my backpack – actually, pretty much everything I own is already in there.

This is clearly not the car belonging to the inconsiderate fucker who sped past me earlier, which is a shame. That'd be karma, wouldn't it? Leaving someone walking alone in the snow on a day like this, only to get a prang a few minutes later. I sort of believe in karma, though I won't admit it to Lil.

Yin and yang, positive and negative, do a bad deed and a bad deed gets done to you. It makes sense. The world turns full circle eventually; I'm living, breathing proof of that. Two days ago I was so sure I was about to break even at last, get on the upswing, close to being free for the first time in all these years. Until what had happened with Rhys. To Rhys. Because of what he'd done when he was supposed to have been *my* boyfriend, and what I did when the horns and thorns broke through my skin and the blood rushed in and blotted out all the words in the world.

Is that why Rhys has ended up where he is now? His karma finally caught up with him? Ran him to ground? Slid the knife into his back as he'd slid it into mine? Does that make me happy? If only it was that simple.

In the case of this driver it doesn't appear to be karma, just carelessness. From this side it's obvious the front end is dented badly, the bumper compressed against the stump of a fallen tree, which, in turn, is compressed against the tyre. It doesn't look drivable, which is a shame as I was half-thinking about nicking it. I can break into and start up almost any vehicle – one of the few 'essential skills' Purvis taught me. I might have 'borrowed' it for a few hours and left it down at the railway station, no harm, no foul, but that's not an option.

The driver must have skidded on the ice, tried to correct it, and locked the brakes. There are slushy skid marks in the snow, veering from the centre of the road to the verge. I'm not surprised. The tyres are bald as an egg. There's a huge rust hole by the bonnet edge on the right wing and I doubt it has anything like an MOT. I'd have been taking my life in my hands getting into this death trap.

While I'm mulling over what to do next I realise I'm being watched. The instant clarity takes the form of the usual cool click behind my eyes. I don't turn around immediately; I don't want to look alarmed. Instead I pull my phone out of my pocket and pretend to play with it for a few seconds, holding it up as if looking for a signal, before half-turning. I raise my eyes rather than my head, scanning the road and woods. Where are you? What do you want?

I spot him in seconds, just off to the left, in the tree line under the snow-drooped canopy of sagging branches, a guy in a big parka jacket and woolly hat, long hair poking out the sides. There's a rifle over his arm. It's not pointed at me, just resting there. He gives a curt nod and wipes his nose on the sleeve of his jacket. He moves back and forth slightly, foot-to-foot, twitchy.

He's standing behind the remains of a low, dry-stone wall but I can see the black tube of the rifle barrel clearly. A poacher, maybe? A farmer? It's hard to tell his age from this distance, could be anywhere between twenty and forty. Like the wood and stone of the cottages they live in, these guys don't wear well out here in the scouring elements. The farmers and their families are a law unto themselves anyway. They do things their own way, by their own clocks, and you're never quite sure what or when that will be.

I saw the first-hand outcome of it once, two of them going at it, all fists and spit, in the yard behind the cattle market, over a lost bet on something that was never resolved. Those old guys carry their grudges around for years, their resentment worked into the blood of the land and the grime of their hands. I should know. It was ingrained in my own father. Every so often he'd let fly, then me and Mum would scramble to get out of the eye of the storm, words only, never fists, but they can still destroy, keep you scared.

No one expected the scrap to lead where it did that day, for Mr Porter to grab the axe and take a swing, leaving Old Happy's thumb hanging off, spouting red blood. I hadn't minded that so much, the sight of the sticky warmth enveloping his hand, it was more that, at thirteen years old and the only girl there, I'd been automatically expected to clean it up. That was the role Mum always occupied; stitcher, mender, soother. Violence was part of the world of men, and it was always us – the girls, wives and mothers – dealing with the clean-up, cleaning ourselves up, because we had no weapons to give us an advantage, no gang of our own to provide strength in numbers.

I swore I'd never end up like Mum. I've found my own gang since, my own weapons.

Old Happy hadn't gone off to hospital that day, the old guys never did. No one went to the police, either. If you thought someone was rustling your sheep you rustled them back or shot at them as they fled into the top field, hoping to pepper their arses with pellets. After you'd kicked off and cleared the air you buried the hatchet, even if it was the one they'd swung at you.

But the guy with the rifle doesn't look like he wants to kick off, standing in the trees opposite. Whoever he is, he's a classic loner type, probably lives in one of the nearby farms. He might have a Land Rover parked nearby, which might mean a lift, but do I really want to get in a car with *him*? Scratch that, bad idea.

'Not your car, then?' I ask, cocking my head at the rust heap by the side of the road. He shakes his head. 'Am I heading the right way for the connection to Carmarthen, mate?'

He waves ahead, the way I'm going, and mumbles something. The trees rustle in the windy silence, snow shifts.

He's still making no move towards me, which is good, though I'm on my toes, ready for fight or flight if needs be.

Not that I *want* to fight some crazy, random weirdo in the middle of a forest. I'll leg it well before he gets over that wall, if he shows any sign of approaching, take the path of least resistance, *this time*, because it suits me, because I have bigger fish to fry.

He stares at me for a bit longer, gripping the rifle barrel tightly, then says something that might be in Welsh, waving his hand towards the car. It's been a long time since I've used my second-hand Cymraeg, though they made us speak it sometimes at school, the daily, '*Bore da, plant* – good morning children,' and the sing-songy response, '*Bore-da*, Miss-sus Thom-as!'

Only Dad ever made any real effort to speak it at home, but I don't understand the words any more and I don't care. As long as he leaves me alone he can lurk around the woods as much as he wants. The woods, *y coed*? Where did that come from? Still, not much use right now. Time to move on, to go, *y mynd*, I think.

I'm not particularly pleased he's seen me, though. I'd hoped to leave unnoticed in the light of yesterday's action and adventure, slip back into the winter without witnesses and no one to describe or identify me. But then who would this guy tell, even if he has something to say? He doesn't look like the civic-minded type. Who would be out here on a day like this anyway? Only someone up to no good, myself included. And who would believe him?

As I shift my pack higher onto my shoulders he says something else, waving towards the car, hitting the side of his head three times as he speaks, making a half step in my direction, but I just nod in return, give him a half-salute of the hand and move on.

Creepy fucker! I glance backwards after a few steps, just to make sure he's not following, but he's merely standing there in the trees as I quicken my step into the fast-fading light.

The Old Man – 10.30 a.m.

He knows he must have fallen into a doze because the bedroom window has grown darker. A reflection of the room has replaced the high dome of sky and the heater smells of hot metal and dust. He half wishes it would start to spark or smoulder, set the rug alight then the sheets, then the blankets. He'd go up like a bonfire for sure, writhing amid the flames, twiggy old limbs burning away to ash in a final blaze of glory.

But not today. He doesn't want that today. He's awake and waiting. Ready, not really watching another repeat of a *Two Ronnies* Christmas special on the TV, but trying to make sense of the dream he'd been having moments earlier ... of way back when ... of the day Brian had walked into the bar and seen ... everything ... nothing ... everything ...

He crushes the thought. He doesn't want to recall the details of the second that cracked the world open and swung them apart for so long. They don't matter now, the whys, the whats, the whos. He'd rather think of the good times, many of those right here, in Brian's old room, tucking him into bed under this ceiling, safe inside his pirate quilt covered in galleons and doubloons.

Brian had liked the sea even then, so much so that, when the storm hit and tossed them apart, he'd surrounded himself with it for thirty years. He's imagined Brian more times than he can count, marooned on his little metal island amid the towering waves, deafened by the wind, deaf to any call to or from home. So different from that summer when he hadn't ever seemed to stop talking about boats and they'd lashed the battered kayak to the roof of the Fiesta, paddled around the salt-splashed coast, peering into rock pools, the water impossibly clear and glassy.

They'd been two years in the pub by then. Once, long before the tarmac ribbons of road had stretched out into West Wales, delivering its flow of cars and buses, the pub had served as the coach road to and from the coast. Well-used for centuries, it was a thread of continuity, a link to the past he was continuing. He liked that, and honestly, living at the pub had been so much better than living with Rose's mother or in the leaky flat above the butcher's shop with the iron smell of blood and sweet sawdust in his nostrils, the suspicion of smirks from the shoppers.

He'd liked being a landlord, liked the regulars who walked down the lanes from the surrounding farms, wrapped in their padded coats with their collie dogs. They never gossiped about him, at least not in his hearing, as long as their pints were poured and no one touched their billiards and the dominoes on their boards at the bar.

Summers were best, warmed by the sound of laughter, the running feet of kids on bus trips. They'd taken pretty good money every holiday season, though Rose had often gone to stay at her mother's through the winter, blaming the damp air of the valley floor, taking Brian to be closer to his school and friends.

Then, that winter when Brian was seven years old, she'd told him she wasn't coming back, that she'd met someone else down at the market, a greengrocer – *the* greengrocer for God's sake, as if there was more than one in a tiny place like this. That old fart with the neat beard, fifteen years her senior.

He'd felt he should protest.

'You're still my wife,' he'd screamed, as she stood with her last suitcases on the doorstep, Brian in the grocer's car, face fogging the glass, not because he wanted her by then but because she was the part of him that was normal, respectable. They were the landlord and his wife, a unit, but she'd just sneered and said quietly, 'You're not a real husband.'

At least Brian had come to stay for summer weekends, holidays and half terms, his bike flung down outside on the flagstones after cruising with those clean-limbed kids from the village, eight, nine, ten years old, so full of life. It made his heart swell, watching them playing war or cop stakeouts in the tall grass of the old graveyard opposite, creeping, hiding, ambushing, so free of the awkward perils of puberty, when it all starts to get so complicated, so gorgeous.

Of all of them it's Gary's face he sees now – Gary with his beautiful blond hair, his thin, stringy muscles turning, that summer, into those of a taut young man of fourteen. He'd watched him, covetous of his youth, his budding

confidence in his own beauty, his edges sharpening, shoulders broadening, a head taller than Brian and almost taller
than himself.

That was the summer the boys spent languid hours lying
on the flat slabs of the tombstones, shirtless, sneaking
cigarettes. Brian was always burnt and sun-sensitive, with
xylophone ribs, not like Gary with his tanned and
tightening torso, but Brian could make things work with
his hands and his mind was a razor blade. While they ate
the chips and egg he'd make for him in the pub kitchen,
Brian would talk about science, astronomy, the stars, far-
flung journeys around the world and into the universe,
geological expeditions underground, through centuries of
compressed fossils.

He'd accepted early on that Brian found the thought of
taking over the pub one day unthinkable, but Gary was a
good apprentice, fascinated, attentive, making a show of
wanting to help, learn how to change the barrels, flush the
lines. When he'd take Gary down into the dusty old cellar
they'd leave Brian sulking upstairs, because there was
something he'd loved in the cool quiet down there, with
Gary watching his every move, eager to learn – 'let me try,
let me try' – helping him lift the barrels with his smooth
brown arms.

Had Brian thought Gary was the son he'd really wanted?
But Gary wasn't that. The want had been different . . .

Something had shattered in his heart when he heard that
Gary had died, so many years ago now and so very young.
In a way he'd lost two sons that day; Brian had returned to
the pub only once afterwards, on the day he'd turned
sixteen, to tell him he was taking that job up north on the

oil rigs, but that he'd send money to him and his mum as often as he could. That was thirty years ago, or thereabouts, and in between . . .

He doesn't want to think about it too much. How something so crucial had been misunderstood.

How has Brian changed in all this time? Will he recognise him? Is he hard inside where he himself has become soft, wood-shaving thin, full of handfuls of dust? He'll find out soon enough. He thinks of the letter, safe in its hidey-hole, and that's when he hears it, the thump, thump, thump on the door.

He's here. It's time.

The Law – 10.30 a.m.

By the time we get back to the nick, and are putting the kettle on to thaw ourselves out, the local radio has gone crazy about what's happening up at the farm. There are very few facts in the breathily excited reports as yet, mainly because even we know bugger all and CID will want to keep it that way for a bit.

Luckily for us our local radio has a listenership of about sixteen, but we're buying time. With something like this the feeding frenzy begins quickly and nothing can sate it, the rare headline pearl of a violent death will soon have them hovering like buzzards, scenting carrion.

Jim and I are glued to our police radios, determined not to miss anything, though there's something slightly surreal about it all, waiting under the watchful eye of the grinning two-foot-tall Frosty the Snowman on the counter top, ready to break into a rendition of Jingle Bells' if we press his belly.

We're not supposed to say anything to journalists, of course, not us in the rank and file; we're deemed incapable of coherent public speech. There's always a press officer, Paul or Alison, on duty down at regional HQ for that, but it's no surprise that the few journalists eager enough to have made it into the office today, despite Christmas party hangovers, have decided to sod protocol and chain-ring each and every police station in the book.

Jim knows all the old hands on the local paper and Western Wave radio and often passes them little titbits and tip-offs, off the record. It's harmless stuff usually, just to keep them sweet, but he's tight-lipped today, with good reason.

'If I knew anything more than the fact that we're investigating an incident involving a serious assault, believe me I'd tell you,' he says, lying with convincing indifference every time he takes a call before putting the phone down and adding something like, 'This stink is going to stick for a long time, love, mark my words. The proverbial has hit the fan.'

Carron, our straight-shouldered, steel-haired receptionist, is uncharacteristically flustered, dealing with calls too, but mostly from her extensive network of friends and family, eager for an insider update. Obviously someone has seen the crime-scene tapes going up, the police cars rushing past with their blue lights and slushy urgency, and the word is spreading through the area like pandemic flu, airborne and eager.

They'll be scared out there already, in the village, on the outskirts, as the rumours spread, the old ladies, the wives, the chattering friends and families, and it's a nice feeling, to be on the inside, I mean, not to be a civilian any more, not to be alone.

They'll all be asking right now, Who could have done

this? Who could be next? They'll be nervous as cats on Bonfire Night because this has the hallmarks of someone unexpected, something unknown. It won't be anyone local, they'll be insisting. No one round here would do something like this. They'll be jumpy and alarmed, but I don't need to be either. Whoever did this, the feral animal is responsible for that cowardly scene at the farmhouse, whoever his friends are, I'm part of the biggest gang in town now, and we're more than a match for them.

The filth, the rozzers, the pigs, that's us and we're proud of it. Whatever our core clientele call us when we spoil their fun, turn out their pockets, seize their drugs or nick them for drunk and disorderly, they'll all be glad to see us today, out in force, en masse, because they all have mams and nans and aunties.

Though they like to make a show of being the alpha dogs, with their steroid- thickened necks and smack-stringy scowls and sniffs, they always change their tune when the real big bad wolves come padding around. Who're the pigs then? Who's ready for the slaughter? And there are always wolves, aren't there, by their very nature, looking for a nice easy meal, a quick smash and grab, a take what you have, licking their lips.

'Little pig, little pig . . . let me in . . .'

Like the knock on the door that must have come last night at Ridgeback Farm. A knocked door must be answered, just like a ringing phone, even if you're a little old lady, alone in a house in a dark, dark wood, and surely you know nothing good can come of it because only two sorts of people knock on strangers' doors in the middle of the night, us and the other sort.

So who are we looking for? That's the real question now. And why have they done this here, to these poor old people?

When the buzzing radios fail to give up the latest details of what's happening up at the farm, Jim gets to work tapping up all his acquaintances for information. He's always reminding me that real police work is not about showy pursuits and rough-and-tumble raids, it's not even about elegant investigations and subtle opponents, it's about knowing who to talk to and when, and how to find out what you need to know.

You don't even need to leave a desk to do that, he insists, and, true to his word, in less than ten minutes, he's learned that the old man has been taken to Aberystwyth General for a check-up, woozy and in shock. His wife is going too, but to the morgue.

So speaks PC Tom Flower, the first man to answer the phone at Bethel outstation, who happens to be the first officer on the scene at the farmhouse that morning. He's writing up his first account at the nick before heading to the bells-and-whistles incident room they're setting up at Central. It seems the old man had been unconscious for a while before he came round and managed to raise the alarm, explaining to the first sleepy 999 call-handler that he'd returned from a night away to find 'intruders' in his house.

PC Flower hasn't taken it well. I can tell from the thickness in his voice. Both me and Jim know the farm is on his patch, that's why Jim rang him first and, as he reminds us, he's been up there regularly over the years, following up complaints about the local kids who think it's a great laugh to throw stones at the old couple's collection of garden gnomes, daring each other to creep up the path, knock on the door and run away.

Like the other village kids, each with their own source of amusement, or thinly veiled antisocial behaviour, their taunting voices always disappear before we can grab them by the scruff of the neck and unofficially slap the silly out of them. Tom clearly feels bad for the old couple, who always had tea in the pot and a Welsh cake ready for him.

Despite his apparent uselessness in catching the little shits who made their lives hell, they'd never once sworn at him or called him a stupid bastard, and he'd never expected to find the nice old lady like that, slumped in her own blood and excrement.

In his words, what had been done to that old lady was 'inhuman'.

'Jesus,' says Jim, putting down the phone to cover the sound of Tom choking up. 'What the hell is wrong with people these days? Nice old pair like that, not much joy left in their lives, trying to live out their last years in peace and some bastards do this. Sorry, love. Makes me despair, it really does. There are some soulless people about. Something missing, you know, up there and in here.'

He taps a finger against his forehead and then his chest to illustrate the point.

'Any idea who we're looking for?' I ask. 'It can't be locals, surely?'

We get a partial answer after Jim has dialled the eastern parade room where, as luck would have it, the duty phone is answered by Dai Evans. He's one of Jim's oldest compatriots, and he relates his own bit of the unfolding drama, how he'd stumbled across 'that useless twat, Billy Fisket' in the country lane near Oldstones about an hour ago, 'gibbering and covered in blood'.

Dai had apparently been on a routine patrol earlier – i.e., he'd nipped down the garage for his usual breakfast bacon roll – when he'd found a bloody great tractor parked in the middle of the road. When he got out and waved to the man in the cab to get the fuck out of the road, he'd seen a none-too-concerned Jack Davies from Highbrook Farm, 'You know, the one with the massive forehead and plug ears,' standing on the verge.

'What's up?' he'd asked Jacky, to which Jacky, never a man of many words, pointed to the skinny lad crouched on the verge and said, 'I was just about to go and call nine nine nine, Dai. Stupid fucker came running down the hill, hell for leather, and ran right into my rig.'

Dai tells us how he immediately recognised Billy Fisket, at this point done with running, sitting shivering in just a T-shirt and jeans. He was nursing a cut lip, a bruised eye and a suspected twisted ankle, and he was constantly muttering something like, 'She didn't deserve that. It weren't right, just weren't right'.

'Jesus Christ, Jacky,' Dai said, 'sure you didn't run right over the top of him? Look at the state of him.'

'Nope,' said Jacky, reportedly cool as a cucumber. 'All that,' gesturing to the boy's dark-stained clothes and hands, 'I reckon that ain't *his* blood.'

After a quick look and prod of Billy and his clothes Dai reckoned he was right.

'But you don't think Fisket has anything to do with the farm business, do you?' says Jim when Dai proceeds to tell us Billy is under arrest at Central as we speak, 'That he did that to the old girl? That useless twat?'

I know right away why he's incredulous. We all know Billy Fisket from his regular appearances in the morning round-up sheets. He was also a few years below me in school, a bit of a no-good who bunked off a lot and whose dad sometimes worked out at the garage on the crossroads. When my dad was filling up the Land Rover we'd often see Fisket senior on the petrol pumps, occasionally smoking a fag, causing my dad to yell at him to put it out.

Nowadays I regularly hear Jim moaning about Fisket junior, who evidently inherited his father's brains. He's the classic annoying little bugger who pops up from time to time, drunk and pitiful, like a skinny, smacked-up mole that needs to be constantly whacked down.

I can't help but wince when Jim clicks on the most recent mugshot on the computer: the picture of Billy paints a thousand words. It's all there, the wasted cheeks and glassy, mackerel eyes; the pitted skin, a cautionary tale of the dangers of substance abuse and lack of vitamin D. At twenty-one years old we both know that Billy is as thick as two short planks, or three long ones; kind to stray dogs; a fan of motorbikes and quad bikes, Stella lager and fry-ups.

He may have been nicked for drug offences and petty burglary so many times it would've convinced smarter men to consider changing career, but he's never been involved in violence before.

'Seriously, Dai,' says Jim, 'there's no way this guy takes the lead in something like this. I mean, I saw the old girl.'

'Well, that's the good part,' says Dai. 'He's pretty much

confessed already. We can't shut the stupid fucker up. Hasn't even asked for the duty solicitor yet. He's in there now, pouring his heart out to that CID twat, Morris. I guess even Billy is smart enough to realise this ain't no soft community-service stint – it's murder, innit? And he's nicked, except he ain't going down alone.'

According to Dai, within two minutes of getting into the interview room under Inspector Morris's imposing gaze, Billy had named someone called Riley Finn as his partner in crime. 'Some Birmingham scumbag with a rap sheet as long as my arm.'

The perpetrator, the initiator, the killer, says the movie voice in my head as Dai confirms Riley Finn is currently unaccounted for.

'Well, the balloons will go up now', says Jim, putting down the phone, 'for this Riley Finn person. I expect we'll get reinforcements from East Division too as soon as they can make it up from town. Get your big boots on, lovely. It's gonna be a long night. We're looking at a manhunt.'

It's that word that does it, 'manhunt'. It makes it real, sets off a flare of heat and anticipation in my gut and a slew of images behind my eyeballs, including shots of flaring torches and yelping sniffer dogs chasing a sweating Paul Newman in *Cool Hand Luke*, and Tommy Lee Jones in *The Fugitive*, on the trail of Harrison Ford's Dr Kimble, issuing orders to search every doghouse, hen house and outhouse until he gets his man.

'Riley Finn? Don't think I recognise that one,' says Jim, and I know he's relieved this probably isn't anyone local, anyone whose mum, dad, brother or cousin he knows. If it's an outsider it means it's not one of us, thank God, and we can still think of ourselves as good people in a nice village who look out for each other.

I also know there's no way he's going to wait patiently to be 'officially briefed' about our new suspect when the CID eventually get around to us. So while I peer over his shoulder, he logs on to the creaky intranet system to get ferreting.

Though I can't pretend we've had much experience of hardened criminals in Pont, it quickly becomes clear that Riley Finn is in a very different league to the likes of Billy Fisket. Straight away Jim discovers that Finn has no address listed in the area, no open file with previous arrests or cautions in our county, only a one-line reference to an incident a few years back, a fight in a Cardiff pub.

The note is brief, but we can see that in 2004 one of our less-than-salubrious local boys, Tom Dooley, went on a 'cash and carry trip' to the capital – i.e., with pockets full of money for drugs to carry back to local junkies – and he'd been caught with enough smack in his jacket to land himself a 'supplier' conviction.

It seems that Finn, who, when we follow the link, has an extensive file on the system for offences in Birmingham, had been suspected of being one of the people who'd 'supplied' him with the packets of white powder, and there was mention of an altercation that resulted in Dooley almost losing an eye and two of his fingers.

There's only one out-of-date mugshot attached to the file, but when Jim clicks it open we both sit back in surprise.

'Hmmm. Well, that's not what I was expecting,' says Jim, and looking at the picture of Finn I have to agree.

It's not a politically correct thing to say but most of our

'frequent flyers' share a persona, a certain look. They practically have a sign above their heads saying 'resident of God's junk drawer' in big, flashing letters, as Inspector Morris delightfully puts it. They're the sort of person you'd cross the road to avoid, or at least clutch your bag a little tighter and quicken your step if you saw them.

But this is no drug-addled Billy Fisket on the screen before us, not by a long measure, this is a respectable-looking passport-style photo of a pleasant person in good health, someone you'd happily give the time of day to on the street.

His curiosity sparked, Jim phones an old colleague of his who defected like a filthy traitor to Cardiff in 2002, lured by better pay and a vastly increased chance of promotion. Inspector Amanda Willis happily fills in the blanks for us and tells us that a hammer had been found under a table in the pub on St Mary Street where the drug swap took place, and that the wounds to Dooley's smashed fingers matched its head, as did the fragments of recovered skin and blood.

She explains how the case fell through after a witness initially said that Finn had used the hammer on Dooley, but withdrew his statement the next day, claiming he'd been confused and drunk. Finn's prints were not on the hammer but it had been a cold day and Finn had been wearing gloves.

An off-duty copper had turned up in time to see Dooley writhing on the floor and Finn sitting down to a half-finished pint. Dooley also completely denied Finn's involvement, insisting they didn't know each other and just happened to be at the same bar.

Inspector Willis is clear about the fact that she's convinced Finn was responsible but couldn't make anything stick.

'Anecdotally, the hammer is a weapon of choice for Finn,' says Willis, who's pretty much lost all of her Welsh accent since leaving Pont. 'I spoke to the lads up in the Midlands at the time, where Finn did a stint for assault a few years back. Actually, must have only recently got out. There was something behind the eyes with that one, Jim, something not quite right. If Finn's about, you watch yourselves, OK?'

So this isn't a one-off moment of madness we're dealing with. Despite the innocuous file photo, Jim and I now know we have what's commonly known as a nasty piece of work on our hands, someone who would beat up a frail old woman without a second thought and who would definitely attract the tag-line 'dangerous offender; do not approach' on any police appeal.

'Personally I think the prison system has a lot to answer for,' sighs the Inspector. 'We try to bang them up, but then they're just left to roam society unmonitored because they need the bloody prison spaces for someone else.' We both nod, though she can't see us, because we know it's true.

It's a regular lament, the failings of the justice system to send down the people we nick, the inability of institutions to rehabilitate or punish those we convict.

'Doesn't look like your average psycho, right?' adds Willis. 'Goes to show, it's not just the shitbags that have shit kids. That one had all the chances in life; came from a good family. Drugs, though, you know the story. It messes with their heads, though I suspect Riley had something going wrong up top long before anyone reported it to us. No doubt all those lovely anger-management and counselling assessments they get inside now will have cleared Finn for release on licence, but we all know how skilled sociopaths are at lying, telling some dumb psychology student what they want to hear, right?' We nod again.

After the call ends, with Christmas wishes and remember me to so-and-sos, there's nothing to do but twiddle our thumbs for a bit until our collar numbers are called and we're released from outstation exile. With time to kill I boil the kettle again, my thoughts drifting towards what'll happen to me next week if Riley Finn, probably well on the way to being out of the country now, is nicked in the next half hour on the Severn Bridge, denying me the opportunity to demonstrate how courageous and indispensable I can be to this investigation.

I'm actually wondering if I'll still be in the force this time next month.

OK, so no one has specifically said anything about bringing charges against me after the Bryn Mill incident, but they won't say it outright at this stage. Embarrassing messes like the one I made four weeks ago are dealt with in-house for as long as possible, so no skid-mark linen has to be washed in public before a bunch of IPCC idiots who haven't left an office for years.

But I know, with every tick of the clock counting off the hours until my hearing, that the prospect of my being quietly booted out of the force is a real one. What's almost worse is that if it's proven I've failed to do my duty, to be an effective agent of the law before I'm barely out of my probation period, it'll prove my mother right – and how will I ever live with that shame?

I'll never be able to forget the look she gave me when I told her I wanted to join the police force. She'd barely glanced up from her raw-handed potato peeling to warn me, with a slow shake of her head, that I was making a mistake. Her exact words were, 'For God's sake, Lissa, isn't it time you grew up? Take hold of your life and stop living in a fantasy world! This is real life not a movie.'

At first I'd thought it was her own smarting lack of ambition talking; I put it down to 'inherent gender bias' as we call it on the force, like 'institutional racism', her engrained prejudice coming into play because I'm not being a dutiful daughter and following in her domestic footsteps. I always thought she'd be far less disparaging if my brothers Tom and Andrew had ever said they wanted to join up, instead of adding their bulk and slow brains to the family farm business.

My father, soil under his fingernails, oil in his hair, sticking a screwdriver into the stubborn tractor engine for the hundredth time that month, was more resigned, saying simply, 'If it's what you want we'll support you, but no shortcuts, girl. I don't care what you do if it's what you want, but don't mess around any more, do something properly.'

Not like a lazy smart-arse with her head in the clouds, as usual, is what he'd meant. Not like the kid who'd always snuck off to gym club or drama club, or to read more bloody books and watch videos when there was actual work to be done, while her brothers pulled their weight.

I'd ignored them both. I keep on ignoring them, though

I still live with them, so technically it's a phased, part-time ignoring, outside mealtimes and chore times. The point is, they've clearly never been able to grasp what I've known since my sixth birthday, that I'm meant for something better, something more dramatic. more cinematic than Pont will ever offer.

Given the chance I know I can do something great, but I also know that if I want to escape a grimy future of toiling on the farm with shit on my shoes, hair stinking of wet hay and prematurely wrinkled like a walnut, I'll have to make it happen for myself, write my own story and write my own role in it.

How can I explain to them that pulling on my police uniform for the first time was like putting myself into character, belting up a better, stronger version of myself? The clothes and the warrant card, the cuffs and the baton, magically combined to convey a sense of power I lacked in all other ways, the power I needed to show what I could do, without the university education other people not living in the arse end of nowhere, but in a decent area with wealthy parents seem to take for granted.

Qualify, transfer, shine: that's been my simple career plan. Solve a big case. Make a high-profile arrest. Save a life. Arc like a bright star in the police firmament, right into a string of promotions and a glass-walled office in the Metropolitan Police, with silver pips on my collar and stripes on my hat. I just needed the opportunity.

It helps to be pretty, too, and pleasant and amenable. Being pretty makes people think you are good and happy and confident. It also helps to be 'the face of the future', though I hadn't called myself that, obviously. It was the phrase my recruitment officer used when I signed up, not shy about admitting that our rural force badly needed to fill its imposed government quota of female officers.

Embracing 'positive discrimination' they'd called it, which seemed like a contradiction in terms, though I didn't argue. I needed all the help I could get to enact my escape plan.

Staring at Billy Fisket's sad photo on the screen I'm doubly determined not to end up a Pont failure statistic when things suddenly start to move; an urgent request for a press release and media appeal pops up on the incident log that's been constantly running in the background, and there's also a call for all the road closed signs and cordon tape in the area to be wrangled into place, for requests to go out to support agencies and the council road teams.

Most notably a firearms response team is being called in from Carmarthen and put on standby – the big boys with their big arms, bigger swagger and massive guns are on their way. There's no doubt that for the first time ever we have an active manhunt on our hands – a killer on the run.

Wanting to be ready when we get the call, I pull on my big boots with the double thick rubber soles and check my belt kit. The situation already has a nice cinematic quality to it – a bloodied Billy Fisket in the cells and a homicidal fugitive fleeing into the gathering storm – and all the makings of a great crime story.

Forgetting the dead woman on her kitchen floor for a moment, forgetting the grieving husband in the hospital, I sip my tea and allow myself a little smile. The day looks promising for once.

The Hitchhiker – 11 a.m.

'Thanks for stopping,' I say, my best smile aimed at the open-a-crack window of the car that's shuddered to a halt in front of me. I'm doing my best to radiate an air of unthreatening reassurance; I hope it's working.

At each crest of the road for the last two miles I'd been expecting to see a cluster of town houses, a triangle of lights signifying a Christmas tree on a high street, but there'd been only winter gloom. Just when I was finally considering turning round and heading back to the village I'd heard the familiar sound of tyres on tarmac, seen the headlights and thought, Enough playing silly buggers.

The car is heading the wrong way, back towards town, but I really need to at least ask directions, or get a lift to somewhere else. I should be well away from here by now instead of going round in circles. So I'd put myself square in the road this time, forcing the battered Ford Focus to slam on its brakes to avoid me. It feels like an ambush, which it is, as the woman inside promptly stalls her car in panic, clearly not happy.

She's relieved, though, when she sees that the alarming hitchhiker who almost caused her to crash is a woman too, not a lurking madman, though women can be all sorts of things these days. We pitch in, sleeves rolled up with the lads. Some of the toughest lads I know are women – Lil, for example.

Now that we're at a standoff I give my best reassuring wave as a welcome breath of heat comes from the gap in the car window as she rolls it down. Before the woman can think of refusing me I shout, 'Thanks for stopping,' jogging around to the passenger door and pulling it open with a forceful swing of my arm. I'd had a feeling it wouldn't be locked, people are trusting in these parts. Stupid buggers.

'All right if I jump in?' I ask. 'I'm going wherever you're going. Great!' before the woman can reply. 'Though, pop the boot for my bag first, will you?'

For a second I think she's going to object, try and pull the door shut, skid off and leave me. She's eyeing me up and down, my snow-wet boots, my stained outdoor jacket. I know I don't cut a sophisticated figure, so I up the wattage on my grin, which has the right effect because the woman relents and says, 'Boot's full of junk. Shove it on the back seat.'

Before she can change her mind I pull open the back door and shove my pack in, clocking the child seat encrusted with crumbs and what looks like a few ancient M&M's as I do so. Good, a mummy. So far, so easy.

'Cheers. Thanks so much.' I nod, as the woman hauls her own bag protectively into her lap, dropping it into the footwell behind her. I slide in, slamming the door on the snow flurries that try to follow me, realising I've just trodden on a toy rabbit and some pieces of a chunky plastic jigsaw puzzle. There are several empty pop cartons in the footwell, too.

'Much obliged,' I say, laying on a shiver of cold and rubbing my hands together while I look her over. She's wrapped in a tatty pink parka-style anorak, too big for her, shiny with wear. She's a skinny thing, roughly the same age as me, I'm guessing, mid-twenties, with dark eyeliner that's smudged a bit. She looks like she hasn't had much sleep in the last few days – that makes two of us.

'Where are you headed?' I ask, though it's obviously only one way in the first instance, the wrong way, back towards town.

'I was going home,' she says, jerking her thumb behind us, 'but there's a bloody massive tree down back there, right across the road – can't get the car through. I had to turn around.'

'Kids to pick up? Boy or girl?' I ask, cocking my head towards the child seat in the back.

'Oh.' Her face doesn't soften when she says, 'A boy,' then adds, 'four years old.'

'Just the one, then?'

'Yes.'

Kid-talk is always acceptable car-journey conversation with mummies, it's something to chat about to this woman with her pink, shiny parka and pink lipstick. Sighing, she reaches to restart the car, the stall initiated by the emergency stop.

'I'm Lee by the way,' I say, to exchange pleasantries and establish a sense of camaraderie. It's good to do this as it makes people think you're a safe bet. They lower their guard if you give them a name. Any name will do.

'That makes me Rebecca, then,' says the mum, turning the ignition key.

I know my driver's name already. I can see the plastic nametag with the local-authority crest clipped on the parka's pocket next to a grinning Santa brooch covered in faded glitter. The woman catches my glance and grins unexpectedly.

'Becca, to you then, I guess, as we're travel friends now.'

Travel friends, right. I don't like the name Rebecca, it sounds biblical, starchy for some reason, and I like Becca even less. Becca is a name for a make-up artist or gossip columnist. If I was called Rebecca I think I'd change it to something else sharpish, so people would take me seriously. That's why I never use my proper name any more. It never really suited me.

'Glad you came by, Becca,' I say, putting out my hand.

She takes it reluctantly and drops it immediately as the radio crackles in and out, fighting its own snow-static. There's something on the news, an update about a road closure, but I can't hear where. There's something else too, about a police cordon going up. Great! That's all I need right now, coppers on the prowl. Luckily Becca reaches across to change the channel, but it's muttering something similar. It's all over the news.

'You on home visits today?' I ask, to keep my new chauffeur distracted.

'What?' she snaps, grinding the key in the ignition slot so hard I wince.

'I saw the card in the front window – you're a nurse, right? Guess you guys are busy in this weather?'

Becca looks at me for a moment then smiles.

'Aren't you ever so eagle-eyed? Yes, I'm a nurse.'

OK, good, I can work with that. That's how I'll think of her from now on. I feel less stupid saying it than using the name Becca. We are what we do, right?

The nurse turns the ignition again, but the engine splutters before it dies.

'Must be the cold,' she says redundantly. 'Shit. Come on. Come on! I have to get back home.'

'OK,' I reply, practising my patience. 'Try turning the radio and the lights off, now put your foot on the clutch. Now turn the ignition again.'

It sputters and, for a moment, looks promising, but then it dies again just as quickly. 'Do you think you're out of petrol?' I ask.

The nurse stares wearily at the gauge, before slamming both hands on the wheel. 'Shit! I don't believe it. Bloody typical.'

So much for my lift. I suck in a breath as my patience prickles, suddenly growing horns and thorns. I repeat my mantra silently to myself as we both sit in the car, staring out of the windscreen at the swirling snow. Jesus Christ, can this day get any worse?

'We should probably start walking, then?' says the nurse after a moment. 'Can't just stay here,' but she makes no move to do any such thing, peering through the windscreen again.

I'm not sure it's a good idea myself. It might be better to shelter in the car for a bit, until it passes over. It's getting steadily worse out there, the sky lowering its white head down to the treetops, but then again, who's likely to pass by and help us out now if we don't help ourselves? We might get a phone signal if there's a break in the trees, maybe we could call the AA, but I hardly want that – I don't need more people seeing me today. I pull out my phone yet again, but there are still no bars, which ends that option.

'Do you have any signal?' I ask, though the nurse is shaking her head as she looks at her own phone.

'No charge on it. Stupid really, I just forget to plug it in all the time.'

No fucking petrol, now no phone charge? I'm already regretting flagging this dopey bird down. I really don't want to be carrying a dead weight for the rest of the day. I contemplate getting out and saying, Well, thanks ever so much anyway, and fucking off back to town on my own. I could make it at a fast pace, before it gets too late. Then again, people often underestimate the elements and their own frailty before them, and how quickly things can go wrong if you don't stay on your toes.

The whole world is balanced on a precipice, teetering, tottering, left, right, backwards, forwards. The rope frays a little more with every decision, the grip slips as the wind picks up.

I realise the nurse is eyeing me intently, waiting for me to take the lead by the looks of it, before making a suggestion: 'I'd like to get to a phone,' she says. 'Not far beyond that downed tree is a pub, I think. Looked pretty shut up when I last passed, but we might get lucky. It's a mile or so that way, maybe.'

She points onwards, and I generally thinks that onwards is better than backwards, but she seems a bit vague for my liking.

'You *think* there's a pub? You're not sure?'

My patience is pricking my insides now, a handful of reverse porcupine quills drawing blood under the skin. I hear Pam say, Breathe in, breathe out, and I try to obey.

'Well, this isn't a way I come that often. I got called out for work.'

'This isn't part of your rounds?'

'Not really, I'm covering today – you know, the snow. People can't make it in. So, what are you anyway, a detective with all these questions?' She grins at her own joke. 'Are you out here wandering the roads because you couldn't get to work?'

'No, I'm . . . between jobs right now.' Not that it's any of her business.

'Home for Christmas?' She jerks her head at my pack in the back seat.

'Yeah.' Sure, if you say so.

'Gotta love it, Christmas. Nice for the kids.'

'Quite,' I say, thinking that a pub, even a closed one, would provide some shelter.

The nurse suddenly looks nervous and I realise I'm probably scowling, my foot tapping the floor of the footwell. I often make people nervous, it's one of my assets, but I make an effort to stop the drumming and smooth out my face.

'Safety in numbers?' says the nurse, seizing the initiative. 'Better if there're two of us, right?'

Of course she would think that, this pretty, dainty little thing, gripping the wheel with skinny wrists it would take just a second to snap. I make myself breathe, then, after a moment, force myself to smile as she flicks the headlights off. By mutual silent agreement we both unclick our seatbelts and open our doors onto the afternoon.

At once, the car fills with icy air and white powder, and I sigh as I open the back door once again, pulling out my pack as the nurse scrambles to get her bag from the footwell. She's stopped with the bloody car canted half out into the road, but there's not a lot we can do about it.

'We should probably push this to the side,' I suggest, gesturing to the nurse to get back in and steer while I shove from the back, but she cuts me off.

'Leave it. No one's coming this way tonight.'

'You did,' I mutter. I don't want a car in the middle of the road to attract unwanted attention but the nurse doesn't look like she's keen to cooperate. Fuck it, let's get going.

As we set off I think I hear a low buzzing in the woods above us, off to the left, high up, over the far crest of trees. I listen carefully. Could it be a helicopter, up in this weather? Surely not? No one would risk it. Unless they're above it, above the worst of the cloud . . . But it could just be the wind in the treetops, or a motor of some sort. Anyway, it's gone as quickly as it came. We pull up our hoods and start to walk.

The Old Man – 11 a.m.

Something has happened. Something is very wrong.

It's not good, this feeling of being afloat. A dark sea of some sort shifts under his bed, rolls and pitches. It's also inside his head, the roiling sea, so he can't make his eyes stay still, fix them on anything solid.

His first thought, as he struggles to make his slack hands work on top of the bed sheets, is that the bitch has dosed him again. She's done it before, he's sure of that, more than once since the first time, the day he'd tried to get up and get to the phone, to get to the door, to get away. When was that, though? When he'd found her out, yes, what she was up to, but how long ago was that? A month, a year? He can't quite . . .

He stares at the ceiling, at the silver-foil star swirling on its string, listening to the raised voice far below his bed in the main bar. The twitchy oaf is shouting with a red-in-the-face voice below the gapped floorboards. He's pacing, calling *her*, no doubt. No love lost there as far as he can tell, not least because she's a total bitch.

He's not heard the twitchy oaf retaliate until now, but he's seen it coming. It's the quiet ones you have to watch; they lose it, lash out and fight back. The ones who store it all up and then one day just explode, like Brian used to sometimes. It was always startling to watch, the tantrum, the explosion of little feet and fists. He'd like to see her get what's coming to her and if it's the twitchy oaf who does it that's fine with him.

He tries to shift his right arm, to get to the stick by his bed, but it seems impossible to make a fist, so slow, so slow. He can only raise his head an inch or two now, to see the object of his attention . . . Of course, the lad must have done it – doped him. Was it because he'd been screaming, trying to get out of bed again? Shouting, 'Who the fuck are you? Who the fuck are you?' while the twitchy oaf kept on insisting he be quiet, 'Come on now. You'll just make it worse.'

'Why are you here?' he'd tried to sputter. 'This is my home. You don't belong here.' Because he doesn't know this lad, does he? Though there's so much the stroke has taken from him; his mind is a jigsaw with missing pieces, faces change without warning, names slip their tags and run away from him into dark corners.

'Be quiet,' the oaf insisted. 'Lie back, for God's sake.'

Why had he been trying to get up in the first place? Was it because he'd heard the front door? A knock on the door, downstairs? Yes! But was that today? Or was that before? He thinks he'd managed to raise himself up onto his arms, though he couldn't work his voice into more than a croak, to call out and say, 'I'm up here. Please come.'

There'd been shouting then, angry voices and angrier feet on the stairs. Then what?

Is it still today? Has he been asleep?

His eyes wander towards the bedroom door, then towards the window where the snow dances against the blackness. He hears a dog howl outside in the afternoon. Strange, because he doesn't have a dog any more. Tigger was a terrier but Tigger is buried out back; Tigger with his speckled white belly and silky brown ears. Tigger liked bits of bacon . . .

Is it time yet? He can't seem to remember. Is someone coming? Is he expecting someone?

He thinks he remembers a dream, or a fragment of one, about Brian, coming back to see him at last. In his dreams Brian is always a young man and he arrives at the pub unexpectedly. He brings a pretty wife who holds his hand and they all hug. Then a mop-haired little one peers out from behind Brian's legs and he says, 'And this is your granddaughter, or grandson,' he doesn't mind which, because the child has Brian's ginger bouncing curls and the soft wife's easy smile. Then Brian leans over him and says, 'I love you, Dad. I'm sorry I was away for so long, but I'm here now. I know you meant no harm.'

He's woken from these dreams in tears, many times. This dream was different, though. Brian was old in it. He'd looked like a middle-aged man, as he would be now, somewhere at least, out there on his oil rig in the Scottish sea. His ginger hair was almost all silver-grey and he was pretty fat, heavy in the shoulders and under his chin, his hands plump and pink.

In the dream he looked like he'd been crying too, his eyes sore and red. He had a bristly, unshaved chin. He'd leaned in and felt his breath and then felt Brian's lips on his forehead, Brian's tears dripping onto his skin. It was an odd dream.

He stares at the silver-foil star above his bed, wishing he could rip it from its all-seeing spot, put out its mocking eye, but right now it would be like trying to pluck a real star from the sky. It's about as far away and just as impossible to reach.

'Season's greetings,' she'd said, 'Christmas is coming,' when she'd hung it there, the bitch, smiling as she did it. She wasn't being pleasant. It was just another jolly cruelty. That's why she'd brought the old carrier bag up to his room and fished the shiny bits of Christmas stuff out of it.

Following the star on its string she'd added a balding rope of red tinsel to the dresser top, twined two gold ones around the bedposts and added a moronic, grinning Father Christmas on the windowsill. Then she'd carried in that bloody balding three-foot donkey, part of the nativity scene he'd resurrected each year, out front, to amuse the kids, and plonked it by his bed. She must have dug it and the bag of decorations out of the cellar, poking around.

'And look what else I found.' She'd grinned, pulling a rumple of yellowed paper from the bag. 'A nice Christmas card. Probably the only one you'll get.'

He'd recognised it immediately. On the front was a crayoned Christmas tree. Inside sat a fat robin with a bright orange breast whose paper beak opened and closed on the crease of the card.

'Dear Mam and Dad, Merry Christmas, love from Bri,' she'd read aloud in a mock affectionate voice, 'Aw, very sweet. Happy memories. Shame you spoiled all that, you old perv.'

She'd held it right up to his face so he could see the writing, the effortfully pressed red pencil on the paper. Something had broken open inside him then, bleeding liquid into his chest. He'd tried to wave it away, grimacing, turning his head, trying to cough out the pain.

'Now, now, don't be a Scroogey old git.' She'd smiled, teeth sharp as blades, enjoying herself.

'Let's put this nice card over here, right where you can see it.'

She'd placed it on the windowsill, next to the photo of them all as a family, when they'd still been a family. June sunlight on the trees; Rose, young next to him, actually smiling; Brian leaning against him, his shock of red hair against his white, bare leg.

'This place needs some cheering up,' she'd said. 'We'll make it our top job, spruce and a clean, all ready for the festive season, for any Christmas callers. And if you're good there's a mince pie for you later. Yes, it's a bit early, but who knows how long you have left. Why wait, right?'

Of course, she doesn't actually want him to pop off too soon. That would put paid to her nice little habits, wouldn't it? If he's lucky she'll go first, fall down some icy steps and break her neck. Ten years ago it would have been the work of a moment to fling himself out from under the sheets and throttle her.

She'd probably known what he was thinking at that moment because she'd just laughed. The threats of the old are the emptiest of them all.

He tries to look at the card now, but he can't quite focus

on it, or on the photo. The faces and edges are blurry, everything is softening again, slurring out of shape.

Something has happened. He knows that much. But he's underwater once more and the light is fading away.

The Hitchhiker – 12 noon

I want to keep moving, striding out, making time, but as we trudge along the tree-lined road the nurse is slowing me down. Her pale-blue Converse lace-ups aren't helping things; they're not exactly a practical choice of footwear for a day like this, and I wonder why she didn't check the weather forecast in advance.

I don't understand her, this girly girl beside me whose shoes have shiny stars on them but whose coat smells faintly of chicken soup. In my opinion nurses should look like nurses, even if they're making home visits. It's not as if they're off to the pub to drink wine spritzers, or off to the shops for a packet of fags.

I'd like to say, Well, if you don't mind I'll just scout on up ahead a bit and you can catch up later, but I don't. The nurse is right, sometimes there's safety in numbers. If the police are already looking for someone, they aren't looking for two people, travelling together.

I try to pick up the pace a bit, pleased to see the nurse matching me as best she can. I'm surprised we haven't bumped into the driver of the other car yet, the rusty heap from a mile back. Chances are they would've walked this way too, as they obviously haven't turned around to meet us on their way back. Of course, they could still be up ahead, making good time instead of mincing along.

'You see anyone walking along here earlier? When you were driving?' I ask. 'Did anyone pass you.'

'Nope, no one. Why?' panting a little from the effort of stabilising her rubber soles on the slush.

'You sure? There was a car back there, no one inside it. Someone stuck or broken down.'

'I've seen no one but you. What are you doing out here anyway, all on your own, in the dark?'

There's a touch of accusation in her voice, the unspoken criticism, It's not safe, not for a girl on her own, and I feel a scrape of annoyance at what's implied: that I'm being irresponsible, hitchhiking on a lonely road like this. My patience chafes the roof of my mouth as I swallow the words, You know fuck all about me, love. I'll fare a lot better than you if anything goes down today. No petrol, no phone charge, no walking boots in your car. If I weighed eight stone soaking wet I'd make sure I never got stuck on a winter road without back-up.

Complacency is a killer, that's what Purvis says, Purvis who self-styles himself as a Zen master guru with a bit of bullshit, Jap-slapping, Kung-Fu-warrior crap thrown in. His assembled philosophy mainly entails pairing pearls of received wisdom with kicks to the nuts. He likes to think he's a bit like Buddha, if Buddha wasn't averse to kicking the shit out of anyone who crossed his path. He's not here, of course, so he can shut the fuck up.

'Couldn't get a lift,' I say, in delayed answer to her question, though I've taken so long to reply she's already lost interest. 'You like being a nurse?' I ask, changing the subject. Can't quite see this one giving bed baths and slopping out bedpans, but maybe it's a case of needs must – we all have to earn a living, and in a place like this the options aren't varied. Maybe she's a single mum, one of the many around here. At least she has a job. Sure the countryside can be pretty as hell when the rain isn't coming in sideways, but it can also be twice as hard.

The nurse looks at me for a moment, like she knows what I'm thinking, and then she smiles. 'It's a vocation. Caring for people.'

Before I can think of a suitable reply, she adds, 'See? Told you so,' pointing ahead through the swirling sheets of snow.

I follow her finger to where, a few dozen yards ahead, the road narrows and the overhanging branches of the trees crowding alongside it create a natural tunnel. Towards the end, almost lost in the gloom inside, a vast old oak has crashed across the lane. As we approach, and the lattice of boughs above gives us a welcome break from the blowing snow, I can see it must weigh several tons; its trunk is more than a yard across, ringed with the circling of centuries.

A chaos of roots bars the way at one end, a head of smashed branches at the other and it's clear that no car is coming through from the other side of that tonight. We both stop short, catching our breath, surveying the damage and the decision it's about to force on us.

'Pub's just down there on the other side, about half a mile I think,' says the nurse, panting.

'You think?' I say, though I have an inkling she might be right. Something about this hill is vaguely familiar.

'These woods, they all look the same, OK?' a note of defensiveness bristles in her voice. 'I told you, I don't know this area that well. It's no more than a mile, I reckon.'

Not wanting to take her at her word I answer by finding a foothold and hoisting myself up the side of the trunk, planting my feet firmly and peering down the road on the other side. Beyond the branches it descends into a narrow valley, a trace of grey winding through the black and white relief of the closely wooded fields. Across the sharp dip it climbs steeply back to our level, Roman-straight, a pale ribbon, slick with snow and ice.

I can imagine a legion of jerkin-wrapped, sandal-shod soldiers marching in formation down that hill, cold and hungry, helmets glinting in imaginary moonlight.

Evidence of ancient occupation is etched all across this country, the long-abandoned forts and almost-echo of tramping feet, attempts at conquest defeated by the stubborn landscape and the gleefully untamed people with their sullen, savage ways.

I always think it must have been quite an exile, to be an invader stationed here, at the rag-end of the Roman Empire, dreaming of fields of golden grain and goblets of wine. The incomers always get a foothold eventually, though. Times they are always a-changing. Everything is in flux – the tide washes in and then washes out. Every country was once someone else's.

It doesn't bother me. I suppose I've never really thought

of this as mine, as home. I never really felt part of it, as if I was treading on strange soil, breathing unfamiliar air in an unnatural habitat.

Squinting through the soupy semi-darkness of this December day I think I see, among the bare trees, maybe half a mile below, the graphic broken lines of what looks like a roof. If we get down there without breaking a leg it looks like our best bet.

With a touch of heavy melodrama a flying disc of daylight moon flits into view above the valley through a break in the snow cover before the swirl resumes. It could be a sign, if I believed in signs, an omen, a signal from the universe to light us on our way. Onwards. But the universe takes pleasure in being obtuse, obscure. Or just being a bit of an arsehole.

'Well?' asks the nurse. 'What do you see?'

I see that we have a choice, climb over the tree trunk and head down the hill, or turn around and walk maybe two hours back to the village bus shelter and the community hall. The nurse pulls her tatty parka closer as I hold up my phone, waving it into the air one last time, willing the ether to reveal its electronic signal. The nurse raises her perfectly tweezed eyebrows and shakes her head before I ask, 'OK, are you up for it?' cocking my head up and over the trunk.

By way of reply she picks up my massive backpack from the base of the trunk and shoves it up towards me with a grunt. Then she walks to what looks like the most likely handhold and scrambles up, using the knots as footholds and the branches to heave and pull.

I'm impressed by this sudden grit. She's stronger than she looks and I think about saying well done, until the pocket of her anorak tears open on a broken spur and a trickle of brightly coloured sweets slips out alongside a lip gloss.

'The treats are for the kid,' says the nurse with a sigh.

Course they are. I know bribe currency when I see it. Everyone can be bought with the right one. Adult currency isn't so different – cigarettes, sex and alcohol, all the tools to help you melt out of yourself, to escape reality for a while, or at least blunt the edges. My weapon of choice is whisky, older the better – one of them, at least.

'You coming or what?' asks the nurse, her feet already thudding on the snow on the other side of the trunk.

'Watch out,' I warn, dropping my pack over onto the road where it lands with a hefty thump.

'Jesus, what have you got in there? It weighs a ton.'

'Just clothes really, some of my stuff.'

'Doing a runner or coming home from one?'

I stiffen. That comment is a little too close to the mark, though the nurse can't know that. She's smiling.

'Sort of both.'

'Been backpacking or something – a little bit of travelling? Gap year thing?'

'Been studying away, that's all. Bag's full of washing. Let's get on.'

I'm not about to share my experiences to pass the time. It'll only freak the nurse out if I tell her the truth and say where I've been for the last two years, one month and twenty-six days. And before that.

I set a challenging pace again, hoping she'll be too out of breath to ask any more nosy questions. The snow's deeper and undisturbed on this side of the tree-fall. Scuffing our way onward for what seems like an age we eventually reach the valley floor, and there it is. The trees peel back without warning to reveal the front of a long, low building squatting in the darkness.

It's a pub all right, but it's totally missed the whole gastro-pub refurbishment movement. You certainly wouldn't be tempted to pop in here for a rare rib-eye steak and a cheeky Rioja. Its days of pushing out chicken and chips in a basket are long past too. It doesn't even look occupied, let alone open to the public.

The only other building nearby is a chapel, tilting at the roadside directly opposite. A canted iron fence rings the churchyard, high with bushes, so just their tops crest the wild growth.

A quick glance at the pub confirms that all the windows are dark. The old pub sign, which must once have hung on the rusted chains hanging from the iron bar over the lintel, is propped against the front wall bearing the words 'Y Seren' or 'The Star', its blistered yellow image, once picked out in gilded paint, guiding the weary to a place of rest and refreshment, now faded to murky yellow.

Star of wonder, star of light, star with royal beauty bright, I think, lyrics dredged up from seasonal radio overload as I give it a professional appraisal: a safe place for the night, good for a kip, once-over. The structure itself looks intact, no obvious holes in the roof or collapsed window frames, but it's old and ageing badly, the far wall bowing slightly away from its base.

Judging by the squat floors and trestled windows it dates back to, maybe, the eighteenth century. A stagecoach wouldn't look out of place halted at the old hitching post, and with an unexpected smile I remember a story Old Happy told me once, when he still had two thumbs, about a mail coach travelling from London to Aberystwyth that was attacked by a lion, an actual lion, all majestic mane and mighty roar.

The beast had escaped from a travelling zoo and burst from the trees to maul the seventeen-year-old postilion and shying horses. The brave passengers fought it off and killed it with pistols and clubs, enabling His Majesty's mail to be delivered, not an hour late. In Old Happy's words, the moral of the story was to 'expect the unexpected and be prepared to do it'. A good motto, as it turns out.

For years afterwards he'd grin with his browned stump teeth and say, 'Look out for lions, little girly. Be ready.'

As I jumped into the back of Dad's jeep the story of the terrible lion always tinged my travels with the possibility of fur and fangs – a cautionary tale about what you might meet in the dark woods.

'Lions, tigers and bears,' I mutter, comforted that at least tonight I'm probably the most dangerous thing abroad in the dark.

I glance down and spot a road sign that still just about reads, Halfway, a timely reminder for travellers that they are exactly at the midpoint between where they are going and where they are coming from – wherever that is!

This is pretty amusing in the light of what's happened over the last twenty-four hours. In many ways I'm at the midpoint of my own life right now, a sort of existential crisis you could say, wholly unexpectedly. It's just as far to go on now as it is to go back. It's time to make a choice, to choose a direction, and here I am in a place that seems to exist only for that reason – where people stop for a moment on their way but never stay.

Perhaps the universe sometimes has a sense of humour after all. If I get out of all this I must tell Lil.

'Christ, what a dump,' says the nurse, interrupting my train of thought. 'Just the sort of place you want to call into for help on a winter's night, I *don't* think. Who the hell lives in a place like this anyway, in the back end of beyond?'

Good question. Only the dead seem present and accounted for in the churchyard opposite and on the weathered marble war memorial next to the pub dedicated to 'The Fallen'. I draw my hand across the plaque, dusting off some snow, revealing the men of this parish, twenty-seven names, thick with Welsh consonants, Ap-Llewellyn, Rhydderch, Pryce. 'How the mighty are fallen,' I whisper to those congregated in this hollow among the hills.

'If you're done talking to yourself, how about we see if anyone's home,' says the nurse, impatiently walking the length of the pub, making a huffing noise every few paces.

At the far end of the forecourt there's an old mews entrance with a car parked under the arch. It's newish-looking, a sensible four-by-four and, by the tracks at my feet, it's clearly been parked quite recently with some foresight, out of the snow that's beginning to drift up over the rear tyres and number plate.

'I think someone's home,' I say.

'Yeah, bloody Count Dracula probably.'

As if on cue, a dog hidden somewhere in the back gives a great, wolfish howl.

'Seriously?' asks the nurse. 'That dog sounds really pissed off.'

We both tense, expecting to see a slavering jaw attached to the hound of hell lollop out of the darkness – it's that kind of place. When none appears I make up my mind instantly, think, Sod this, and walk to the heavy wooden door.

'Let's try our luck,' I say, taking a firm grip on the iron knocker, raising it and letting it fall, once, twice, three times. The metal on wood crashes like cannon shot through the silence.

Knock, knock. Who's there?

Spiky snowflakes pepper our clothes and eyelashes while we wait for an answer as, in the woods behind us, a great cloak of crows explodes with shared cries into the lowering sky.

Then inside, something moves.

The Old Man – 12 noon

It's colder than ever now. He needs a blanket but no one has come to check on him for ages. He's so very sleepy but he must stay awake because there's something important he has to do. He has to get out of bed, but he's not sure why – and he's so very tired. He has to try and focus on the room around him, save his strength, be ready for when *she* returns.

Lying there, he's flushed with hot embarrassment to think how it had taken him almost six months to realise what she was doing. He'd first suspected when he'd seen the new gold chain around her neck, when she was always pleading poverty, always moaning about the kids and mouths to feed, the bills to pay, as she puffed his pillows and spooned soup into his mouth.

He hadn't said anything immediately, he hadn't wanted to get on her bad side over a mistake, to accuse her outright when he had no real proof, just ferrety suspicions, scratching away at the back door of his brain. It would be terrible to accuse someone of something like that, of being a thief, if it was unfounded. He knows better than most how it feels to be faced with unjust accusations, the subject of sneering lies.

He'd felt awkward about even mentioning it – shouldn't there be more money left in the grocery fund, enough for another week, surely? Weren't there five fifties in the envelope this time, not two?

He could easily have been wrong, his mind wasn't exactly reliable, but he should have known, it wasn't just the stroke.

Of course she'd had an answer for everything, saying the post was late when he'd asked if the monthly amount had come, then making out they'd already had the exact same conversation the day before, wide-eyed and slightly concerned that he'd already forgotten: 'I told you. I already paid it in for you.' Her wistful smile implying his memory was finally failing, that he was going dotty, senile, losing his faculties – poor chap, poor old dear, how sad.

Then she'd kept saying she couldn't find his Post Office book when he'd ask to see it, that they were sending another one out to him, that it was all under control, she'd sort it for him, with Mr Blass in town. He'd heard impatience creeping into her voice then, felt it in the rough way she'd helped him onto the bedpan. She'd soon started to let him know that she could make things hard for him if he kept on 'misbehaving', if he insisted on 'being awkward', on being a 'bad egg' all the time.

She didn't say it outright. There were more subtle methods – bringing him food he didn't like if he was rude to her, forgetting to put the fire on before she left, leaving him shivering all night. By then, after the second stroke, he was more or less confined to his bed, his limbs clawed and disobedient, but his mind still ranging through the hours, pacing inside his skull, frustrated, caged behind the effort of the sounds his lips tried to make.

She'd started to dope him up at the end of the summer. Maybe it was just to make her life easier at first, but there was that time when the doctor called, the day after he'd threatened to complain about her, to say what he thought she'd been up to. He'd heard her talking about him, standing at the foot of the bed while he'd drifted in and out of a sticky, narcotic sleep.

'Well, Doctor, he has his good and his bad days,' in her best fake, compassionate voice. 'This is one of the not-so-good days.'

He'd felt her smiling, flush with fake pity, patting his ankle through the blankets, 'Here are his charts, all up to date.'

How could he tell anyone about the little impatiences and indignities he's endured since then? Over the weeks and months?

'Look, you dirty old fucker,' she'd exploded after the doctor had left, after he'd come round from his heavy sleep, after he'd lost his temper like a child, shouted – well, gargled with sloppy fury – pumped his legs in a geriatric tantrum, 'Bitch, bitch, bitch.'

'Let's not pretend I don't know what you are,' she'd spat. 'Kids need new shoes and clothes and I need to pay for the fucking gas and electricity and all the food that's scarfed down. So you can try and tell whoever you like. No one will believe you. I'll just tell them you're rambling and going senile at last.

'Which of us will they believe? What are you going to do with that money anyway? Hire Thai rent boys to wank you off in your dribbling old age? I'd bet fifty quid you haven't been able to get it up in years. Now shut up and stay still or you'll make things worse for yourself. You've got it good, you know. More than your kind deserves, and it could be much worse, I assure you of that.'

Things were clear between them after that, all pretence dropped. The unfairness almost overwhelmed him. How dare she call him a dirty old man! He'd railed in his head and through his gummed mouth and it had brought on a worse turn than before.

Now that reinforcements have appeared in the form of the twitchy oaf, he's a prisoner either way, but it won't be for ever.

Someone will come. Brian's been sending his cheques regular as clockwork for years – even if he hasn't wanted to speak to his father he hasn't forgotten him. Maybe it was those last letters the old man wrote, when he could still hold a pen, that got through to him, swayed him into wanting to come back. He'd felt he had to make the first move, before it was too late, then, weeks later, the lifeline had arrived: a letter in return. When Brian gets back he'll give that bitch and the twitchy oaf what for.

But when is that?

A pain seizes his chest like an iron fist and his neck twists into a rope of agony. Oh Christ, not again, please! There's nowhere near enough left of him, he can't lose any more. He has to be ready, but ready for who? He has the terrible feeling he's forgotten something important. He's waiting for something important but his thoughts are unravelling. The sea calls again, the sea of losing himself.

Brian likes the sea. Brian likes to take the red kayak out around the rock pools. He should probably start on Brian's tea soon. Chips and egg. He'll be home from his adventures with Gary any minute, grubby, laughing, starving. What's for tea, Dad? He'll start peeling the spuds in a minute. He just needs to sleep for a little bit first . . .

The Law – 12 noon

OK, it's only twelve o'clock but I'm already bored. It's normal apparently, for the momentum of the hours to slow down after the first fuss-rush of the opening ninety minutes of an incident, at least according to Jim, because I wouldn't know. He says we've entered the hiatus between the initial discovery, the securing of the crime scene and the slower stages of the follow-up inquiries.

'Patience, love, they'll call us eventually,' he says, seeing my restlessness, and I hope he's right.

There's no doubt we're well out of the loop here, excluded, on the back foot, struggling to get any more concrete information about what's happening now we're into slow-time waiting for updates to drop on the incident log. Then, by luck, one of Jim's ex-probationers pops his head around the door, tasked with collecting all the extra road-closed and scene-management boards that are stored in our unused back room.

'Hey, ladies, what's cooking?' asks PC Ty Podmore, a podgy bearded bear of a nice guy I'm quite fond of. He's clearly gay, but not annoyingly proud of it so, as far as I know, no one gives him any gyp about it. I actually find this a bit annoying because at least once a week some old dinosaur always asks me to make him a cup of tea or calls me hun, but I tell myself it's only temporary. When I'm an inspector they'll all have to call me boss or ma'am.

'A big fat slice of hurry up and wait,' says Jim in response to Ty's hail. 'Unless you can enlighten us further, dear Officer Podmore?'

As it happens Ty's just bursting to tell us how, twenty minutes ago, he'd had a nice chat with the desk sergeant at Central, where Billy Fisket is being interviewed. (I strongly suspect Patrick on the desk is his current boyfriend, but that's none of my business and, luckily for us, Pat is a motormouth.)

'Apparently Fisket is blubbing in the interview room as we speak,' says Ty, huffing arms full of kit from the back room into the boot of his four-by-four as we watch.

I'm ready to lend a hand if strictly necessary, more than a bit jealous that he's actually getting to do something in all this, no matter how small, as he continues.

'Well, Pat says Fisket's pouring out some stupid fucking story about a big take, one last big job. That's what him and this Finn character were up there for, apparently, at the farm. They supposedly met up in Birmingham, while Billy was on licence up there, hatched this stupid plot because he'd been running his mouth about the old dears being secretly loaded.'

'What? The Lewises? Seriously?' asks Jim, voicing what I'm thinking.

'Yeah, I know. Billy himself doesn't seem sure why they'd

still be living in that wreck of a house if they're sitting on a secret nest egg, only that the old pair had supposedly minted away a fortune or something! Can you believe it? Looks now like it wasn't just an opportunist "break and take" after all, but a planned job. Albeit the world's dumbest one – but that's Fisket for you! Moron!'

So here it is, the first hint of the all-important motive we've been waiting for this morning, the reason why there'd been a terrible knock on the door of Ridgeback Farm last night, rather than anywhere else.

Now I'm desperate to learn more about Billy's 'plan', which was responsible for this morning's horror, but it seems Podmore is on the clock for Inspector Morris's team and that's the only new stuff he knows. Declining Carron's offered cuppa and accepting the Kit-Kat I press into his hand, he rushes off into the afternoon snow, leaving us to hurry back inside, noses and fingers already frozen.

'For fuck's sake! That Fisket's a stupid bloody bugger!' explodes Jim as we ruminate at my desk. 'What was he thinking of? Why was he messing around with someone like this Finn character? What did he think would happen?'

He slumps back into a chair before slamming the desk so hard that Carron spills her tea. 'Yes of course the old dears are secretly loaded and have tons of shit worth stealing! Like all old recluses living in houses that are falling down around their ears, they simply *must* have a fortune in cash to spare, or a bag of gold sovereigns tucked under their mattress. I mean, come on, the Ark of the bloody Covenant is probably stashed away in the cow shed, right? Even the bloody loot from the Dolau gold robbery has most likely been stuck down the back of their old settee for fifty years.'

The Dolau armed robbery is, of course, second on the Pont infamy list under the Bedford Row deaths. As kids, me and my brothers had regularly gone looking for the missing Dolau gold hoard, spending summer's evenings on the beach, in the woods, pretend pirates with bandanas tied around our brows, digging out hopeful little piles of sand or earth.

Since I'd first heard the tale from my dad I'd fantasised about solving it. Every copper has, I suspect, especially Jim, because everyone knows his dad, ten years a retired inspector now, had actually been a young PC on the scene.

I've never tired of hearing how, once-upon-a-time on an airless August afternoon, a man in a balaclava walked calmly up to the counter of the jewellers on the high street with a pistol in his hand, ordered the woman at the desk to fill a carrier bag with gold chains, rings and bracelets, before opening the safe. The haul that day included a custom-made brooch for a special private customer – a one-of-a-kind creation with ruby red eyes glowing like fiery suns, though I've always suspected this is a canny elaboration of Jim's, or Jim's dad's.

What isn't disputed is that when the bag was full of booty, the bold robber thanked the woman politely, told her to count to one hundred, fired one flamboyant pistol shot into the wooden flooring and walked out, vanishing into thin air.

'Jesus, that was a proper job,' says Jim, apparently lamenting the loss of the good old days of the bloodless robbery. 'Things were different then, people were different.

No need for all this blood and spite and greed. Whoever the hell he was back then, he had the balls to carry out a plan and no one got hurt.'

'Cos no one got in his way, maybe?' I suggest, but Jim, unwrapping one set of his two rounds of lunchtime turkey sandwiches, makes no sign he's heard.

'Course this palaver will knock that day right off the top of our infamy list now,' he says grimly. 'Bedford Row too, probably, cos that was a *domestic* at heart. Sign of the times, I guess. Poor old buggers. They barely had enough cash to pay their bloody council tax. If Fisket thinks there's money up there, why didn't he keep it to himself? He didn't need a strong arm like Finn; he could have just gone up there wearing a pair of tights over his face and demanded it. What would the old couple have done?

'Jesus, I bet Inspector Morris is just loving this! His fat head is probably exploding in the interview room right now. Bet the urge to slap that silly twat across the face is almost too much for him. Frankly I'd like to do it myself. With my retirement coming up I still might. It's not as if they can fire me now, is it?'

I don't say anything because I know Jim would never do anything to endanger his longed-for pension, but the sentiment is real.

'There's always one, isn't there?' he says sadly. 'One idiot planning a dumb job that turns into a massive balls-up and the little people pay.'

He's right, of course. Some things never change. There's always one idiot looking for an easy score, one last big job. I mean, it's the staple motivator of almost every heist and gangster flick ever made. Though in this case it's hardly on a par with nicking the Mona Lisa from the Louvre or pocketing a ton of gold bullion from the Las Vegas Bellagio, it's all relative. Anything over a thousand pounds would seem like a fortune to dole-bothering Billy, and probably worth the risk. What he obviously hadn't taken into account was that in every gangster flick ever made, something always goes horribly wrong.

Maybe it's not entirely Billy's fault though, being just 'soft as shite', as Jim puts it. Billy has had it all stacked against him since the day he popped out of his junkie mum – a drunken father, a council-house upbringing, all the clichés shared by our local scumbags. I'm not saying I believe in the popular 'nature versus nurture' bleeding-heart liberalism pumped out nowadays – I mean, people are born with choices and many simply make bad ones – but maybe Billy realised too late that he was in deep trouble.

Do any of us really know we've reached the point of no return before it's too late? Did I, at Bryn Mill farm four weeks ago? I mean, why the hell did Sergeant Biggs take me along in the first place? An inexperienced kid on a warrant? That's what the Federation rep is arguing in my defence, and he's pretty convincing, despite his sweaty hands and feeble comb-over.

He's half persuaded me it's the truth, that I was 'badly briefed and ill equipped', that it could have happened to anyone. I'd simply 'succumbed to inexperience, to a moment of ill-judgement'.

I did not panic. I absolutely did *not* freak out.

OK, I should have listened when the sarge said stay outside, instead of ploughing on in – *our heroine confronts the suspects and leaps into action* – but you don't think you're going to be *that* one, do you? The one who chokes and freezes. The one who trembles. The one who runs. Because, despite all the rehearsals I've done in my head where I lead the suspect home in handcuffs, I've never practised the one where our heroine is shit scared, or our heroine hides in the face of danger.

When did Billy, home for Christmas most likely, realise all hell was about to break loose? Too late, I suspect, just like I had. Except that he's sitting over there at Central now and I'm sitting here. Both of us waiting for the outcome, for what happens next.

The Hitchhiker – 12.30 p.m.

'Bloody hell, where the . . . ?' begins the man who pulls open the pub door before the words die on his lips, hanging in the frigid air for a few seconds before his mouth snaps shut.

Surprise! I think, raising my hand in a bright and breezy hello before saying, 'Hi. Nice day for it!'

'Oh!' says the man finally as the nurse steps out from behind me and gives him a limp little wave, too.

He's tall and broad under the bulky old army coat, might be in his late twenties or early thirties, but he looks sweaty and out of breath, as if it's taken quite an effort to get to the door or he's come a long way to answer it.

As I take the measure of this man I step back to give him some extra room. In the space of just two seconds I can see he has that cornered look in his eyes, which can mean all sorts of things, none of them good usually, or maybe he's just pissed off because we've interrupted him watching the rugby and having a lager; there's alcohol on his thick breath.

I can see a light on behind him, somewhere at the end of a short, wide flagstone passage, but coldness seeps outwards through the pub doorway, despite the swirling snow gathering around our feet in mini drifts. We're less than a sentence in and my hopes, not high for this encounter in the first place, are plummeting with the temperature.

I already dislike this unshaven, almost wordless man on the doorstep, whose left hand is bound in a grubby-looking bandage; he has a cut on his cheek that needs cleaning. He still hasn't said anything, and his silence reminds me of the silence between grown-ups and children when they don't know each other. Well, it's time for a grown-up to speak.

'Sorry to bother you,' I say, super polite and breezy, 'we broke down at the top of the hill. Do you have a phone we can use, please?'

He takes a long time to answer, staring first at the nurse, then at me, then back at the nurse again.

'No, no phone,' he says eventually.

'Oh, OK, well, the snow's getting pretty bad now. I think we're stuck here. Would you mind terribly if we came in for a bit, so we can think what to do next? Maybe you could try and run us to the next town? In your car? If it's not too much to ask,' which, of course, it is.

I cock my head to the side of the mews where the car, with its solid tyres (and suspected four-wheel drive), is sitting.

'No. I mean . . . I can't. I can't leave. No petrol in it, anyway,' he adds.

And just like that, I'm sure he's lying, though I can't really blame him for not wanting to act as a taxi to two random women in this weather. Chivalry is one thing but there's such a thing as taking the piss.

'Just you out here, then?' I ask, eager to keep him talking because he looks like he's about to shut the door in my face.

'Yeah.'

He glances behind me again at the nurse, who exaggerates her shivering, rubbing her hands together. His pupils widen. Yeah, I get it. She's the cute one, but I'm the one with the brains.

Peering ahead, down the road, the nurse says, 'We don't want to be any trouble but it's not a day for walking.'

'You two . . . you're on your own?' says the landlord after a ridiculously long silence.

'Yep,' I confirm. 'She picked me up back there, thank God, but, you know, the weather . . . And there's a tree down up top.'

'Yeah, I picked her up on the road,' adds the nurse. 'Well, she kind of threw herself in front of me. Look, could we just come in for a bit,' she asks, blowing on her hands. 'It's cold as a witch's tit out here.'

'Where's your car then?'

'It ran out of petrol up top.'

He gives the nurse a long, hard stare, taking her in from head to toe before asking, 'You from the town?' in my direction.

'Yeah,' answers the nurse. 'I am, and she's home for Christmas. You the landlord here?'

'Landlord? Yeah, well . . . This place's been shut for a few years now. Not open no more.'

'Well, we can't go on in this right now. Can we stop here for a bit?' asks the nurse, adding a smile.

'We're not open. This ain't a pub no more. I don't really think . . .'

'Just for a bit, then,' I say, tired of polite small talk. I step forward, as good as pushing past him into the hall, leading with my shoulder but saying pleasantly, 'You're a star! A star in The Star! I'm freezing to death. Bit out of the way out here, aren't you?'

I keep talking so he can't protest, edging past him into the pub, cocking my head for the nurse to follow sharpish. 'It'd drive me nuts being out here alone. In here, is it?'

The man doesn't exactly resist as I point towards the light at the back of the passage so I don't wait for his approval. The nurse has taken her cue and is right behind me, one hand already on the door, pushing it shut from the inside, throwing the thick bolt back into place.

'Thank God for that,' she says, brushing snow from her coat, stamping her feet in an exaggerated fashion. 'I'm Becca by the way, this is Lee. And you are?'

'Becca? Yeah. Er, I'm Brian.'

'Nice to meet you, Brian,' she says. 'You're a lifesaver.'

I'm grateful she's making the pleasantries and distracting him, because it enables me to step forward with purpose, leading the way into the old bar without further invitation. As expected, it hasn't seen a customer in years, the décor is a time warp of every era from the early Victorian age to the 1980s, when time seems to have ground to a halt, dug in its heels and stuck fast. The whole place smells of damp and old beer, and what I suspect is beef Pot Noodle. I've eaten enough in my time to recognise it at ten paces – breakfast of champs.

I don't like this pub. It's hard to say why but I just don't, and that's more than enough reason to be on guard. Paranoia has never killed anyone yet, as far as I know. It's always better to be suspicious than to wish you'd listened to your instincts later. People ignore their instincts all the time. They'll get into a taxi even though the hairs on their neck scream at them not to, they'll stay in their seats when they smell smoke and should head for the door, all because they're afraid of seeming rude, looking foolish or, worst of all, making a fuss.

Lil showed me an article on it once, how people who survive the worst, who escape disasters and tragedies, don't worry about how they look to others. They're the ones who've learned to question everything, the ones who react, who run at the first sound of gunshots; they're the planners who took the time to check the fire exits in their hotel before they were drunk and dazed in the middle of the night and the air was thick with smoke.

I'll check all the exits in a minute, but for now I can see the door and there's no one between it and me except the nurse, which wouldn't be any sort of issue.

I can smell something else in here too, under the whiff of Pot Noodle, but it isn't smoke, it's earth and iron – 'earth stood hard as iron, water like a stone'. The landlord's hand is bleeding quite a bit, the wrapping spreading with fresh red stains.

'Nice old place,' says the nurse with a fairly convincing smile. 'Guess we're the last people you were expecting on a day like this. Bet you don't get many visitors.'

No shit! But I can't blame her for making an effort as I dump my pack at my feet and do a brief survey of the room. There's a pile of mail on a beer barrel by the door.

One lamp with a wonky shade illuminates the bar where an electric fire is burning, and the radio fizzles with voices and music. There's a plate of toast crumbs, an empty mug and a half-empty plastic cup, the source of the Pot Noodle smell probably, on the floor by a balding wing-backed chair. Two empty cans of Carlsberg lie on the floor.

There are no Christmas decorations in here, no Christmas tree. It's unlikely the landlord's Jewish so he's probably just a miserable bugger – each to their own. There's a carrier bag of groceries abandoned by the armchair, spilling a couple of cans of tomato soup and a box of mince pies. The old bar tables and chairs have been pushed down to the end of the room by the fireplace, the grate full of rubbish – it clearly hasn't hosted a blaze in years.

I take all this in in seconds, and much more, filing it for future reference.

'Glad to find you here,' says the nurse chummily, still talking. 'It didn't look like anyone was home.' She clearly doesn't want him to kick us out just yet, either.

'Yeah, it's really coming down out there now,' I add.

'Could be a whiteout soon,' says the nurse. 'Looks as if we might be snowed in before long.'

It must be clear to anyone with a brain that she's angling for an invitation to stay but he doesn't make one. He doesn't ask us to sit or enquire where we're trying to get to. This is either a criminal lack of curiosity, bad manners or he just *really* wants us out of here.

He looks somewhere between alarmed and baffled, rather than just pissed off. He clearly doesn't want to meet my eye but can't quite stop himself from looking at the nurse. His gaze lingers on her for a second or two, then flicks away again, down to his feet, up to the ceiling, before repeating the process.

I can see why but he doesn't have to be so blatant about it. Yeah, she's very pretty with her cheeks flushed from the cold like that. She has that look that makes men's eyes linger; a pixie face, bobbed dark hair – elfin would be the word – and those cool grey eyes and the dark mascara. Her pink lipstick has a high-shine quality, too pale but emphasising lips that could be considered pouty.

I hate this kind of girl, always have. I'll never be one of them but I don't want to be. Sure, they have their own skills, of sorts, ones they've honed over time, breathy, pouty, survival instincts of their own, but they're no match for mine.

The nurse is unzipping her coat now, revealing the top of a tight black sweater, her breasts pushed snugly into the v. She's wearing a rather trendy, expensive-looking leather jacket as well, unexpected under the pink mass of the parka, and I suppress a smile at this little hint of rebellion winning out over the rest of her mummy ensemble. Small acts of defiance, eh? I know about those.

'Nice place you've got here,' she says to the landlord again, pushing her chest out just a fraction, her mouth sliding into a smile.

There's something a little unravelled about that mouth. Those lips have pinched themselves around a fair number of cigarettes, I'll bet. I thought I'd smelled a faint memory of fag ash earlier. The car had held it, as had the nurse's hair. No one smokes with kids in the car, surely?

We wait in silence as the nurse's patter dries up and the wind coils around the building. We need to give this guy something to do right now, so he doesn't cause trouble. The universal leveller rarely fails so I ask, 'Any chance of a cuppa?'

He seems about to refuse when the nurse adds, 'One sugar if you've got it,' with a sudden smile, flashed purely for his benefit, 'and I could murder a biscuit.'

It works. He relaxes just a fraction.

'Yeah, OK,' he says. 'Wait here.'

He heads through the door by the bar, and a few moments later a kettle starts to boil.

The nurse rolls her eyes. 'He's a rare one, isn't he?' she says, sitting down on a wooden bar chair. 'What the hell is his problem?'

I roll my eyes back in agreement but don't sit yet, carrying out a small circuit of the room while the kettle gathers steam. There's a second door to the left. I'll check that out in a bit. The curtained windows must overlook the front approach and the road but I know, from being outside earlier, that they're all shuttered.

Eyeing the framed photos on the wall, I lean in towards each of them for a closer look. There's one from the 1970s, a man with two young lads, one sunburnt to a pink flush, one sun-bronzed and golden. In another, older one, a woman is holding a ginger-headed bundle in a shawl, outside the pub in better days, where the background is painted and primped with flowers.

The other pictures are generic black and white shots of the local area circa 1975 and a reproduction tint of, what else, Constable's *Hay Wain* in cheap, faded acrylic. I can't help but smile when I clock the watery reproduction of the marauding Lion of Aberystwyth, a pencil and colour sketch from a book by the looks of it, cut raggedly, as if by a child's hand. I wonder if, long before I was a scared listener, a Young Happy had spun his tale of the fearsome lion to the children of this pub.

I hope so. It's not a bad legacy, and a place like this would surely have been an exciting if slightly frightening place for a child to live. A pub has chatter and laughter and great nooks and crannies for hiding in, but it also has strangers and dark, drunken moments, a type of impermanence that shifts with the whims of its customers. I'd have preferred to live here, though, than on the farm, on balance. A farm has a steady rhythm but you never really forget that that rhythm of the seasons is the rhythm of birth and death. Of growth, sale and slaughter.

As my review of the room reaches 360 degrees the landlord reappears with two chipped mugs of something weak and brownish. He plonks them on the table nearest the nurse and we each take one. It looks insipid but smells OK and at least it's hot. There's no biscuit.

'Brilliant, cheers,' I say, as the nurse takes a sip and warms her hands on the mug. The landlord watches her every move and wets his lips with his tongue. He hasn't made one for himself.

'Any chance of a stronger tot?' I ask. 'To warm us up? I'll pay of course.'

His mouth tightens. 'You mean a *drink*?'

No I mean a sniff of cocaine. 'This is a pub, right?'

'Yeah, but the taps are off, been off for years, like. Sorry.'

'But you still have your spirits, some of the Laphroaig left,' and I gesture to a couple of bottles on the dusty shelves behind the bar to make my point. The labels are faded but

I know what most of them are anyway. The Laphroaig is a good bet if the bottle's got a tight cap. That stuff will outlast the apocalypse.

'One for yourself?' I attempt humour, but it doesn't raise a smile. Jesus, this guy needs to brush up on his customer service, no wonder the place ran into the ground if this is his idea of hospitality. Purvis is always saying he'd like to run a pub. Nothing fancy, just a spit and sawdust place for drinking, darts and old-fashioned blokes with dirty playing cards and smutty jokes, but it's a lifestyle, isn't it? Open for the customers' pleasure, whenever it suits them. Enforced pleasantries, like I'm making now with this dopey guy when I could just take the bloody bottle myself. It's not as if he could stop me.

This isn't necessary, though, as he sighs and casts about for a glass, his hand wavering between the bottles before pulling one down, twisting off the top, sniffing and making a face. It's not the Laphroaig but beggars can't be choosers.

'Like one?' I ask the nurse as the landlord makes heavy weather of wiping a tumbler with the end of his grubby sleeve. She's chosen to sit in the gloomiest corner of the bar, at a hard table facing the door. She couldn't have picked a spot further away from the barman. It's where I would have chosen to sit, over the softer cushioned benches by the empty fire. Occasionally something twitches in her face, as if there's a bad smell she's being forced to endure, but she nods her head at the offer of a drink.

'Yeah, why the hell not, thanks.'

The landlord is still keeping a close eye on her. He doesn't look at me much. I'm evidently not that interesting, probably because my tits are safely tucked away under my old khaki parka. That's OK. I like to be of no interest, even a source of disdain if needs be. It increases the chances of avoiding trouble – it also helps you maintain the element of surprise.

I crane my neck over the bar while the landlord's back is turned towards the liquor shelves, getting a second glass down. There's a landline phone on a low shelf, the old-fashioned, plastic kind with a rotary dial base unit and heavy handset. There's a wire running from it up the bar and into the back somewhere.

'Phone not working, then?' I ask as he slops a miserly tot into two cloudy tumblers.

'Uh, no. The line's out, since the storm last week, been trying to get someone out . . . to fix it.' He shrugs.

'Out here all alone and you don't have a mobile?'

'No credit on it.' The story of the day.

I take the glass from the landlord, swallow a mouthful and drop the rest into my tea. Warmth spreads out into my chest and throat.

'You're all on your own?'

'I like being on my own,' he adds.

As if on cue there's a thump on the low ceiling above us. We all jump but I don't show so much as a spasm on the outside, my hands just drop to my sides, ready for action, a reflex just in case.

All our eyes fix on the cracked plaster above us as a second thump sounds, weaker this time, and a little floury puff of plaster is dislodged. The nurse catches my eye and then looks at the landlord, eyebrows raised for an explanation, but he looks down at the bar and starts to wipe a cloth over it as if nothing has happened.

I raise an eyebrow at the nurse this time.

'Is someone upstairs?' she asks patiently. 'I thought you said you're alone here?'

'No, well, yes. Just my old dad. He's in bed. He can't come down no more. He's a bit . . .'

He twirls his finger in a circle by his forehead, making the universal symbol for gaga, loopy. 'He don't recognise nobody no more. He's got Alt-zheimer's, you know,' he continues, stumbling over the word.

'Well, that's a relief,' says the nurse. 'I mean, I thought for a moment you had ghosts.'

I sense a hint of sarcasm in her voice, but she smiles in a girlish way at the landlord. 'Bet an old place like this has a few ghosts. White ladies? Highwaymen?'

Oh my God, she's trying to flirt.

'No ghosts,' says the landlord.

My veneer of good humour is starting to wear thin, my patience raising its hackles as a growl forms inside me. This man-of-few-words act is getting old, and the novelty of the tea and whisky and being out of the raging cold is fading. As soon as the weather lifts I'll be out of here. The quiet woods seem preferable to this creepy place. If the worst comes to the worst I can even pull my kipping bag out of my backpack and bed down somewhere. Maybe at that motel back there. One of the rooms might still be dry enough.

I like the cold anyway. The sun's fine if you're lying by a swimming pool somewhere but not when you're stuck for days on end in close confines with other people, sweating, scratching, snoring. Like in C block, the cold water was always warm coming out of the taps, so I couldn't even cool down when it was my turn to take a shower. When you can't change your clothes whenever you like you make friends with your own smell; it's not such a distasteful thing. You get used to it. But the sweat of others, that's something else.

And the heat makes people's brains swell, cooped up together. Like the time I just knew Lilli-Anne was going to go ape-shit with little Val because she'd taken some chewing gum from her bunk. One packet of chewing gum could be enough, though it wasn't really the chewing gum, that was just the trigger, the sort of trigger you see anywhere, in any city-centre pub on any Saturday night. The dynamic shifts quickly from fun and banter to fists, the aggression always there underneath.

I realise I'm clenching my hands into fists, making them hurt, so I rub them gently to ease them off. The conversation lapses as the landlord slumps down into his chair and the nurse says, 'Guess we all stay put for a bit then.'

'Suit yourself.' He shrugs, so she sighs and picks up a copy of the *Mirror* from the table and starts to leaf through it.

Silence is fine with me. I put my headphones on low and settle into the nearest chair, appraising the pub's delightful décor, particularly two old pistols crossed over the fireplace. They look like cheap 1970s reproduction shit, but there's a rusty hatchet by the fire. If a scrap were to break out here and now, in this room, the hatchet would be a better bet than the pistols. The smooth wood of the handle looks like it would be nice to heft.

I used to chop wood on the farm. I never thought of an axe as a weapon then. Nothing was a weapon then. Now everything is, and I've tried to explain to Pam that it's when a weapon is in my hand that the best clarity comes. It's when the moment of the day, hour, minute, shrinks down to its essential essence – the choice presents itself – to hurt, maim, to wipe the smile off someone's face. Anything is a weapon, my fists, my teeth, a bottle, a glass, easily broken to expose shards.

In that moment it's not that I *want* to kill. I'm sure of that. When the weapon is snug and tight in my grip it's as if a great calm comes down from above and they really see me – the ones on the other end of the look – and I see them. Like the fox in the road earlier, our eyes lock, something passes between us. Who is hunter, who is prey?

That's the choice. I don't *want* to kill but I can, though it's not what people think it is. It's not an urge, an instinct. It's a decision, always. Do I, or do I not? That's what separates people from animals, from each other, their power under control, to use or not use. I've seen what an axe can do to a human body. I'm not eager to use one. Too clumsy.

I drain my tea and take a deep breath as the fire in my hands spreads to my chest and head. Then I settle down to wait. And watch.

The Accomplice – 12.30 p.m.

Billy Fisket doesn't like the look of the copper – the massive one with the bad breath looking at him like he's shit on his shoe. After today he knows that's exactly what he is, he's known that all his life really, even before his mam started yelling it at him, followed by the teachers, then the kids, who were happy enough to spend some time with him as long as he had cans of beer to pass round or a packet of something to toke up or snort.

But he wants him to understand, this Morris bloke, how it happened, and about the old lady . . . he wants him to know he could never have hurt her, done that to her face, to her fingers. He has a nan of his own, after all. And he never touched the dog either: 'I mean, what kind of fucking animal hurts an old fucking dog, a nice little dog too, never even barked or tried to bite. Too soft, see,' he says, trying to get the point across once more.

Inspector Morris waits, with something resembling patience, while Billy babbles on, snivelling through snot strings, wiping his hand across his nose. He knows that

Fisket realises it's all over, now that they've taken his bloodied clothes, fingerprinted him, stuck a plaster on his head and the lawyer's arrived.

He's been talking for the last ninety minutes, non-stop, even without his lawyer present, but this is official now, on the record. He's just waiting for the duty solicitor to sit down and stop fussing with her briefcase, so he can start the tape and they can begin.

'Get him some tea and a tissue or something,' he says to the uniformed officer stationed by the door, before pressing the button on the recording unit and saying his name, the time and date for the record: 'Start at the beginning, Billy.'

So Billy does just that. He tells them how he first met Riley Finn, not up in the Midlands after he finished his three months in prison there, but before that, during the twelve months he was first in foster care over by Aberdarren, after his mam took that overdose. All the kids he hung out with then, round the back of the abandoned garages, knew about the Finns, the proper posh family who'd been lords of the manor or something like that, a couple of hundred years ago.

The other teenagers talked about the big house they'd had down Monmouth way, until they lost most of their money after the big crash in the 1980s, that's what everyone said because that's what their mams said to each other.

Still they weren't as poor as Billy and the other pot-head, shoplifting, bunking-off crew he hung around with, just 'new poor' and feeling life was hard as they'd had to move to a shithole in Wales to live with a dotty old aunt on her crumbling farm because they were broke. The aunt's house was still bigger than the whole street where Billy had lived as a kid, though it was falling apart a bit. You could see the missing slates and the closed-off end with the boarded-up windows from the school bus that took them right past the front drive each day.

Riley would come sauntering down to the road, cool as anything in old-looking trousers and a jacket, but good trainers and a posh watch. No one said anything funny or smart about it though, cos no one wanted to get their heads kicked in or their jumper set on fire with a lighter, like Tom Phillips had for calling Riley knobhead and English cunt.

The mother and father were always coming to the school, bringing stuff from the farm for charity days and harvest festival, vegetables and their own cheese and shit like that, trying to sound all Welsh and saying, '*Bore da*' in a funny accent.

There were already rumours then, though, about Riley. Mrs Pruitt, his first foster mam, was always talking to the other mams in her kitchen about the little things that had disappeared from their houses after young Riley had been over to visit, the odd antique locket missing here, a trinket box or eternity ring there, not lowering their voices in front of him because he was invisible and meaningless: 'Hocked for cash for booze and drugs, you know. Shame too, such a nice family . . . of course they're not really from here . . .'

Of course, Billy explains to the baffled inspector, who's tapping his pen impatiently on the table, waiting for him to say something relevant, there were worse stories too, more reasons why you didn't mess with Finn, like the not-being-very-nice-to-animals stories, kicking or throwing stones at cats: one kid even claimed her cat went missing not long after Riley had been seen trying to catch it down the playing field.

Then there was that thing with the pony or donkey that was all hushed up – after that hoo-ha Riley disappeared overnight.

'But tell us about how you and Finn planned the job,' says the inspector, eager to get to the relevant material. 'Start there, Billy. Start with the planning to go to the farmhouse and rob the Lewises.'

'I am,' says Billy, 'I'm explaining why I went along with it, cos I knew what Riley was like. But I never meant to do it.' Billy sighs because he knows how it sounds, cos it's what every scumbag like him always says to the pigs – 'It weren't me!' – when they're nicked, but in this case it's true.

So Billy explains how he was serving his third post-prison burglary probation in Birmingham, where his mam's cousin had put him up in a room. Billy's cousin Rowan works in a pole-dancing club (though Aunty Mary thinks it's a wine bar) and she'd got Billy some work on a burger van outside. That's how Billy had met Double-D-Cup Gemma, who liked an end-of-shift extra cheese, extra onions, at the van.

Gemma had apparently shagged Billy a couple of times and he wanted her and her awesome tits all to himself. He'd thought he could impress her if he made out he was part of the same bunch of hard bastards who ran the club with drugs and prozzies thrown in. That's how he'd ended up bragging to her about his 'one-day, grand plan' to make a fortune, thinking it would improve his chances of a regular shag.

How was he to know that Gemma was a *friend* – and on-off other half – of Riley Finn, who, as it happened, was also living up there on probation.

If he'd known he'd have run a mile, but after he'd told Gemma about the farm, one day Gemma said, 'Someone to meet you, Billy, from your old home town, land of my fathers and all that,' and there was Finn, large as life and always hanging around the van and the club with drugs to offer and trouble to dish out. Everyone was talking about it, about Riley's rep, you know, the drugs, the prison time and the GBH, and how Billy was in the shit for sticking it to Gemma.

Then one night Finn said, half pissed in the strip shop's back room, 'So tell me about this old couple, Billy boy, that Gemma said you know. Tell me about this farm and the money that's up there. Don't keep a sweet deal to yourself now, you owe me something for hitting up on my Gemma.'

'So I just played along, to keep Riley sweet,' says Billy. 'I dunno how it got as far as it did, all right? It was just something we used to pretend about as kids, that the old boy and girl had some treasure stashed up there and we were always trying to find it. I was just trying to sound like I had the biggest bollocks, so Riley wouldn't kick the shit out of me and do whatever it is mentalists like that do when they've moved on from setting people's school jumpers alight.

'I didn't have no stories about beating the shit out of no one, did I? I never thought anyone'd really take it serious. I was just tryin' to get a blowjob. In the end I just fucked off home for Christmas, like, glad to be out of there and out of Riley's way.'

By the time Billy gets to Finn's surprise arrival in Pont, late the night before, Inspector Morris has already had to turn the tape over in the recorder and Billy's on his second cup of tea.

'I was well-scared, wasn't I,' he explains, 'because, well, you would be, wouldn't you, sitting down to *The Royle Family* Christmas special and a nice mince pie, then having that nutter turn up on your doorstep out of the blue, yelling, "Ghost of Christmas presents", or something. Riley was already half pissed, psyched up, talking, talking, talking, insisted we "borrow" a car from down the street. Well, I didn't want to say no, did I?

'Riley was rambling on about coming home, about some inheritance and birthright, about how these old farmers always have loot, they just hide it well, and repeating, "Don't take no excuses, right, Billy boy! Don't let them play ignorant. No fuss – quick, quick. Get the handy hammer from the glove box. The sight of the handy hammer always gets their tongues going. I never travel without it."'

'The handy hammer?' says the inspector. 'So Riley brought that along? Tell us about that.'

So Billy admits he'd seen Riley's handy hammer before, seen what it had done in the strip pit's back room to some cocky twat's splayed fingers over an unpaid fifty-pound debt.

When they'd finally parked up at the end of the lane by Ridgeback Farm, Billy was hoping like hell no one was home. Surely the pair of old dears would be too scared to answer a knock on the door at eleven o'clock on a winter's night, but after a few minutes the old woman appeared in her nightie.

'"Snow put you off the road?" she asked,' says Billy, 'then Riley stepped forward and shoved her back into the passageway, saying, "Shut the fuck up." The old woman was totally confused and kept saying, "What do you want? I don't understand. You shouldn't be here. Take my pension. It's on the table, just take it," and stuff like that. "I don't want your fucking pension," said Riley. "You know what I want, what you're hiding and you're going to tell me where it is, aren't you? Like a good old girl."

'Then Riley pushed her through into the kitchen where their elderly dog was sleeping in his basket, shoved her down on a chair by the kitchen table, saying "Let's make this quick. I'll count to ten, then you tell me where it is."'

Billy describes how the old woman protested as the count began at number ten, looked blank by number four and started to cry when Riley reached number one. She kept asking what they wanted as Riley's foot began to tap on the flagstone floor, faster and faster, a storm gathering, until the old lady got a slap on the face, then another.

'I kept saying, "Don't, Riley, for fuck's sake, don't. She don't know what you're talking about. Her mind's wandering, like. She's about a hundred years old for Christ's sake," but Riley wasn't having it and kept saying, "That's not true, is it? You're being a clever old bitch and pretending to be senile for his benefit, playing the sympathy card. But I know better, I know all about clever old bitches like you."

'After a while the old woman, obviously just wanting to say something, anything to calm Finn down, had whispered, "There's money upstairs, in the top drawer, front bedroom. And there're medals in the bedside drawer."

'Riley said, "Well that's a start," getting into the whole thing by then, enjoying it,' says Billy. 'Riley told me to go and check it out, see what was up there. Check under the mattress because old buggers love hiding shit under mattresses. Well, I didn't want to leave the room, did I? Didn't want to leave the old dear alone with Riley, not for one minute. So I said, "What are you going to do to her?" And Riley just gave that smile and said, "Nothing, you stupid twat. We're just having a friendly cup of tea, all civilised, just catching up on small talk."

'So I did as I was told and had a good look, but there was nothing but junk and crap up there. Then, when I came back a good while later, the old woman was tied to a kitchen chair with the cord from a lamp and Riley was swigging from a bottle of whisky.

'"Jesus, what the fuck?" I said, and Riley said, "She just wasn't being helpful. Don't want her running off, do we?"

'"Running off?" I said. "Where to? She can hardly fucking walk."'

'"Oh, I dunno, I know her type. I think she's a sneaky old bugger. Well? What did you find?" So I put the hundred quid's worth of rolled notes I'd found in a drawer and some medals that were in a posh presentation box on the table.

'I didn't want to give them to Riley, like, but by then I didn't want to go back empty-handed, did I? It didn't make a difference, Riley just called me a twat and a retard, pocketed the cash and said, "Do I have to do everything myself?"

'Then Riley left me in the kitchen and went to search, and I listened to the sound of smashing and stuff splintering and breaking upstairs.

'Fucking mental, man, it was scary mental. It went on for ever. I kept telling the old lady it'd be OK. I tried to loosen the cables on her wrists a bit so she'd be more comfy. I gave her a drink of tea.'

'But you didn't untie her?' asks Inspector Morris, interrupting.

'Fuck no! Riley would've killed me. I gave her a drink of water and some sips of tea, OK? I told her it'd be all right.'

'But it wasn't, was it, Billy?' says the inspector.

'No.'

It takes Billy a few seconds to gather himself before he describes how Riley returned to the kitchen even angrier than before, how he couldn't believe it when Riley had grinned 'like it was Christmas', which it was, and pulled out an old gun, waving it about, pointing at the kitchen pots and stuff.

'Riley was well-pleased saying, "Look what I found in the back room. Nice old pistol. Is this a collectible? Looks like it might work. There're bullets, too. But I don't need a gun to make you tell me what I need to know, do I?"

'That's when it happened,' says Billy, welling up again. 'The handy hammer came out of the bag and Riley said, "Let's focus our minds here. If you lie to me one more time, if you pretend you're a wandering old biddy and don't know what I'm talking about, I get to use my little friend. The old woman started whimpering then and Riley yelled, "Shut up! Stop that bloody racket now!"

'That's when the poor old collie pricked up its ears from where it had been watching, all quiet like, in its basket, joining in with howls to wake the dead. That was all it took to tip Riley over the edge. The collie was the first to get it. Riley yelled, "You can shut the fuck up too," and took the hammer to the top of its head. It was an 'orrible sound that, like a nut cracking. Felt proper sick, I did. Then the old lady's voice cut off and she started to pant and struggle. The dog wasn't dead just then. It lay there all stunned.'

Inspector Morris waits as Billy struggles to continue, his face showing no emotion, no judgement in front of the suspect, as he's been trained to. 'And then what happened?' he asks eventually.

'I said, "She don't know nothing, for fuck's sake, Riley. She'd of told us by now." So Riley said, "Maybe, you dumb fuck. I saw the way she was looking at me. She thinks she can play me. Everyone thinks they can play me." So I said I'd made a mistake – it was just a story I'd heard, kids bragging and making stuff up, but Riley just said, "Let's find out, then," and grabbed the old girl's knobbly hands, spreading her fingers across the chair arm and said, "Which finger do you like the least? It's not like you use your hands much to clean this shithole, is it? You won't miss one."

'Then the hammer came down on her littlest finger. The howl that came out of the old lady was fucking horrific. By then I wasn't looking no more. I couldn't. Riley just sat there waiting, silent, staring at the old girl all the time while she said, "Please don't," and, "I don't understand. Why are you doing this?" After a bit Riley said, "Maybe you're right, Billy boy, maybe she really doesn't know, but she's not here on her own, right? What time will the old man get back? Shall we ask him where the good stuff is? Bet he knows."

'That's the first time I thought of the old man,' says Billy, 'when the old woman said, he'll be gone till morning then started whispering, "Please no, please no. Don't hurt him." I was proper freaked out by then. I didn't want to sit there all night waiting around, and I didn't want to see what Riley was gonna do to the old man neither, when he showed up. I didn't sign up for any of that, so I said, "Riley, let's just get out of here while we can. I made a mistake, all right? The story was bullshit. Let's get the fuck out of here."

'Riley wasn't pleased and started yelling "A mistake? You did make a mistake, Billy boy. Do you think I'm going all the way back empty-handed after all this? The old man will give it up. In a few hours he'll tell me what I need to know. Anything to eat in this dump?"'

Billy goes on to describe the next few hours as Riley munched through two cheese sandwiches and half a packet of biscuits, swigging at a bottle of whisky while Mrs Lewis cried quietly, her eye swelling into a fat blue ball where Riley had hit her.

'I was trying to think what the fuck to do. I couldn't eat nothing, like,' says Billy. 'I just felt sick. The old girl's head was slumped down. I asked Riley to let me untie her. Her hands were going all fat and red. It was horrible. Riley just said, yeah OK, but she wasn't to move off the chair. That's when I got the blood on me, from her hands. She was clinging onto me, wouldn't let go, I had to pry her off.

'Riley lay down on a little settee by the door then and dozed off for a bit, but I couldn't sleep. I was shitting myself, covered in the old girl's blood. I was thinking about how the hell to get out of there, thought about creeping past and out the front door, but it was right next to the settee, and the hammer was in Riley's hand. I was worried about the old girl. She was woozy like, going in and out of a doze. It got bad fast when Riley came to, muttering about wasting our fucking time and swigging more whisky.

'The dog started to growl and yelp then in its basket, and Riley yelled, "Shut the fuck up," a few times, but it just kept making these horrible little noises. Then without warning Riley jumped up, wrapped the cord of the lamp around its neck and throttled it, just like that, stringing it up in the window for the old girl to see. To make a point, saying, "Tell me what I want to know or you're next, you old bitch."

'It was the sickest fucking thing I've ever seen, that little dog's eyes rolling in its head. I couldn't look. Course that set the old girl off wailing twice as bad again, so Riley smacked her to shut her up and she flew off the chair onto the floor, a little bag of bones really. Then Riley kicked her in her ribs. Then she went quiet at last.'

At this moment in the interview Billy breaks down and cries into his already soggy paper tissue. The tape is suspended for three minutes while the inspector gets him a glass of water and the lawyer asks if he's OK to go on. When he's ready, Billy manages to describe how he suddenly found some of the courage that had eluded him since birth, or at least a sense of immediate self-preservation, jumped to his feet and grabbed the handy hammer, brandishing it at Riley, who'd sat back down to finish the last bit of sandwich.

'I yelled, "I've had enough of this, you sick fucker. I'm fucking out of here, and if you know what's good for you you'll fuck off too." Then I shoved the table and chair between us before Riley could get up and whack me, lobbed the hammer across the room and bloody ran for it.

'I was down that passage and out of the front door like a flash and I never looked back the whole time I was running, though I heard Riley howling like a mad thing behind me, swearing and promising to kill me. I wasn't waiting to find out, was I? I didn't really know where I was going, didn't even realise that I had the car keys in my pocket. I just legged it across the field into the trees, out of sight.'

Inspector Morris sighs at this, a sigh that says, without any need of annotation from the transcriber, What is wrong with people?

It's what they're all thinking and Billy knows it as he explains how he kept on running until he was properly lost on the snowy hills, wandering through the woods for a good couple of hours before dawn, getting muddier and colder by the minute. Finally, around nine o'clock, he'd stumbled down the steep banking towards the road and slammed into the side of the tractor.

'I never hurt the old girl,' he says, staring dry-eyed now. 'You have to believe me. And I never hurt the dog neither.'

'I think we'll take a break there,' says Inspector Morris, before he gives in to the urge to say something that may, in the future, be held against him, or possibly to smash the snivelling little shit right in the face.

Once outside he takes several breaths to steady himself, pops a mint in his mouth and drags a comb through his hair. Now he has to deal with the worst bit. Now he has to speak to Osion Lewis, the old woman's husband.

The Hitchhiker – 2 p.m.

I'm already tired of waiting. The afternoon is slipping away, our options narrowing with every minute the temperature drops and the light falls. The nurse is looking bored, still thumbing the newspaper, but also keeping her eyes on the landlord behind the bar, who's trying to give the appearance of dusting and tidying things he clearly hasn't felt compelled to dust or tidy in a decade. Then she looks at her watch, gazes around with mock resignation and says with a lazy grin, 'Looks like I'm cancelling my opera plans for the evening, then.'

I can't help but smile for once, all things considered, adding, 'Guess I should call the ambassador then, and tell him I won't make supper,' just to play along. We wait for the landlord to speak, but he doesn't join in, so to break the silence I ask the nurse, 'Husband at home, waiting for you to show up?' but she shakes her head. 'Someone will be keeping an eye on your boy, though?' I add, remembering the conversation we'd had in the car earlier.

'Oh yeah, the babysitter will be cursing me by now, I expect.'

She fishes in her bag and pulls out a battered packet of cigarettes, but it's empty. Sighing, she pats her pockets for her purse and pulls it out, finding a note.

'I've got a fiver if you've got any fags?' she says to the landlord, but he just shrugs and shakes his head.

'Any pictures of your boy in there? In your wallet?' I ask, not because I want to see her kiddie snaps, just for something to pass the time that's stringing itself out like high-street bunting.

She hesitates for a second, thumbing through the bulging wad of receipts and cards in her purse before eventually nodding and handing me a creased snap of a fat, tuft-haired boy and a dark-haired girl. Neither child looks like her. Neither is attractive. In fact, the fat kid might be the plainest boy I've ever seen, his features squished together like someone's squeezed a lump of clay in their hand.

'Cute kids,' I say with what I hope is the right kind of smile. 'Is this a cousin or a friend? The girl?'

'What?'

'You said you had a son so I was just wondering who the girl is.'

'Cousin.'

'How old is he again?' I gesture to the chubby boy.

'Four.'

Jesus, he's a big lad for four, soft though, soft around the middle. Too many Mars bars and hours on the Xbox, most likely. 'Growing up fast,' I say, because it seems like the thing.

For some reason the nurse looks amused. A smile tugs at the corner of her mouth and I wonder if she's laughing at me. Perhaps it was too obvious what I meant – fat little bugger. Or maybe she's just surprised that anyone gives a shit. Of course I don't really. I don't have much to do with kids. No opportunity, even if I was interested.

'Can I see?' asks the landlord to my surprise, but the nurse is already pulling the photo from my grasp and replacing it in her purse.

'Don't want to bore you with endless kiddie snaps, do I?' she says, before adding, 'What about you, though? Wife? Kids? Girlfriend? Boyfriend?'

'No, no wife or kids. Just me.'

'How do you make a living out here? I mean, now the pub is shut?'

'Dole. Benefits, you know.'

'No private income then? You know, rich daddy upstairs? Waiting for the inheritance?' She winks. 'I guess all this will be yours one day then? You could sell up?'

I'm not quite sure why she's so interested all of a sudden. Personally I'd tell her to mind her own business if I was the landlord, but he just shrugs and says, 'We'll see.'

'You, student lady? Significant other expecting you home tonight?'

'Nope, free and single.'

As the conversation drains away into the damp air the nurse gives up, puts the purse containing the photo of her chubby darling back in the bag at her feet, zipping it up and tucking it protectively between her still-soggy Converse once more.

'Any snacks in there?' I ask to break the awkwardness of a situation that's even more uncomfortable than it was five minutes ago.

134

'Sorry. Those M&M's back there on the road were the last of them.'

I have one more muesli bar in my backpack, but I'm saving that for emergencies – always keep a little something back for every eventuality. I'll pick my moment in a bit and ask our host if he can stretch to some toast or something. Surely he can spare that. Right now he's decided to disappear somewhere, upstairs probably, so I get up to change the radio channel while he's out of the room. Christmas classics have been droning on into the premature twilight for the last hour but, Bah, humbug! or not, I have to draw the line at a choral version of 'Little Donkey', sung to death by some kids really overdoing the high-pitched sentiment.

I hate donkeys. I've never understood their appeal, never wanted to ride one at the beach, even as a little kid. Donkeys stink. They're usually crawling with flies and fleas and dripping matted shit from their back end. They also explode like watermelons. I can vouch for that.

Believe me, I wasn't pleased to see it, though on the day I found myself standing in the pink, misty aftermath of the world's stupidest prank, at the ill-judged distance of about five feet less than necessary. It was no joke, picking bits of matted fur off my clothes, trying not to inhale vaporised blood. That donkey cost a lot – in money and in trouble. Purvis's fault, naturally.

You can't be sentimental about animals, Dad used to say when I was a kid, when slaughter day came around or when one had to be put down, but he was a fine one to talk. I heard him whispering to those cows of his all the time, in the black secrecy of the morning hours, in a softer tone than he ever used with me or Mum. Maybe that's why I hated their sleepy bovine faces so much, their dull unquestioning acceptance of their fate.

A cow is a formidable side of flesh, especially in motion. En masse they can easily trample a whole group of men, yet they'd never joined forces, tried to push down the fences and flee the fields. I'd hated them for that, and for going meekly towards their last trip in the trailer, to be stunned and sliced before they were slabbed on restaurant plates or shrink-wrapped on supermarket shelves.

Cows have beautiful eyelashes, you know, long lashes like 1950s bathing bombshells. When I was about twelve there was a baby heifer with the longest lashes I'd ever seen; her lashes had made me want to cry as I looked into her big brown eyes. For a split second I thought there'd been a moment of understanding between us, but when I opened the yard gate and tried to shoo her out, she just stood there, swishing her tail until I lost it, threw myself into the little cow's flank, punching the hard side of her brown warmth.

I don't think Dad or Mum realised I was crying when they pulled me away, before Dad took the belt to my backside. It was the only time he ever actually hit me.

Something broke in me that day, I think, broke between us all. I remember yelling, 'I wish you'd both just die so I could sell this shitty place and fuck off out of here,' and then he'd tanned me some more so I had to sit on a cushion for three days. I hated the cows even more after that, but not as much as I hate fucking Christmas songs.

Turning the old-fashioned knob through the small range of radio channels, it's a choice between the ripe old cheese of Wham's 'Last Christmas' or Aled Jones trilling 'We're Walking In The Air' from the fucking *Snowman*. I feel a violent urge to punch something, even though Pam's calm and patient voice whispers in my ear, 'Breathe, in, out; in, out . . . once more. You are the passenger. Let the moment pass by the windows of the train. Leave it behind. In, out; in, out. I am in control. I am the fucking train driver. I am moving onward.'

The wind is dancing around the pub now, jeering and picking at the warped window frames, finding plenty of ways in. Above us the floorboards begin to creak and crack with the weight of someone walking to and fro, and I'm guessing the absent landlord is up there, seeing to his father. As I register the sound of water running, from somewhere overhead, juddering through the ancient pipes I realise I need to pee.

'Toilet?' I ask the nurse, glad of the physical distraction, 'I need a wee.' Mostly I just want an excuse to do something, to wander around and explore without it looking too obvious, and it's an opportunity to investigate the toast situation.

'Hungry?' I add, cos suddenly I could eat a donkey on toast.

'Yes to both,' says the nurse, eagerly getting to her feet and shouldering her bag. Clearly she's the kind of woman who can't go anywhere without her body armour mummy shopper. Or maybe she just doesn't trust me. Fair enough. I've stashed my own backpack by the chair, locked with a good, strong padlock, the key is in my pocket.

'We might need a tetanus shot when we find one,' says the nurse. 'A loo, I mean. Same goes for the toast, but I could eat a horse right now. After you, then, lead the way.'

We head through the most obvious door, to the right of the bar, along a short corridor in the direction of the kettle we'd heard earlier. There's only a low lamp burning on the floor to light the way, but I can smell the whiff of old chip fat at ten paces – you never get that out from under your skin, I know from experience on kitchen duty.

As soon as I push open the door I see a large, low space filled with cabinets and cupboards that must once have been the hub for whipping up pub grub. A huge, scrubbed table sits in the centre. A rusted slab of a chest freezer, still working judging by the little green light on top, sits against the back wall. Out of habit, I wander across, lift the lid and peer in.

'Hope there isn't a body in there?' says the nurse, only half-chuckling, and I know why. This is the sort of place where Mr Twitchy the landlord might stash the bodies of any late-night travellers who happen along, after dismembering them first, naturally. But there's no stash of silently screaming severed heads in there, just a few boxes of potato waffles, the inevitable jumbo bag of frozen peas and some tubs of economy vanilla ice cream.

At the bottom, rimed with spectacular frost shapes in boxes that look like they passed their sell-by date sometime in the early 1980s, is a pile of minced-beef pasties and Findus crispy pancakes. There are a load more boxes dumped on the flagstone floor too, defrosting slowly into sloppy puddles.

'Corpse free,' I confirm, letting the lid drop, and the nurse smiles.

The table in the centre is piled with magazines, the sink displays a few dirty dishes and empty beer cans. A first-aid kit, at least thirty years old, is open on the counter top, its contents recently rummaged, a blood-stained tea towel next to it. The landlord's hand has received some attention here, or was about to, and I wonder what caused the accident, reminding myself to ask him. Also to ask him how he got the little cut on his cheek.

The old eight-ring hob is thick with congealed fat and the large oven looks like a serious fire hazard, with a snake of frayed wires leading to an ancient, overloaded four-point plug. An antique-looking washing machine seems to need emptying, the next basket of washing ready to go, smelling tangibly of piss.

The rubbish bin is piled with microwave ready-meal boxes and empty cans of peaches and rice pudding, nursing-home fare for the toothless and dribbly – the gummy indignity of old age that await us all, sucking soft, syrupy fruit and children's food. God spare us! It's better to burn out than fade away, right? As Purvis is always saying, though he thinks Kurt Cobain invented the phrase for his suicide note, rather than it being a Neil Young song lyric.

I don't suppose it matters who said it, the sentiment is sound. Take the old guy upstairs who must be waiting to die, anything to be free of all this, maybe dreaming of a rare steak and chocolate gateau. My stomach rumbles in sympathy and I'm glad to see there's a half-started loaf on the counter, next to a newish microwave and a crumby toaster. It's cheap sliced white, but better than nothing. The nurse opens one of the overhead cupboards and I spy a jar of Marmite. Jackpot!

'Love it or hate it?' asks the nurse. 'I bloody hate the stuff.'

I love it. It has a high barter and swap level. A jar will go for a couple of packets of fags easy. I secretly think all people who hate Marmite have a flaw in their character. I'm not sure I can fully trust anyone who doesn't like Marmite – dinner of champs.

'Guess we'd better find the loo and the landlord before we just tuck into his loaf?' I suggest.

'A well brought up girl, eh?' The nurse grins. 'OK, let's stay on his good side, if he has one. Though either way, I intend to demolish that loaf when we come back.'

I nod as I move to the back door of the kitchen, spotting a key in the lock and testing it right away. The door opens with some resistance onto a mews forecourt at the back of the pub, densely covered with snow, the old cobbles only visible under the square of shelter provided by the porch.

There's a second yowl of a dog as the door creaks inwards, echoing off the walls of the enclosed space, which explains the Hound of the Baskervilles effect earlier. Stepping outside I can see the culprit, a great, shaggy German Shepherd tied to an old kennel under the slope of the mews roof.

It's straining at the chain and yelping at the upstairs windows, then back at us, carrying on like it's not used to visitors. Maybe this one's a biter, a handful, because someone's been happy enough to leave it out here in the freezing cold, howling. Dogs are pack animals, you have to show them you're the alpha dog, so I stare it down for a few seconds, approaching slowly and steadily, then, when its ears and shoulders drop out of an aggressive stance, I reach out and put my closed hand on its neck.

'What's up, boy?' I say. 'All mouth, no trousers eh?

No need for that racket.' Adding, 'Good girl,' in a whisper, as my hand finds a collar carrying a round metal disc with the name Tessa punched into it.

'The music they make, the children of the night,' calls the nurse from inside the kitchen doorway, in what might pass for a Transylvanian accent. 'Mwah, ha, ha! That's from *Dracula* I think.'

'Yeah, Bram Stoker, I know,' I answer, 'but he's talking about wolves when he says that,' just in case she thinks I'm a thickie who's never read a book or seen a film.

'Oooh,' says the nurse, 'top marks! You studying English then? Doing a postgrad?'

'Yeah, anthropology,' I reply, not missing a beat, ignoring her raised eyebrows as I scan the area. It's true in a way – I study people.

I'm relieved to see there's a way out of the back forecourt if needed, a small door in the garden wall, now I can relax a bit, the exits are all covered. The snow is getting steadily more aggressive, the wind barging up against the side of the pub, slapping into my face with stinging persistence.

'Come on in so I can shut the bloody door, will you?' snaps the nurse, hugging herself in the doorway as the wind shrieks. 'It's Arctic in here already. Is that bloody hound properly chained up?'

She looks relieved when I nod, as the dog whimpers and lies with her head on her great paws, looking up at me with eyes full of hope that I'll take her inside. But I can't, so I leave her where she is, closing the back door on her resumed howls so we can continue our search for the loos. Heading out of the kitchen, there's no sign for the toilets, so we follow the dark corridor round to the right, past an old plaque bearing the words 'dining room'. A blood-red curtain is pulled across the doorway, furred and blackened with mildew. When I part the curtain I can see the room is piled higgledy-piggledy with dark wooden tables and chairs.

We pass a bricked-up doorway next, which, if my radar's correct, would once have taken us back through to the bar – looks like it was sealed off a long time ago and it appears to be a dead end. But around the next corner we find a flight of stained wooden stairs, the old, shallow kind that used to accommodate women, servants and maids, wearing long trip-hazard skirts.

There's probably a main stairway on the other side of the building, but somehow we've come around the back way. It's something of a maze in here, with low ceilings and flagged passages.

'Shall we try upstairs?' I ask.

'After you, professor,' says the nurse.

I turn my back on her so she doesn't see the annoyance on my face as I lead the way.

The Law – 2 p.m.

While I'm sitting at my desk, starting to think about one of my pending files, Jim has finally decided to call Susan Bell over at the hospital. We ran out of official colleagues to pump for updates about half an hour ago, but Dr Susan is an old friend of Jim's who he's known since primary school.

They're down to a skeleton crew at the cottage hospital at this time of year too, just one unlucky pathologist is on call for any sudden Christmas suicides, but Jim knows they'll have rushed Mrs Lewis's PM through, top priority, to confirm the cause of death, and Sue's now had just enough time to do the postmortem.

'Jesus, Jim,' she says on the speaker phone, 'you should've seen the old dear. Her face all swollen up . . .' She swallows and takes a breath. 'Honestly, what a mess. It's been years since I saw anything like this.'

And neat and sensible Sue with her tiny hands and huge glasses knows what she's talking about. She's seen her fair share of carnage because, according to Jim, she was a high flyer in their day, went to Oxford Uni then med school, then went on to consult for the Metropolitan Police. For some inexplicable reason she came back to Pont about five years ago, by choice, to finish her career at the hospital, and she's clearly extremely annoyed that this sort of crap has followed her home.

'This isn't assault or even GBH.' She sighs, the sound of paper rustling as she leafs through her notes. 'This is at least attempted murder, in my humble opinion. I mean, you don't do that to an old dear and expect them to get up and shake it off, do you? Fucking animals; I thought I'd seen enough of this shit in London to last a lifetime. These were supposed to be my twilight years; coronary failure, old age, the occasional tractor accident, that sort of thing, not this sick shit.'

'Yeah, it's not good,' says Jim. 'So the assault definitely killed her, it wasn't a heart attack or something? Natural causes, I mean, on top of the assault.'

'Not unless you call doing a tap dance on someone's ribs and fingers natural causes,' she clarifies. 'Four of her ribs were broken. There was massive trauma inside; her lungs looked like pulped brisket, smashed bone, she'd bled out inside. Kicks to the ribs – I reckon someone put the boot in – and then there's her fingers, maybe a stamping, but something blunt-ended could have been used.

'Look, I can't stop. The grandkids are coming over at four for Christmas-cookie making, God bless 'em, so I've got to rush. I'll put my report in later, but I hope you're going to get the bastard!'

'We're going to try, Susie love,' says Jim. 'OK, well . . .'

There's a pause as neither wants to say Merry Christmas when there's nothing merry about the mood right now. Eventually Sue says, 'Well, take care, you old fart,' which at least raises a corner of Jim's mouth into the place where his smile is usually found.

'You too, speccy four eyes,' he replies.

After he hangs up we sit for a moment thinking about Sue, about her array of medical tools and what she's been doing with them for the last three hours in the morgue. Though we're both thinking it, we know there's no point in asking the forbidden questions right now: Why do bad things happen to good people? and Why do the harmless often come to the worst harm?

Jim always tells me I must resist the temptation, that there's simply no room for sentimentality in an incident room when you're martialling resources or looking at lurid crime-scene photos. You don't ask if the victims suffered or knew what was happening to them.

Of course you know there's a real person attached to each case, that a trained liaison officer is with the grieving family, treading carefully with compassion around the wheels of bureaucracy, but the victims are at one remove, cut-out characters with their own tick list roles to play, because they have to be.

Except it's a bit different today. In the aftermath of this morning it's hard to maintain a professional distance. The violence that's ripped through the darkened farm two miles away would be terrible if it had happened anywhere, to anyone, at any time, but that something so undeserved, so visceral, has happened here, in a place like Pont, at Christmas, is unthinkably perverse.

I keep trying not to see the image of the cracked-egg head on the kitchen floor, keep trying to pretend it was merely a scene from a movie I saw, nothing more than special effects make-up and trick lighting, and I know Jim is trying not to think about the old lady sewn up on the mortuary slab, cold and alone.

Carron is just about keeping it together. She's been to the toilet twice today already for a discreet little cry but I don't have that luxury. I'm not a civilian with all their expected weakness and sentimentality, their safe cocoon of ignorance. I have to wait until later when no one is looking to even think about letting my emotions surface. That's why it's safer to distance myself – *our heroine grits her teeth and bends to the task in hand* . . . that sort of thing, compartmentalise.

If it's difficult for me it's a gargantuan task for Jim, who's grown up under the older people of the village, alongside their children, whose children have since grown up with his. He's so attuned to their web of communal histories, to the gossip and news of the market and high street, the school visits and house calls, that he could pull on any strand and reel in the story of each person at the end of it in seconds.

I know he wants to talk about it, to tell me about Polly Lewis the deceased and Osion Lewis the widower – the real people with distinct names and histories, instead of the cardboard cut-out victims the newspapers will make them when we officially identify them.

'You should have seen them in their younger days, love, Polly and Osion,' says Jim, leaning back in his chair, ready to tell a story. It's a mark of respect to pay attention, even if I didn't know them, to be part of the naming of the dead, to bear witness to the reckoning.

'You wouldn't have recognised them then,' says Jim, 'so in love in that spick-and-span farmhouse, which smelled of baking any time of the day you happened by. Smashing jam tarts, she made, always just out of the oven.'

He tells me a rural tale of a devoted couple who kept a small head of cattle on the top meadow of the farm left to them by Mr Lewis's father. How, before their baby was born, when she was almost forty – 'a blessing, at her age!' – Polly had worked in various jobs in town – cleaning the bank after hours, serving behind the counter in the Post Office – to make ends meet. Cheerful, chatty, always a good word to say about everyone, Polly had a liking for colourful silk scarves and lily of the valley toilette water. Osion was a quiet but hardworking farmer, who did rugby coaching in his spare time and was a very proud dad.

'I remember her about in town, wheeling that monstrous old pram,' says Jim, eyes staring through me, back into the past. 'Like something out of Mary Poppins, it was. Big old black thing, probably the pram she'd rode in herself as a nipper. Puffed up with pride and love at what she'd made, the definition of doting. Good-looking kid that one, too, though to be honest, grew into a bit of a shit later, bit of a bully, like. Sixteen and handsome, cock of the walk, with that sneer kids have? That boy had it in bundles.

'He'd stare at you with his baby-blue eyes and say, Sure, *cunt*-stable – I was only in my twenties myself then – but I don't know who took the charity box money, or sprayed the village hall with white paint, or whatever, smirking because he knew I couldn't prove anything.

'A mother never believes it though, does she?' he adds, shaking his head. 'Polly never thought her little angel was anything but that. And rightly so – thank God for mams, I say,' and as he talks I try not to think of my own mother, her permanent blanket of disapproval, her tight mouth ready to criticise.

'The boy died young, well not a boy, a young man almost, a terrible thing,' recalls Jim. 'Drowned in the brook one night, on his way home from a friend's. Some sort of fall, drunk on home brew they reckoned. There was a funeral up on the plot at the farm after. Broke my heart, it did. Everyone came, for the Lewises' sake. They closed off up there after that, kept to themselves.'

He strokes his neat crop of almost white hair and smiles and for a moment I can see the young and keen PC he must have been.

'She was a character though, Polly. I remember how she'd come into town in their ancient car, this antique yellow Ford Cortina thing, held together by rust and luck. She must have been in her sixties by then, but she seemed much older to us. Mrs Death, some of the younger boys in the nick called her. She couldn't park that bloody junk heap to save her life. We'd just see it abandoned in the middle of a full lane of traffic, while she was getting her pension or nipping into the shops.

'How she didn't kill herself driving that thing, or mow down someone else is a miracle. In the end her licence was taken off her. We didn't really want to but the shopkeepers were complaining it was a safety issue and so on. Then she got this boneshaker bike until her hip gave out. Bright yellow bike, big old motorcycle helmet, skinny legs flying.'

But we both know that's not how Polly Lewis will be remembered now, colourful, eccentric, balancing a shopping bag on her lap, wind lifting the ends of her hair and whipping her trouser legs. She'll be reduced to the horror of her end, the victim of Ridgeback Farm.

'Stupid bastard, Fisket,' says Jim with sudden ferocity. 'Him and those other shitty kids were always up at the farm, back in their day, like their fathers before them, little pricks, causing trouble. I had words with Billy's mother no end of times, but she was a raging alcoholic by then and he was already in and out of foster homes – had a file as long as my arm by fourteen. Stupid stuff, mostly. Shot a sheep in the arse with an air rifle, you know, what the dope heads round here call "just a laugh".

'They broke into that old pub down past Caerau a couple of times too, you know, The Star, the one everyone has always called The Halfway, cos that's where it is. We caught Billy and his mates messing around, trying to get in and turn the barrel taps on so they could get pissed. That old kiddie fiddler, George Rhydderch, was in and out of hospital that year and they gave him a hard time for a bit. Then they got bored – attention span of a gnat and all – and found the wonder of drugs . . .'

Jim probably has plenty more to say about Billy, but we're suddenly interrupted by Carron saying, 'Shhhhhhh,' and flicking the volume of the old Roberts radio up midsentence. Then we hear the first of the official news appeals we've been expecting for the last hour, the word finally moving beyond Western Wales, rippling out into the rest of the wide world.

Our bog-standard press release asks anyone with

information, or any potential witnesses, to call the emergency incident-room number immediately. The only mention of the old couple is that they've suffered serious assaults and been 'named locally' as the farm occupants behind the police cordon. Then there's a short sound clip of Inspector Morris's wet-gravel voice saying he can't confirm anything else at this stage. He gives a basic description of Finn, warning everyone not to approach the violent offender under any circumstances.

The hunt is officially on. The media appeals will surely turn up some sightings now, with everyone watching the roads and rails as far south as the Severn Bridge, as far North as Wrexham. The appeal says Riley is most likely on foot, and now I'm itching to get on mine and join the fun, especially when DS Matthews reappears in the doorway, dusting snow from his clichéd, fur-collared donkey jacket, like something out of a 1970s cop show.

Marching in with the words, 'Any chance of a coffee, love?' to Carron, he's obviously in something of a tizz, gracing us and our tiny outstation with his presence very reluctantly to send some updates to DI Morris via the internal computer network.

With the boss tied up in interviews he's in charge of the scene at the farm and wants to open up the electronic logbooks without having to go all the way back to Central, which is at least forty minutes away.

As Jim logs him on to his archaic PC we peer over his shoulder, hoping this is a good opportunity to learn something useful. There's a chance now that we'll be given a task, however bureaucratic or minor, that will include us in the day's events. It's clear he's putting out leave-cancellation notices across the whole area and issuing a request for support from neighbouring forces. This definitely means no divisional turkey roll, bingo session and Christmas piss-up at The Owain Glyndwr this evening, not that I was going anyway. I'm not exactly flavour of the month right now.

'Anything new to report, Sarge?' asks Jim. 'Any sign of Finn? Any sightings from the patrol cars?'

'Too soon for any of that really,' says Matthews, not looking up from the screen. 'Couple of false alarms from the border boys, that's all so far.'

'What about Fisket? Anything new there?'

He looks slightly annoyed that the police tom-toms have already telegraphed the news of Billy's role this far out into the sticks, but he knows how officers pass info around, and he particularly knows Jim's limitless contacts, so he doesn't reprimand us.

'Little shit's in with the inspector now,' he says grudgingly, fingers flying on the keyboard. 'Fucking tosser.'

'What's with this Finn character?' continues Jim, not easily deterred. 'I mean, what's up with someone like that? And are we looking for a getaway car?'

'No, we think our suspect's on foot now, their car was left at the farm . . . look . . . You'll get briefed with what you need to know when we're ready. Don't you have some work to be getting on with?' he asks, turning around and giving us a pointed look, forcing Jim, who was doing his best to read all the logbook details over his shoulder, to make a face at me that says, 'What a twat!'

For the next five minutes we're forced to retreat to my desk, trying to look busy, but the DS is finishing up before we know it. With his usual dramatic urgency he gets to his feet, throws back the coffee Carron made him, and possibly spat in, and yawns before ordering, 'Right, you two, don't move from your desks or go sloping off anywhere for the rest of the day. Stay put until I return to sort out the rota.'

As if we need him to tell us we'll most likely be called for the shift changeover later, to replace the others freezing their arses off at the scene since this morning. They're already well overdue a meal and wee break at the road closure too. People forget that police officers occasionally have to take a whiz and scoff a sandwich just like they do.

Now it looks like we and the other officers who've been left out of the action throughout the day, will land the unglamorous task of being the evening replacements. It's a coin toss as to whether or not the road closure or house cordon is preferable, and I envy Jim his woollen cape, made in the days of beat walking and 'all's well' night patrols – the cheap nylon zip ups they give us now don't keep a hamster's fart at bay, let alone the winter wind, and either way I'm going to freeze my tits off.

'Stay put!' says Matthews again, just because he likes the sound of his own voice. 'Right? Especially you, Leg-it! At least now you should understand what that means, I reckon.'

As he scowls I feel like I've been kicked in the guts. I can't believe he's just called me by my 'nickname' to my face, in front of Jim and Carron, and I don't think he even realised it. The arrogant prick! What happened to innocent until proven guilty?

As he grabs his car keys and a Kit-Kat from Jim's desk, swaggering importantly out into the afternoon, Jim and

I carol, 'Yes, Boss,' and flick a simultaneous two-finger salute at his back.

'Don't take any notice of him, love,' says Jim kindly. 'CID are all wankers.'

Watching him drive away I'm no longer in anything resembling a productive mood. My chances of getting properly involved in this breaking case have just plummeted to zero. It's not supposed to be like this. I'm trying not to think about how I, *the face of the future,* will now have to spend the night standing in the snow, ferrying cups of coffee back and forth to the real investigators from the flasks in the van.

This is not the image I've been trying to nurture. It's hardly likely to make me live up to the promise of the poster girl for Pont. I know I have potential, but so far no one has acknowledged it, and Sergeant Matthews isn't the only one to dismiss me. I got the same look from Inspector Morris last week when he dropped by to tell me the date and details of my pending interview with the Professional Standards board.

As I'd filled in the forms, and he'd explained my entitlement to have a representative of the Police Federation present, I'd thought his contemptuous lip curl was just because he's a seventeen-year mate of Sergeant Biggs, who's still in the hospital. How had I ended up with Morris as my mentor, the worst kind of beer-bellied dinosaur, a relic from a different era?

Well, to hell with him and Matthews and their stick-up-their-arses, respect-the-rank, earn-your-stripes manner, I think, as Jim and Carron pretend to tidy up their desks to avoid catching my eye and showing they're embarrassed for me. I'm not going to sit here like a good little girl twiddling my thumbs all afternoon, I simply can't, not while my head is exploding with humiliation and my hands are twitching with insulted rage.

I might as well save what I can of the afternoon now. Technically, before all this blew up, I had plans of my own, for my boyfriend to buy me some Christmas lunch on the QT. If I can't get involved in this unfolding incident I can at least salvage something good from the day. If I think fast I can still make it to Darren village and back before the shift change, if I'm lucky. It's time to get off my arse and get out of this bloody nick.

The Hitchhiker – 2.30 p.m.

After a count of fourteen, a turn and then another seven steps up, we reach the top of the stairs where the darkness is almost complete.

I stop short for a moment at the sound of a toilet flushing, pulling out my pocket torch and ignoring the nurse's comment of, 'Aren't you the handy one,' from the darkness at my back as we step up onto the landing. It smells less like a mouldering ruin and more like a hospital ward up here, tinged with disinfectant.

There are narrow doors in front of us on either side, presumably leading to bedrooms, but only one, open just a crack at the far end, shows a slice of pale light. By unspoken agreement we head towards it together.

Pushing the door open with my left hand, the first thing I see is a high, iron-framed bed with big, round knobs, like something out of Charles Dickens. It takes me a moment to register the withered old man lying there, almost lost in the tangle of sheets with his eyes closed.

He's not wearing a bedcap or anything but he looks like

he should be, a relic from another era in this ancient bed in this decrepit room. Instantly, I'm ashamed by the sight of him, for him, for his state of decay and for my own realisation that I really wish I hadn't opened the door.

It's not that the room is squalid. The bed is clean enough, the sheets are a freshly washed white and it's warmish, with a four-bar fire on full, close to the bed, but there's nothing homey or cosy about this room. A wheelchair is propped at the end of the bed with a thankfully empty bedpan on the seat, ready for action. There's a vast chest of drawers, funerary and forbidding, and a leaning prefab wardrobe from the 1980s that sits squashed into the far end of the room where the eaves are highest.

The motley collection of tired Christmas decorations adds to, rather than dispels, the sense of decaying despondency, especially a strange, waist-high, balding donkey, missing one hoof but wearing a red Santa hat. This is not a good sign. The donkey seems to be giving me a look. I don't meet the donkey's eye.

The old man's face is turned towards a portable TV perched on top of the large chest. The inevitable Christmas repeat of *The Sound of Music* chitters brightly to its end, credits rolling over the Austrian alps, as the more serious business of the afternoon news bulletin approaches.

But the old man's not really watching the TV; his mouth hangs open slackly. It takes him a minute, and obvious effort, to turn his gaze on us in the bedroom doorway. Straight away I can see his dilated pupils, flat and black – he's obviously doped to the gills. Painkillers, maybe? Though it seems someone is at least partially at home behind his glassy eyes, because there's something there I've seen before, a wordless pleading, a shame at that pleading being necessary.

I try and muster a smile for his benefit as his hands splay on the sheets, fingers buckled. God, I hate the hands of old people, they grip like claws, pointlessly clinging to the last ragged ends of their lives. There's drool coming out of the side of his mouth now, gathering on his chin in spittle strings. I resist the urge to let my smile become a grimace.

Without meaning to I find myself thinking of the old woman's twisted monstrous claw gripping my sleeve again, her pleading face, spittle spraying, the blood on her wrist and the front of her clothes, but it had been too late by then to change it. To take it back.

As I step into the room I can smell the tang of fresh piss. Sure enough there's a wet patch on the blankets where the old man's crotch must be.

'Jesus,' says the nurse, peering from the doorway then stepping forward.

As her face twists into something uncharitable I realise I don't like her at all. I'm trying to hide my own revulsion so she could at least do the same. A nurse should feel compassion for the old, the sick, for people like this. Their hands should be ready to help and heal with a soft, soothing voice, vocation or no fucking vocation, and if you don't feel it, fake it like everyone else.

'You all right there, old fella?' I ask, because it seems the done thing when we're both staring at him like a monkey in a zoo.

He's trying to form what could be a wave with his twisted claw. He can only lift it a few inches off the covers, but it looks like he's gesturing, pointing downwards.

Downstairs? The effort sheens his face with sweat. Frustration blooms on his face as he tries to make his mangled mouth form the words his brain is generating, trapped around his thick tongue.

'S, S, S . . .'

'What's that, old fella? I can't understand you.'

'So, so, so.' The words raise more spittle.

I look at the nurse for help but she's distracted by the TV, flickering on top of the dresser. The sound is almost too low to hear but a ticker of breaking news scrolls across the screen: 'Police search expands following incident'. Then the bulletin newsreader mutters something about a death and a manhunt.

'Turn that off, for God's sake,' I snap. 'A bit of help here?'

The nurse gives me a look to match the donkey's, but reaches over and flicks the knob off, moving round in front of the TV.

'I'm sorry, I don't understand what you're trying to say, fella,' I repeat.

'Any ideas?' I ask the nurse, who looks at me as if to say, Fucked if I know, but then steps forward to the edge of the bed.

'What is it, old chap?' she asks. 'Don't tire yourself out – it's OK. Take it easy. Don't try to talk now.'

'Br, Br, Br . . .' the same meaningless sounds come out. I can't tell if he's pointing downstairs, towards the door or just gesturing out of desperation. He might be saying bugger off for all I know. Yet there's an urgency in his face, in the tension of his arms, something important.

The nurse shrugs, leans in to me and whispers, 'Maybe he wants to take a shit,' pointing at the bedpan.

Nice, I think, then, oh Jesus, I hope not, because I'm *not* up for that. 'You offering to help?' I ask.

'What the fuck are you doing in here?' says the landlord's voice.

The violence in it makes me flinch as he appears behind us in the doorway, pushing me aside, which I really don't like, and I tense in reflex as he walks to the side of the bed and grabs the old man's hand.

'Get the fuck out of here,' he says, shaking with rage, 'both of you.'

He's holding a wet sponge in a plastic bowl with a towel over his arm, presumably to clean up the old man. I realise then that the floor at the near side of the bed is also wet.

'My so, so, so,' splutters the old man, hand flailing again in a small circle. The strain on his face is evident.

'Jesus. You'd better calm him down or he'll have a heart attack,' says the nurse redundantly.

'He already has. Get the fuck out! You shouldn't be in here. Why are you up here?'

I see something in his face that I recognise. It's fear. Fear and shame and other things, perhaps because he's doing his best to take care of his father, or perhaps because he isn't and he's been caught by strangers who have turned up in the dark winter days of his father's life to pass judgement.

I drop my shoulders, deliberately relaxing into a pacifying posture, stretching my hands out towards him, palms up, open in apology. 'I'm sorry. Really. We didn't mean to pry. We were just looking for the loos.'

'Yeah, we didn't mean to upset him,' says the nurse, saying something useful for once. 'Is he OK? Looks like he's had a stroke? Must be hard, looking after him all alone?'

159

Now your bedside manner kicks in, well, better late than never.

The landlord doesn't answer. He just clutches the bowl of water and the old man's clawed hand.

'He doesn't have any other family? You two are alone here?' asks the nurse.

'Yeah, just us.'

'And he can't move. He's bedridden?'

'He can't move much since the last attack.'

'And he can't speak?'

'Not much, no. Not now.'

The old man gestures at us, or perhaps at something only he can see, maybe something lodged behind us in another lifetime. He looks through me as his muscles seize and clench for a second before slumping back into the pillow, his eyes fluttering shut.

'Is his mind going? I mean, does he still know who you are?' asks the nurse.

'I don't think so. He's confused most of the time.'

Jesus, this is depressing. I can't think of anything worse than being stuck here, trapped in that useless body, still having the power of thought, the desire to speak but no way to get the words out. Alzheimer's would be a mercy, really. If I ever get like that I hope someone will put a pillow over my face – someone should do that now for this old fucker. Put him out of his misery. It'd be a kindness.

'Look, just get the fuck out of here,' says the landlord. 'He's OK. He's OK. He gets tired that's all. He needs to sleep. Get out.'

The nurse steps back as he moves towards us, before he can shove her out of the room with his outstretched arm.

'Right, sorry, the loo?' I repeat, eager to beat a retreat.

'Down the end, on the right. Be quick.'

'Bloody hell,' I say, once we're out of earshot along the mildewy upper corridor. 'Poor old bugger.'

'Yeah, shame,' says the nurse with a complacency that must come from seeing similar poor old sods every day. Guess you get immune to it after a while. You can come to accept all sorts of things as normal, as par for the course, I know that well enough.

'Shouldn't there be a home-help here or something? Is he on any of your colleagues' rounds? You know, home care?'

She gives me a patient look.

'I already said he's not on my regular rounds. Not really my area, I'm just filling in. Guess I could check later. Back at the office . . . with Social Services . . .'

Sure. Course you will.

'What do you think he was trying to say?' she asks, her face clouding for a moment. 'He seemed pretty worked up about something.'

'Buggered if I know.'

Eventually we find the bathroom. It's fairly acceptable, despite looking like something out of the 1970s in all its avocado green and brown glory. There are dark rust stains in the plughole of the sink, but there are a few clean towels stacked on a rack above the bath and a bottle of bleach by the loo. It's been used recently, rather heavy-handedly, too, judging by the sharp ammonia mist that lands on my tongue.

The inside-out skins of a pair of rubber gloves lie in the bath. The landlord's at least keeping the place clean. No tetanus required after all.

161

'Wanna go first?' asks the nurse.

'Sure, cheers.'

I know I should really take off my gloves to use the loo, and wash my hands like a civilised person, but it's still 'as cold as a witch's tit', to quote my brittle travel friend, and my hands still hurt like a bastard every time I pull the gloves off. It's too much effort to do it with the care it needs so I don't bother – it's unhygienic but that's hardly my priority at the moment. I don't want to stay in this place any longer than necessary.

If the snow lets up I'll press on and take my chances. I'm better on my own. I'm halfway to somewhere for sure, so it can't be any further to whatever's down the road than what's behind me, that's simple logic. The nurse can come or not, as she pleases.

When I head back into the corridor my companion is watching the old man silently, through the crack in the bedroom door. Spotting me she holds her finger to her lips before padding back to use the loo. Intrigued I put my eye to the crack in the door where hers was. The landlord is sitting on the edge of the bed, looking at the old man. From this angle I can't see his face but his posture suggests a man deciding what to do next. The towel and sponge is in his hands but he's not using them. The clock ticks steadily as the blood from his wet bandage drips onto the floor.

The Old Man – 2.45 p.m.

He forces himself to breathe but his heart's racing and his vision's greying out. Somehow there's snow in his head as well as outside the pub now, as he lies here, sweating, shaking. He's somehow aware of the twitchy oaf close by, hissing, 'Calm down, calm down, for fuck's sake, and keep quiet,' flicking the TV back on and turning up the sound to cover the noise of his struggles.

He wants to tell him to fuck off, to yell it right at him. He wants to ask who that was in the doorway just now and what's going on. Who was that girl who looked like a boy? Dressed like one? She can't be a friend of Rose's; she doesn't have those sorts of friends. Or does she now? Where is Rose anyway? Why isn't she here? Has she gone shopping again in this weather? Stupid woman!

What's happened to him? He can't move much. It's not just his left arm that's limp now. He feels his face drooling, spittle dripping onto his chin and cheek. There's something on the TV again, something about the police. There's been an incident over the way, a robbery. Some bastards have beaten up that old girl, no names given yet but he knows that farm, Ridgeback on the stream.

Looking for lifesavings, probably, the bastards, money for drugs most likely. Bet they broke in and she tried to fight back. He can understand that, the urge to resist, the outrage boiling up, the impulse that stays young, even after your body withers into old age.

That's what's so cruel. He wants to fight but he can't. Can't find his walking stick right now, the one he uses sometimes to beat the floor by the bed to get their attention, to make the buggers – the harpy – come. Not that they always come.

When Brian comes back they'll get it in the neck, for sure . . . Wait . . . Brian . . . is Brian coming back? Is he here already? No, that was just a nightmare. It must have been . . . Oh God, Brian . . .

Everything is jumbled, tangled, his heart racing to escape his chest as he forces himself to breathe as best he can. He realises someone is cleaning the floor by the bed. Why bother with that now? Why does it matter? Why not just let him die in peace?

No one will come looking for him. It's such a long time since he's had any visitors, since he heard the knock on the door and young Blass the post shouting up, 'Mr Rhydderch – George – it's me, Glyn Blass. Haven't seen you for a while. A l-l-letter's come for you. I thought it was important; it c-c-c-came to Dad at the Post Office, so I opened it. He's worried about you, your boy Brian. He says you haven't replied to any of his l-l-letters. Dad always said, before he passed away, that you should make it up. It's time now, surely? To b-b-build a b-bridge? While you can, he said. I thought I should come, for B-B-Brian.'

Time? It's long *past* time, that's for sure, and he'd tried to shout out to him, to say, 'Don't go, Glyn boy, stay, I'm coming. Get me out of this bloody place,' but he couldn't make himself heard through his mangled throat.

By the time he'd got himself to the foot of the stairs young Blass was long gone, but there was the envelope behind the door and he had to get to it before *she* came back, before she took it away.

The effort it had taken to get that far, every muscle burning like he was running a marathon along every yard of the bedroom floor, the sweat soaking him, pulling with his better arm, pushing with his feet. It had taken him almost an hour, edging along the landing, sliding down the stairs on his arse like a kid, the last few feet, easy by comparison. Then he'd reached out and clutched the letter to his sweating chest.

Blass had already opened it because it had been addressed to Blass, sent into his care. That meant he could slide out the paper, even with his limp and useless hand and read the letter inside. He'd devoured the words in the folded square of paper marked 'For Dad'.

He'd never thought about how he'd make it back up to bed, not fighting gravity, not when he was already exhausted, but that hadn't mattered because he'd known then, known that Brian hadn't stopped writing to him like the harpy claimed. That she must have been hiding the letters from him all along, so sure he wouldn't know.

She must have reasoned that if Brian ever came home and asked where the money was, the cash he'd been sending regular as clockwork, then she'd look all innocent and say he'd spent it. They'd just think, What a kind woman, talking care of that dirty old bastard. What a kind soul.

After reading the letter he'd slumped, wet with exertion, against the wall and read the note Brian had scribbled to Blass, also inside the envelope; I'm worried, Mr Blass. You were always a friend to him. Could you pass this on to my dad? He doesn't answer my letters or calls. I've been trying for a few months now.

Hadn't expected that, had she? Hadn't expected Brian to go around her and try straight for Owain, not knowing of course that he'd died? If there's enough time left young Blass might even come calling again. His heart's in the right place, that one, like his old dad.

After he'd read the note through three times he'd folded it up as small as he could and shoved the letter in a warped crack between the door and the wall. He'd wanted to keep it but couldn't risk her finding it when she came back and saw his attempted escape. Besides, he'd memorised it, each word, the ones that mattered. Every time he thinks of those two simple words his heart explodes.

'Dear Dad,' it said. Dear, Dad, 'I need to tell you something . . . something about Gary . . . I did something. It wasn't meant to happen that way. It was really why I had to leave . . .'

The words circle from his head and up into the blackness of sleep. Somewhere in the spaces between he can hear the sound of a sponge on scuffed floorboards, water sloshing in a bowl, washing, but he cannot lift his head to see the water turn red.

The Law – 3.05 p.m.

When she phones the nick, just after three o'clock, Chrissy Williams is clearly more pissed off than worried.

'I was only supposed to be watching the kids until one o'clock,' she whines to Carron, her nails-on-a-blackboard voice audible through the receiver six feet across the room. 'I'm not a fucking child minder. She was supposed to be back by now. I have to get home. My Dave will go mad if I'm not there to get the tea on. Now look at the fucking weather! Probably can't get my car out already.'

'Is this really a police matter?' asks Carron, holding the phone an inch further away from her head and pursing her lips. 'She's a grown woman, and there's really no need for that language, lovely girl.'

'It's a fucking police matter when she said she'd be back by one. I guess she's a missing person, so you have to find her, right?'

'Not exactly, it's only been two hours. I'm sure she's on her way right now,' says Carron as me and Jim roll our eyes.

'Have you rung anyone else to check where she is, or checked in with her boss?'

'Yeah, of course I have, I'm not a retard, love. I rang her manager's number down the surgery and she said the last old fart on today's home visit list was down for a check at noon and she doesn't know where the fuck she is. She's not answering her work or her personal mobile.'

It's Carron's turn to roll her eyes as she takes down some details on her pad. With everything else that's going on a three-hour missing woman is hardly a priority but it could come in useful to me as I've been trying to drum up a non-suspicious reason to leave for the last half hour to make my late lunch date.

We've only been dating about six weeks, so I wouldn't exactly call him my boyfriend, we just got chatting while I was collecting the CCTV following a break-in at his dad's estate agents and I'd seen at once that he was the sort of bloke with a secret thing for women in uniform.

It's not serious, but he's much richer than I am, is generous with meals and gifts and smells really good. He also has great teeth, white and straight, like American TV teeth, and that alone makes him a cut above most of what's on offer around Pont.

This morning the plan had been to go down to Darren village to fetch some paperwork relating to a pub fight, the perfect excuse to drop in at the office and invite myself for a bite of lunch somewhere on his expenses. I've already left him two messages today, trying to confirm a time and I'm a bit annoyed he hasn't replied yet.

It's too late for lunch obviously, but a mince pie and a coffee would go down nicely, and I know Jim won't bat a baggy eyelid if I say I'm going on a nurse-check and pasty/cake/bacon-roll run for the long evening ahead. As long as I'm back by five o'clock, no one will be any the wiser. I know because I've played a bit of hooky like this before.

More than once I've taken the Panda car out 'patrolling', usually along the coast to watch the cold-shrivelled surfers beating the waves on their boards in the bay. Once or twice I've pulled up at one of the deserted picnic areas on my way home from a call to read a book for half an hour in peace and quiet, usually an Agatha Christie, Elmore Leonard, or Patricia Cornwell. Well, I know it's not very professional, but the monotony gets to me and I need the occasional hit of crime excitement to sustain me through the boredom.

It's not that big a deal really, normally so little happens in Pont and virtually nothing happens quickly. No one's been any the wiser so far and I get to keep my sanity. Chrissy Williams's call is a bonus for me as it gives me a legitimate reason to take a run in the car. As I grin at this bit of happy luck, Carron has already called the nurse's boss, written down the name and address of her last appointment and got the number plate of the car.

'I'll check it out,' I say to Jim, snatching the paper from Carron's hand and pulling on my coat. He's still absorbed in Matthews' scene updates on the screen, which he's neglected to properly log out of when I add, 'I'll do a drive around in the four-by-four. See if I can spot this nurse's car. I've got an hour or two to kill. I'll get some snow supplies in while I'm at it. Think it's gonna be a long night.'

Grabbing the car keys before anyone can say otherwise,

I head out into the twilight afternoon on the lookout for Rebecca Nash, missing nurse.

'Stay in low gear,' shouts Jim after me, not looking up from the PC screen. 'And get me a Chocolate Orange and a can of Lilt please. And don't do anything I wouldn't do. Stay on the radio, love!'

'Will do, Sarge. See you soon. Keep the kettle on,' I call back, dreaming of the day when I get to send someone else out for my Coke and Snickers from a nice desk at HQ.

It's already as good as dark as I leave the nick forecourt, buckling on my belt kit, complete with cuffs and pepper spray, just in case. The four-by-four is full of petrol (thanks to Jim's diligence) and like most people in Pont I've driven Land Rovers since I was old enough to reach the clutch. I'm not that bothered about the weather when I reverse out of the yard. We get a snow panic every winter, dire weather warnings, a rash of end-of-days milk- and bread-buying and candle-checking, but then it passes.

Though less than a mile out of the village it seems the forecasters might actually be right this time. It's a big one and I've clearly underestimated just how quickly and completely the snow is coating the countryside, closing off the sky and drawing down visibility to a few hundred yards.

It's pretty obvious I can't get through the back lanes down to Caerau after all as, on a snake-like stretch where the road narrows to a single track, I find myself skidding to a halt behind an overturned trailer, abandoned in the growing whiteout.

I might be able to get around through the mud and sludge at the sides, but the last thing I need is to prang this expensive off-road vehicle to add to my sins. Cursing and grinding the gears, I reverse what feels like half a mile to the nearest passing place and do an exhausting ten-point U-turn.

As my tyres slither back towards the narrow tarmac strip that passes as our main road, the trees close in and the landscape begins to look threatening and unfamiliar. I'd never admit it but the opaque darkness between the trees crowding these hills has always carried a breath of dread for me. As a child, cuddled deep under the bedcovers, I'd often suspected the gnarled oaks and spreading beeches around our farmhouse of creaking and croaking secrets to each other in the night, plotting against me.

Even worse, the narrow cleft of the valley below our farm had reflected the howls and yelps of endless neighbours' dogs, fretting under the moonlight, giving me a deep-seated fear of wolves. Though Mum repeatedly reassured me they'd died out in Britain centuries ago I'd always wondered how she could be sure. One or two might have stayed hidden, foraging for fat children in the dark Western hills, keeping their heads down and their noses sharp for the scent of fear. At four or five, I was even convinced one was hiding out in our attic, prowling under the beams, with lip-smacking, razor-sharp teeth.

As I drive into the growing darkness it occurs to me that maybe those childhood fears were not unfounded, just misplaced. In a way, my mother had lied to me and to herself. As today has proved, there are hungry things prowling abroad by day and night, ready to feed on the weak and unprepared, to huff and puff and blow your house down.

One such thing had come for the old couple at Ridgeback Farm and walked right into that cosy old kitchen, so what else could be lurking out here, maybe on this very road, lying in wait for me?

As I drive I try not to think about how I'm alone in this car in the isolating dusk, very far from my gang of officers for once. It's never bothered me before but, after the events of the morning, the safe shape of the familiar countryside assumes a distinctly wolfish air as I inch along in the snow.

Telling myself to get a grip, I fix my eyes closely on the road ahead, using my technique to distract myself from darker thoughts. *Our heroine is unfazed by the looming, sinister woods that try to hamper her progress, as if in conspiracy against her. Bravely she gathers her calm, faced with a decision. She is reluctant to return to the withering gaze of the formidable Sergeant Price without his chocolate and can of Lilt. She needs to use her wits to rescue the endeavour and come up with a gutsy course of action – a plan B.*

I decide to take a shortcut and follow the farm track that comes out by the ruined motel on the back road. From there it's a straight drop down the valley to Darren. The council will surely have salted the road, and it's a fifteen-minute run past the petrol station, always open and always stocked with sausage rolls and microwavable steak-and-onion pasties.

Yet, as half an hour passes, I find myself still crawling along in second gear, cursing, increasingly unsettled, trapped behind my headlight beams, squinting through the wall of snow. My mobile phone on the seat next to me is stubbornly silent, even though I've been willing it to ring since I set out, for it to be my 'not boyfriend', full of apologies for missing my messages, for dragging me out in this shit weather on a false promise of free food. Right now, I'd actually be grateful to hear his usual greeting, 'How are you, gorgeous?' though, to be honest, I've been getting a bit bored of him lately.

It was nice at first that he's so interested in what I do, that he thinks my job is important, that he, unlike everyone else, seems to think I'm up to it. I was flattered, until lately, when I realised he's often more interested in getting the low-down and dirty on the incidents I've attended than doing the same with me, as you'd expect of all good love interests smitten with the lady police heroine.

Of course, there are lots of people like that around, ghouls who get their rocks off from second-hand tragedy, the rubberneckers crawling along in the outside lane of the motorway past the twisted metal in the carriageway, mouths agape. He's definitely one of those. A real civilian.

'Was it very grim, Liss?' he'd asked once, after I'd gone over to his straight from the scene of a hanging suicide.

'Well, it wasn't pretty, put it that way,' I replied, glugging his expensive Rioja in the corner of his deep leather sofa.

'Come on! Spill the beans. Did that old man really cut his wrists and paint on the walls in his blood? That's what my dad says he heard down The Owain Glyndwr.'

'Don't be stupid,' I'd snapped, irritated by his eager grin. One of us with a flair for the theatrical is enough at any given time. 'That was just graffiti, daubs of red sheep paint. It said, "Fuck you, Laura", a message to his ex-wife.'

Or so I'd heard from Ty Podmore, who'd heard it from

CID, because I'd spent the afternoon guarding the front door with no chance to go inside.

With the news spreading about the Ridgeback incident I'm actually amazed he hasn't been bombarding me with calls today, pumping me for the latest insider info and gory gossip: 'They're saying it's a slaughterhouse up there, Liss? A veritable bloodbath? So who's this fugitive then? This "perp" on the run?'

I know he'll call Finn that – 'the perp' – when he grills me later. He's fond of Americanisms like 'autopsy' and 'pleading the fifth', even though I tease him about it. He'll no doubt be down at the Darren office now, gleefully imagining a Louisiana-style manhunt in full swing, complete with loudhailers and lazy-eyed wolfhounds, from the safety of his office chair.

To be fair, *I* already have, and it's hard not to indulge in a little continuation of that fantasy right now to pass the time, particularly about what I'd do if I stumbled across the dangerous offender Riley Finn in the road ahead, right here, this very minute.

Our heroine screeches to a halt in a dramatic flurry of sleet, police baton at the ready. She follows her flawless instincts and impeccable training, fearlessly exiting the vehicle, approaching the offender with a loud and clear caution, identifying herself as an officer of the law. With her eyes flashing and hair flying attractively, she orders the offender to surrender immediately.

At this point Finn will obviously refuse my command to drop to the floor, necessitating some breathtaking heroics. *Catching her breath and steeling herself for the confrontation, our brave young heroine delivers a disabling blow to the back of the knee and one to the stomach. The fugitive is unable to break free of the expert headlock and, flailing and gasping, crumples to the floor. Our heroine applies her knee to the suspect's back before snapping the cuffs on, and the dangerous offender slumps in surrender.*

Cue my triumphant arrival at Central nick, preferably in slow motion, to a nice soft-rock soundtrack song of my choosing. If Finn is a little more battered and bruised than is legally acceptable I'm sure no one will mind; maverick cops have to break the rules now and then and use unorthodox methods to make sure justice is done.

I can already see Inspector Morris's mouth falling open at the sight of the trussed Finn, revealing his full set of fillings in awe of my skill.

Who you calling a fuck-up now, sir? Cheers ensue.

I'm under no illusions that this is an altogether more palatable scene than the one that concluded my afternoon at Bryn Mill farm four weeks ago. There were no handcuffs and cheers after 'the perp' John Harvey came lumbering towards me with a knife in his hand; the exact opposite in fact.

'Wanna play with the big boys, love?' he sneered. 'Well? What you gonna do, Officer?'

I sometimes wonder, if I'd bothered to read John Harvey's file which the sarge had given me *before* we'd left the nick that day, would I have thought twice about going inside alone? Instead I ignored Biggsy's order to stay put while he went around the back, gave the wooden front door a push and, finding it unlocked, opened it.

Stepping into the cool plaster-damp, dog-smelling gloom I'd thought the outcome would be simple, that Biggsy would come in through the half-open kitchen door, down the passageway across the flagstones and catch Harvey with his feet up.

We had our warrant, had already made a note of the twelve barrels of stolen and illegal red diesel in the back of the van out by the shed; we knew we would make a good arrest. All I had to do was stand back while the cuffs went on before smugly showing the sarge what I'd found in the hall. I was already congratulating myself when big John, 6 feet 3 inches and 22 stones, stuck his head around the kitchen door.

Compared to those minutes of hot, iron-tinged panic, the fantasy confrontation with Finn in the woods is a doddle, so engaging, in fact, that I've forgotten all about Rebecca Nash and the purpose of my errand. And, as I finally come upon the junction by the old Blue Skies Motel, I almost miss the flicker of someone moving in the trees.

The Hitchhiker – 3.30 p.m.

It was the smallest thing that had done it, triggered the countdown. It was sitting behind Rhys on the shelf in the photo – a small green canister, missing its lid. I couldn't read the words on it, but I'd known right away what it was, a grenade of sorts, about to explode.

The image returns to me now as I stand at the pub's kitchen counter, eating the Marmite on toast I've just made with the landlord's dry loaf. The nurse is wolfing down three slices at the kitchen table and has also helped herself to a can of beer, saying, 'Sod it. It's Christmas,' an unexpected move.

I could murder a beer right now, but I don't join her yet. Stealing bread is one thing, stealing a beer has started more than a few fights in my experience. But the landlord hasn't come back downstairs yet so, with luck, we'll have finished eating before he does and can clear away any evidence.

As I stare out at the snow blotting and shifting the surface of windows, I remember how the small square of living room had looked in the photo Rhys emailed me – like it always had except for that single overlooked can of Silvikrin hair spray – the scent of my youth, of crowded school toilets, of unattended club discos and sudden betrayal.

I'd wondered about it constantly, over the weeks, why it was there, who it belonged to, and who exactly had taken that picture of Rhys grinning up at me from the screen.

I'd pushed the thoughts out and away from me for as long as I could, practised my patience until it was raw and blistered, sat for hours on my mind train, letting everything sail by outside, or tried to.

I'd failed. The thoughts simply kept returning, circling the outer globe of my brain, roosting inside, flitting like birds, trying to escape, a niggling trapped instinct. Every so often I'd hear them bashing about up there and wondered . . . kept on wondering . . . their peck, peck, peck eating at my throat and chest, devouring the days, hours, minutes.

Because, to be honest, I'd felt it for a while, the unease in his voice during our weekly phone call, nothing said, rather unsaid, a sense of strained performance under his usual casual questions and replies. Of course it was worse because I couldn't get to him, to thrash it all out in person, couldn't look him in the eye. How could I reassure myself that I wasn't simply imagining things, overreacting, my speciality, flying off the handle, taking things the wrong way?

It's not the sort of subject you can raise in a weekly phone call anyway, not with other people always listening. Not when someone can just hang up, cut the line and leave you hanging from a noose of doubt. Who is she? I wanted to ask. Are you cheating on me, Rhys? Are you bringing a girl to your flat who is leaving her shit around? Are you getting careless because you care less and less if I suspect?

It'd been a while since I'd talked to him properly, with everything going on, about what I might do when I reached the end of my time. I'd pretty much decided there could be a life for me with Rhys in it. A real life, not a long-distance one.

I remember Lilli-Anne, sitting on her bunk in her underwear because it was so fucking hot that day, laughing when I mentioned it, when I talked the taboo talk about getting out and starting over, because no one does that. It's bad luck to say the actual words, tempting fate, because something can always happen, even at the very last minute. When your bag is packed and you're waiting at the gates, in your own clothes, with your own plans, something can happen.

'Well, we'd miss you, girl, but what the fuck would you do out there,' Lil chuckled, 'as an "upstanding member of society"? You know they generally frown on beating the shit out of people out there, right? What'll you do without someone to tell you when to eat, sleep and shit?'

'Whatever the fuck I want,' I answered.

'Isn't that how you ended up here in the first place, doll? I reckon we'll see you again. You won't be able to keep away. What the fuck are you gonna do away from C wing?'

That was her little joke, the 'C' wing thing. Lilli had coined the term from the 'C word', where all the cunts sleep, on the second night after she'd arrived and settled in the bunk opposite. She'd meant it literally, having one herself, no insult intended. She said it was her way of owning it, like the way gangsta rappers have started calling each other 'niggas' – 'appropriate the language of oppression for your own ends'.

'Think you could be Little Bo Peep and look after the sheep?' She'd laughed. 'Can't see you as a farmer, darling, making fucking jam and boxing eggs, even if your folks finally give you that old place, unless they're hiding a fortune in undeclared income or something. Fucking bonus! Still, if it's in your stars it'll flow to you, doll.'

Typical Lil, filth and fortune-telling in one breath.

But the photo changed things. I knew I could only make a choice if I had all the facts to hand, the hard evidence and space to assemble it. I'd thought coming home would give me the room I needed to think, here, in the deadest, dullest place on earth, in the darkest season, where there are no distractions. But then I took my spare key, let myself into Rhys's flat and *boom!* Carnage.

As soon as I saw it I'd wanted to lash out, kick, scream, punch, all Pam's words and warnings wasted in the moments after I'd removed my key from the lock. More than anything else I'd wanted to hurt someone, badly, even though I'd tried to say, Change the story. Choose your next action, the power of my mantra had waned to a wisp of white noise.

Why was I so angry to learn he'd been sticking his dick in some slapper with big hair?

We were all wrong from the start, an idea of something that didn't really exist outside our own heads. Sure, we'd managed a few visits over the years, days, snatched hours, after I first went away and then when he was still here and I was up in the Midlands. All those months, the distance just doable, but everything changed later, with the move to C wing. It had got so much more real then, the world of space and time between us. It wasn't even a long-distance relationship, more one on permanent pause.

Can I really blame him for fucking someone else when he's been virtually single for so long? Patience is finite. I know that. Absence doesn't always make the heart grow fonder, otherwise I'd fucking love this dead-end arsehole of a village I once called home.

There'd been that single week, though, when we'd seemed like a grown-up couple, those seven days doing normal things together, like walking on the freezing pebble beach up at Aberystwyth, warming up with coffees in cafés, holding hands. Just like a fucking romantic couple. When he'd moved into his new flat he'd given me one of his spare keys, 'For when you're able to stay over,' he'd said, pulling me straight into the bedroom and shagging my brains out.

It had seemed like a sweet gesture, the key, but an empty one. The shagging had been quite sweet, though – slow and fast and slow again, and with kisses and wine. That afternoon had been as close to good as anything I've ever known, and lately I'd started to think about it a lot. Of it being part of what could come next for me, for us. Of that little flat, or a new start in a larger one. Of something clean and simple. A quiet life.

But then, yesterday . . . was it only yesterday?

What had I expected? He'd never really said he loved me. Simply saying, 'love you' in that throwaway fashion that ends a phone call doesn't really count, just more useless words spiralling around, more wallpaper. I'd only said it once or twice myself, always when I was blazing drunk, then in emails that came back with the answer, 'you too', or 'take care babes'.

Maybe he'd just come to mean more to me in his absence than in the flesh; the idea of him, my posh boy, *mine*, my going-straight guy, existing as a reserve chute if the main one failed – pull the cord, float back to safety.

I can see how I poured what I'd needed into him, saw my own wishes reflected back at me and mistaken them for a future. That's why I was so humiliated, seeing the flat, what it told me without words – I had been deselected, upgraded to a better model. I felt like a fool, a loser. Soon I'd wanted him to feel a lot worse, and he had.

'Cheer up. It might never happen,' says the nurse, her voice coming to me from far away, though she's just across the table, emptying her can of lager. I realise she's watching me daydreaming and I feel naked in that moment, spied upon, violated by her cool grey gaze. I'd like to toss the empty toast plate into her silly grinning face and tell her to mind her own fucking business.

'What if it's already happened!' I say, instead of beating the shit out of her, which I could do, easily. I turn my back to her as I quietly rinse my plate and knife under the tap before placing them neatly on the draining board.

'Oh, it has, hasn't it? Already happened,' says the nurse, tossing the can in the rubbish in a single well-aimed throw and gesturing round the room. 'I mean, why else would we be here? Why are you here, Lee?' she asks, curiosity in her face now, but we all know what that did to the cat.

If only you knew, I think, turning and walking away without bothering to reply.

The Law – 3.30 p.m.

What was that? I think, as I snap my thoughts away from Riley Finn-catching command-room glory and back to the suggestion of a figure that just flashed by, black on white against the darkening day. Something definitely caught my eye out there, just off the snow-clogged road.

It was only a glancing idea of movement through the fogged windscreen, activating what Jim calls that 'lizard brain' of ours, so attuned to registering the flickering of dark threat. Once upon a time it would have stopped us getting eaten up by something bigger and badder, so he says we should never ignore it.

Though I'm not entirely sure I haven't simply spooked myself, I slow right down and look back over my shoulder to get a second look at the old motel's forecourt. I'm familiar with the Sunny View Motel, a crazy folly, abandoned for decades by all but a few hardy kids and the occasional druggie.

The community bobbies do a sweep of it twice a year,

just to make sure there aren't any missing homeless people mummifying among the rat droppings and birds' nests, though I've never been inside. It's mostly a place where kids mess around, but surely it's too cold for that sort of thing, bongs and blowjobs, at this time of year.

Sure enough, I glance behind me in time to see a hooded shape, head down, dodging under one of the broken door panels along the front of the cabin. He, if it is a he, seems to have dropped something that looks like a big shopping bag. They're not coming back to collect it, which immediately makes me suspicious. People have very little around here, so no one dumps anything easily or quickly.

I hit the brakes again, catch my breath as the wheels began to slide, correct the steering, then wait a few seconds before reversing backwards slowly, level with the dropped bag. Throwing the door open I can see it's a large leather woman's holdall, expensive-looking rather than the usual market-bought PVC or designer knock-off.

A little flowered make-up pouch spills from inside revealing a hairbrush and lipstick. The design's familiar: Chanel – at more than £20 a pop it's not a popular brand locally. I squint up towards the motel and, a few seconds later, see a dark head-sized shape appear at a splintered windowpane before it flies back out of sight.

If anything this looks like a classic bag snatch and dump to me, the reaction of a petty robber caught riffling through an opportunistic grab theft by a passing black and white panda car. If they hadn't panicked I probably would've just driven right on by.

As the engine idles and the blizzard thickens I wonder if I should take a look. This obviously can't be our fugitive, mucking around, wasting time with pocket money and maybe a credit card from a stolen bag. I know Riley Finn is most likely miles away by now and I don't really want to tie myself up with yet another pile of unnecessary routine paperwork before Christmas.

I could indulge in a little selective amnesia, drive on by and cut my losses but, then again, someone who's lost an expensive bag like that will be well pissed off and will certainly report it. They might also be equally pleased to have their property returned by a diligent officer, which wouldn't do any harm.

And, if I'm honest, there's something else that makes me reluctant to drive on and turn a blind eye today: the image of John Harvey, fresh in my mind, how he'd been so unafraid of me with the knife in his hand, unafraid even of the uniform I was wearing and its supposed conferred power.

Shame floods my cheeks as I think of it, and I realise I want to act like a copper for once instead of just rehearsing it. So before the urge to confront this little thieving toerag wears off, I get out of my car and pull on my coat. Squatting in the snow I lift the handle of the dumped bag with one finger, just in case there are prints on it, and can see right away that there's no wallet inside, no ID, no phone – the first things a thief would take.

There's a box of Valium, though, a prescription pad for Carmarthen NHS Trust and a cheap NHS pen, alongside a box of plasters, some hand sanitising gel and a clear packet of blood-sugar testing sticks. It crosses my mind that this is a doctor's or nurse's bag and, as it happens, I'm looking for a nurse.

According to Carron, this motel is on the route Rebecca Nash would have taken to her last appointment and I find myself hoping she hasn't been mugged – or worse. I mean, this isn't a prime car-jacking area – it's hardly LA or Cape Town – but you never know, a woman alone, especially today when all bets are off on the kindness of neighbours.

I pull out my radio, thinking about calling it in and getting Jim's advice on what to do, hoping that by now the nurse has shown up of her own accord and is filing a theft form. But every time I press the call button, the air from the handset is thick with static and the echo of my own voice.

As a force we've always struggled with technical gremlins and low coverage between the radio masts, so I'm hardly surprised there's no signal here, that I'm in a blackspot. I'm on my own for now with a decision to make: take the easy option and head back to the nick or check out what I've found.

Lives turn on such moments, on such decisions. I know that only too well. If I take a chance, maybe I'll get a nice collar from this and a pat on the back by the end of the day. As I stare up at the abandoned hotel I enlist some help, asking what I should do. *What would the Scooby gang do? What would Clarice Starling do?* Then, tossing the bag onto the back seat of the car, I zip up my collar, slam the car door and head towards the motel.

Crossing the cracked car park isn't as easy as I'd thought, not with the snow building into a whooshing tsunami of white, but I do my best to check the area for any signs of disturbance as Jim has trained me to do. After a scan through squinted eyes, I spot several sets of what looks like softening footprints in the snowfall, or perhaps it's only one set of footprints going back and forth between the motel, padding across the car park towards the road and back again in a muddled line.

I know I'm probably only looking at the tracks of teenagers, so I try not to think of John Harvey, how the sheer size of him had stopped me in my tracks, switching off the voice in my head that says, What if it happens again out here? What if you freeze when you're all on your own, without back-up?

Instead I choose to remind myself of Jim's wise words on my first day under his tutelage, 'Give it a chance, love. You can't learn everything at once. Most of us aren't born with a spine of steel, we have to grow one.'

To buoy myself up a bit I mutter, 'What do you think, Scooby? Is there a gang of no-goods at the abandoned motel? Should Clarice go inside and look for Hannibal Lecter or his serial-killer friend? Come on then, adopt an authoritative tone. Announce yourself with confidence.

'This is the police,' I say loudly, striding towards the boarded-up motel door. 'If you're in there, skinning up or smoking weed, come out now and stop playing silly buggers.'

I'm pleased to note that my voice sounds steady and demanding, even though only the whispers of the wind answer my order and my lizard brain steps up again, registering another flicker of movement along the curtain fabric of a window to my left.

'If you make me come in there I will not be pleased, come out now!' I demand, raising my voice even further.

OK. Plan B, then. *Our bold heroine investigates. She enters the motel. Come on, Scooby.*

My baton drawn, my heart rattling just a bit, I approach the broken door panel. I feel a bit better because at least it will be hard for anyone to creep up on me in there, like John Harvey had, to do anything quietly in fact. One look through the broken door shows me the floor is littered with branches from a huge hole in the partly collapsed roof. Of course, that means I can't exactly creep in either, but then, I don't creep, I remind myself, I am an officer of the law.

'Come out where we can see you,' I say. 'You're pissing my partner off and you won't like him when he's not in a good mood.'

Well, a little subterfuge never hurt anyone. There's strength in numbers, even if they're imaginary, and one's potentially a seven-foot cartoon dog or a fictional FBI agent.

When no one replies or shows themselves I take a deep breath – *our heroine steels herself for what might be ahead, ready and alert.*

'OK,' I say, 'we're coming in!' and duck into the motel.

The Old Man – 4 p.m.

He knows he's dying now and that's OK, at least he's not alone any more. Because he *knows*, even if it's just for this second, he remembers. He swallows down the wads of tears rising in his throat because if he lets them go they might pour out around him and drown the room – that at least would be quick, because what's the alternative now?

She'll come back soon, the harpy, clean up this mess once and for all, and what will she have in store for him? What choice does she have? The only question is not *if* she'll finish him off but *how*. Will she smother him, starve him, or just leave him to fail in his own piss, turning the heaters off and letting the winter do its work?

Whatever she chooses no one will come until it's too late and no one will care when they do, now that the lies about him have become supposed truths. That's why she's been able to get away with keeping him a prisoner here for so long. They're all relieved that the box is ticked and he gets his hot meals and once-a-week bath, their civic duty has been discharged.

He starts to cry now. There's nothing else to do, now that he knows what they've done. All of it. The work of the last months, this terrible day, and these last evil hours. None of it really matters. He knows Brian is close and that's something, though he is also gone, long gone, away so much further than the north.

He'll end it here, in his heart. He can't make the words as sounds, but he says them in a jumble in his head, he'll make his confession as if Brian can hear.

So he begins, talking to the silence and air.

I never touched him, Bri. Not in the way that you think. That day, in the pub, his hand on mine . . . He was sixteen years old and he was teasing an old man, wasn't he? What he saw as an old, sweaty-palmed perv? I can see that now, I saw it later, though I couldn't at the time.

It was a game to Gary; I realised that too late. I was the joke at the heart of it. I'd been a joke to him for years. He played up to me, to tease you, to make you squirm. That's why you stopped inviting him round here, by the end, though he'd just turn up anyway when he was bored, when he wanted someone to bait, a spider to pull the legs off.

I knew what they said about me in the village. I tried to be discreet. Sure, I made the odd trip up to Aber where, if you were looking for a certain type of friendship, you could wander up by the ruined castle and look for someone who caught your eye and shared a smile.

That's what we did then, how we hid it. It wasn't like it is now. The rest of the world might've been proudly speaking up and fighting their corner with their rainbow flags, but not in places like this.

How did they know, anyway? The people in town? Was

it written on me, in the way I moved or spoke? Little pitchers have big ears, Rose used to say, and big mouths. Gary was part of that, wasn't he? Though your mother didn't help. I know the things she'd started to say even before she left with her grocer lover – to her friends, her mother, right up until the day she died: a husband who wouldn't sleep with her – one who was, you know, wrong in his ways.

Except that wasn't the only reason she left, was it? She would've left anyway, even if I'd done my marital duty. Even if she'd never caught me that day, laughing with that ten-year-old boy from up Brook's farm, playing skittles, smiling, plucking that strand of hair from his eyes. Indecent, was what she called it, but it wasn't what she thought, ever. She just made it that way to give herself an excuse.

I never touched that kid, Bri, any kid, ever. Jesus, how could I want to? I never touched Gary – not until he touched me. Until he slid his hand onto mine that day, pushed his knee up against mine.

He liked to play with people, didn't he? I heard it said later, years after he was gone. After Gary's funeral, old Mr Blass, who never spoke ill of anyone, whispered to me, 'I shouldn't say it, George, but he was a nasty piece of work that one. Made my Glyn's life hell, teasing him about his stammer, running in and out of the shop when he was minding the counter, "B-B-Blass, h-h-horse's ass," and the like, making his life a misery. Face of an angel; heart of a cruel little prick.'

I thought Gary liked me, Bri, thought maybe he was *like* me for a while. But I couldn't have been more wrong, could I? I'll never forget his face when he said it, 'Jesus Christ!

Have you no shame, you old perv?' Laughing after I'd slid out my hand to touch him back, just to reassure him it was OK if he was that way, it would be OK, pulling his hand away so it was finally clear to me. It's true, my shorts were tight and it looked like . . . you know what it looked like. You saw . . .

'Jesus, old man, I like to fuck girls,' is what he said. You didn't see that part, did you, him laughing as you fled out of the door. You only saw the part before, where he smiled at me and I was smitten. You thought it was something dirty and, in a strange way, you thought that meant I preferred him to you, loved him more. You were just fifteen, and I never really got the chance to explain. What's left to say except that I'm sorry? I'm sorry, Brian. My boy, my son.

There, it's done. His confession completed, his mind slides away again as he catches sight of the TV. A reporter is standing in front of the old Lewis place, up at Ridgeback Farm, reporting that burglary again, the incident they've been going on about all day.

Poor old buggers, as if they hadn't had enough to deal with after the loss of their son? How could the heart take it? Not that Gary had had much of a heart, but maybe beautiful people don't need one. Ordinary people assume so many things about them because they associate a pretty or handsome face with goodness, kindness, best intentions. They can be the worst, though – hiding in plain sight.

He knows Gary wrote those things on the bus stop, on the side of the library. 'Rhydderch fiddles with kids', 'Rhydderch is a bent bastard'.

Poor old Polly and Osh, waiting so long for a son and getting that one.

There's a blurry photo now on the TV screen, of the people they think must have done it, the robbery. Christ! They're saying it's murder, that a woman's dead. That must be Polly! Dear God! Those suspects they're showing, surely one of them is Billy Fisket, that old drunk Ned Fisket's son?

The police are asking if anyone saw anything, saying not to approach the other suspect that flashes up. He's seen that picture before today, but he hadn't really paid much attention to the mugshot earlier. As the words 'dangerous offender' scroll across the bottom he knows that can't be right. He knows that face. He sees it clearly. It's been here in this room, right here.

Panic fills his throat but can't escape. His body floods with the beat of his heart as he struggles to hitch in a breath. The memories, the strands of thought, slide away with the air in his lungs, slippery as the years, streaming from his mind. He's losing the part of himself that knows what the point of any of it is. Perhaps there isn't one.

It's cold and quiet. Where is everyone? Where is he? This isn't his room, his and Rose's room. This is Brian's room. The star pinned above his bed twirls on its string, winking secrets of its own, its purpose unknown. Shouldn't Bri's sailing boats be hanging up there? Is the star there to guide someone to him? Is it for Brian, to light his way home? He thinks he feels Brian's hand in his but he knows this isn't possible. It's just a dream, or a memory, but it's a good one.

'It's OK, Dad,' says the whispered voice, near and far, perhaps even imagined. 'It's OK now.'

The Hitchhiker – 4 p.m.

It's no good. I can't separate myself from the memory any more. The patience train has pulled into the station and come to a dead halt. I have no choice but to get off, take a look around and hopefully find something to kick or hit. As the train doors part behind my closed eyelids I alight again into Rhys's flat, even though I'm really sitting in my hard chair in the bar, waiting for the storm to slacken.

I'd known Rhys wasn't home when I walked up to the door yesterday afternoon. His car wasn't outside and there was no sound as I turned the key in the lock. That was good. What wasn't so good was walking around the flat seeing his familiar stuff – his jacket flung on the coat stand, sports kit drying on the radiator, the expanding DVD collection of Hollywood noir and thrillers he loved so much, knowing I was a stranger inside. Because of the *other* stuff that was there, the *girl-stuff*; especially the matching knickers and bra set sitting snugly next to his Y-fronts on the drying rack, black silk and lacy.

Who actually wears underwear like that? was my first thought. Not me, for sure, was my second, which was the problem.

In the bathroom there was a mini deodorant by the sink, a nail file on the windowsill. On the bedroom dressing table was a hairband and, of course, the green canister of Silvikrin hairspray, medium hold. And where were the remnants of my own past visits? In a carrier bag shoved in the bottom of the bedroom wardrobe with my heavy-metal studded denim jacket, my bottle of Head and Shoulders shampoo, a toothbrush. Out of sight, out of mind.

Something dark had gripped my insides then, twisting with the invasion of the everyday. I knew that this girl, whoever she was, obviously hadn't moved in, but had made her presence known, staked out her territory, a part of Rhys's everyday routine, at least enough to warrant the occasional stopover.

That's a stage beyond a fling, isn't it? More than a few fumbles, a bit of fun? That's the next step on the relationship road? How far along, though? Could I find out? Did I really want to?

I opened the drawers of his desk first, poked around in the paperwork and junk. His computer was the prime target. Raising the cover of the high-end laptop I fiddled with the mouse until the home screen grew light, no password prompt on the screen, just straight into the toolbar.

I clicked through the photo file first and, right away, found half a dozen pictures that must have been uploaded from a digital camera. They'd been taken recently by the look of them, judging by the autumn light shimmering along the unmistakable Victorian seafront of Aberystwyth,

Constitution Hill, housing its camera obscura, rising in the background, quicksilver sea to the left.

There was another shot too, taken here in the flat, and I knew at once who I was looking at, the name of the woman with her hand up towards her face as if to say, Knock it off, though she's smiling and shiny, sleek and camera-ready, as she always was.

It was Melissa Lloyd, her mane of surely processed blonde hair pulled back into a neat, work-like plait. Cocky, confident Marvellous Melissa, darling of gym displays, diva of school plays and rotary debating sessions, as close as anyone had come to being a popular girl, a role model. Oh yes, I remember her, chatty, smart, pretty and she used it regularly, cultivated it, coasted upon it.

I haven't seen Lissa Lloyd for maybe ten years, when she must have been in her GCSE year and I was dodging A levels. We were never friends. Lissa never gave me a second glance, not even in gym club after school on Wednesdays. Why would she have been interested in someone ugly and sullen like me, lacking in the art of flirty smiles and eyeliner application, who preferred the power of the ropes and vaults to the graceful beam and backflips – what purpose would I have served on the great Lissa 'love me' train?

So what is she up to now? Is she a secretary somewhere, sucking up to the boss with her hot tits, teeny waist and cups of weak tea? That'd be about right. Or does she work at the estate agents with Rhys? Is that how they met? What a disappointment it was that Rhys had made such a mediocre and unchallenging choice.

Just in case I'd been in any doubt there was the letter, in his email drafts, addressed to me, then handwritten on a sheet of paper under the dictionary by the laptop: 'Lee, I'm sorry . . . we've drifted apart, I don't feel the same . . .' the rest mediocre and predictable too. I'd have expected a little more flourish from someone who called himself a novelist than, 'There's someone else. Things haven't been right for a long time . . . I don't feel the same.'

Had he thought an email would be too informal? Too callous? An old-fashioned, slightly cheesy touch like a letter would be just like Rhys.

He was right though, wasn't he? It'd been years since there was anything like fireworks or fever clinches between us, the memory of which might have warmed him enough in my absence, to keep his hands off the nearest short-skirted slag. But Lissa had been on hand and what's easy is always comfortable. Lissa had always had both those qualities.

How could I have expected him to be loyal? That wealthy, well-spoken lad I met slumming it at a grunge gig in Aberystwyth during my sixth-form year, the one I sneaked off to with the meat-packing boys from the factory. How the hell had we ended up in his dad's flash car, borrowed for the night, halfway through the live set, more than half pissed on filched vodka, fumbling, exchanging fluids?

After that I was his 'bit of rough', I'd known that, introducing him to the pastimes of smoking and drinking, so rebellious! He'd talked all the time, mainly about how he had a horrible job lined up after college, at his father's chain of estate agents, which he hated the idea of because secretly he wanted to be a writer. He'd talked about his stories all the time, though he'd never let me read any of them, so I was never sure if he was actually any good. I suspect he wasn't.

I knew all along that I was his little 'fuck you' to his parents, a bad girl – or his idea of one. Four months later he'd left for an accounting course in Cardiff while I'd stayed home until I could sit at least one A level. I'd thought back then that maybe I could make it through to college somehow. I'd always read a lot, even though I didn't show it. I was thinking maybe psychology or anthropology, until that stupid fucking incident when the police were called.

That night shattered it all, forced my decision on me, snatched away others. I couldn't just stick around, stubborn and seething, waiting for the fallout.

We kept in touch for a bit, me and Rhys, hiding it in letters because people still wrote them then. Later, I'd known it was impossible, that Rhys would want a nice, proper girl to take home to his parents. And there's nothing proper about me, not in the ways it matters. Proper girls spray their long blonde hair with Silvikrin. They work in schools with primary-aged kids in primary-coloured classrooms. They love children. They love to cook.

They don't have tattoos, or if they do they're little flowers and henna patterned shit, not a Welsh Dragon, roaring. They don't glug whisky straight from the bottle. They don't take a bottle to the back of someone's head in a pub. Not ever. Not even if it means a man gets to force his hand down into your jeans unresisted and pushes you into the alley at the back where the rubbish bins are and you can't push him off.

That's what I did to that animal. I defended myself. That

sweating, pervy bastard who was friends with Rhys's father and old enough to be my dad.

I'd seen him once before at the estate agents, smarming up too close behind his uncomfortable-looking secretary, hand on her shoulder. It was Rhys's dad's perfect chance to make sure I was out of the picture at last, to make me leave, quietly, by promising to make sure no charges were pressed against me, for the assault, as if it was my fault.

It wouldn't have been so bad if Mum and Dad had stuck up for me, but they knew my temper. It wasn't the first time I'd been in trouble with the police, for drunk and disorderly, for being gobby and aggressive, brought home sulking in the panda car. They believed *him*.

I didn't wait to see what plan they'd hatch for my disposal, I just packed a bag and left home – at eighteen I was a free agent. At least I know that man will carry the scars to the end of his days. His drippy wife and perfect kids will have to look at them and hide the fact that they know the truth about daddy's little habits. People need to learn that you can't just take what you want without consequences.

Standing in Rhys's flat in the snow-gloom afternoon, I'd imagined how Lissa Lloyd might have to learn that soon too. How nice it would've been to take a bottle to her face then and there. So much for the plan she'd smashed to pieces with a flick of her blonde mane. The biggest laugh you can give the universe is to make plans, just like Lilli-Anne said.

Rhys, *my Rhys*, had been writing me out of his plans while he wrote Lissa Lloyd in, but the worst thing was still waiting for me inside his laptop, open in a Word window behind the photos. It took me just twenty seconds to recognise the story of my life on the pages, scrolling through the manuscript. I couldn't escape the reality of the source material behind the file named 'DRAFT THREE – The Farm Girl'.

It was a terrible title, obviously meant to be ironic, a thick, paper copy sitting in a neat pile on the desk, full of pencil annotations and scribbles. Leafing through I saw the substance of some terrible coming-of-age drama there, of my childhood, my unjust 'expulsion' from town by my 'wicked father-in-law', then what came after: my letters, my phone calls over the last few years, his rare snatched visits and mine, in and out of town so no one would see me or tell his parents.

What a first-class fucking idiot I'd been. All those detailed questions that had made it seem like he'd wanted to know all about me, get under my skin. My stint in Birmingham, then in C wing, it was all there, and I remember him saying, clear as day: 'Tell me more. Tell me about your days and nights, your routines, your meals, the scraps, the lock-downs, the fear, the violence. Tell me about crazy Purvis and damaged Lilli-Anne . . .'

And I had, from Purvis's neck-clicking tic that had always bugged me, to Lilli-Anne's sayings: 'The Chinese symbol for catastrophe is also the same for opportunity', which is there on page twenty-nine.

I'd been so flattered by his interest, that I'd mattered enough, because if I mattered I could be loved. Because I thought he'd understood that the world needs people like me as much as it needs people who milk cows and till soil. In the world beyond the fields people like me put the edges on society, hold it together, draw its lines. The sheep need someone to keep the wolves off, even if it's one with a knife or a gun, but the wolves are hard to spot and sometimes you need to be one to beat one.

Except that reading the pages I wasn't a wolf any more. When I read the chapter about what happened to me in the car, to Purvis in the fire, I felt tears prickling my eyes. Actual tears. Who'd have thought it? I haven't cried in years, maybe never, not since the little heifer, certainly not through the agonising weeks in bed, bound in bandages, sick with morphine dreams, that Rhys had turned into a plot twist.

Of course I hadn't indulged my tears for long. I'd taken a different approach. I fixed my eyes on the opposition and fetched what I needed. After a quick forage, I grabbed the matches, the lighter and the hammer from the pantry cupboard before phoning Rhys on his mobile so he could hear me work. Once I knew I had his full and complete attention I smashed the laptop with the hammer and set fire to the manuscript. Then I left, pulling the flat door closed quietly behind me.

I hadn't meant for the whole flat to go up in flames. Or Rhys for that matter . . .

The Law – 3.45 p.m.

As I duck inelegantly through the half kicked-out door of the motel I'm careful to avoid the jags of wood and split melamine panelling, thinking, Tetanus, and also, I hope there aren't any monster spiders in here.

Once inside I can see the old reception desk with its moulded countertop still in place, but most of the other fittings have fallen to the twin assaults of damp and rot. Still, it must have been a cheerful place once, a culture clash in prefab blue and white, someone's misguided ambition to bring a little American glamour to the heart of Pont.

I've always wondered if, during its heyday, anyone slept in the boxy, efficient rooms, imagining themselves making a stop on the open highway towards the broad-planed, sun-bleached cowboy West of America, though I doubt it, and from the many road movies I've seen, that isn't much to aspire to unless your idea of a good time includes cannibals, murderous hitchers and psycho hoteliers.

Cutting the thought dead not to freak myself out any further, I shine my pocket torch down the corridor to my left just in time to see a hooded head pop out of a doorway then, quick as a flash, retreat. I wait a moment, startled, before the head appears again and repeats its hasty duck back.

The furtive bob, in and out of view, has a touch of farce about it, a cartoonish clumsiness that makes me think of games of hide and seek, of a kid standing behind the living-room curtains, convinced he's invisible, despite the obvious bulge and his visible shoes.

'I *can* see you, you know,' I say, fighting a sudden, inappropriate urge to grin.

A moment later a gloved hand pops out and beckons me urgently down the corridor as a voice from inside the figure's vast fur-trimmed hood shushes me, finger on lips.

It's such a childish gesture it's impossible not to edge towards the invitation, and I find myself baby-stepping down the corridor, taking care on the old laminate floor that's warped and rippled beneath my boot soles by tree roots as thick as my wrists. I can't afford to trip, fall or do anything obviously dumb and girly, like the movie extra who's the first to get slaughtered in the spooky motel.

The far end of the hall is better preserved than the foyer, the ceiling still intact. I stand well back against the corridor wall as I peer in through the doorless frame to where the figure had been a moment earlier. No sound comes from the room beyond, which is a shell, though it still has its ceiling and is dry.

In the gloom I can see an old armchair in the corner and, around it, a careful circle of domesticity where an old wooden crate serves as a table with a Thermos flask and tin tea mug on top. It's obvious I've found a hideout, or more accurately a den.

I spot the air rifle propped against the crate before I register the man standing behind the armchair. As I open my mouth he raises his fingers to his lips and repeats his hushed warning from the shadows of the corner.

He doesn't seem to want to make eye contact, head down, face deep inside his raised hood, shuffling back and forth from foot to foot, and I tense for a moment before finally realising what's bothering me, what his posture and body language tell me – you don't need police training to see it. He's more scared than I am.

'What's up, mate?' I ask eventually. 'Are you OK?'

'Shhh, please don't shout,' says the voice from the hood, though I hadn't.

'Who are you?' I ask more softly. 'Do you live here?'

He shakes his head. 'My name's Sam.'

'Are you OK, Sam?'

He gives another shake of the head, his hands gripping the back of the armchair even more tightly. I'm glad he's behind that chair, but evidently so is he. I lower my baton and immediately he relaxes a fraction of an inch.

'What are you doing here, Sam? Are you sleeping rough?'

The voice still comes from inside the dark of his hood. 'No. This is my quiet place. It's my quiet place. My quiet place.'

'Quiet place?'

'Yeah. Holiday fun for everyone. If it weren't for those goddam kids.'

He sounds like he's quoting someone else's words and the weirdness of the situation doesn't escape me. I have to fight hard to quash the unhelpful image it triggers, of him pulling back his parka-hood disguise to reveal a grinning clown face or old man's mask. *It's the old motel ghost. Steady, Scoob.* I quash the urge to laugh.

'Goddam kids?' I ask.

'They come in and smash stuff up. They chase me away. This is my quiet place.'

'OK. What's up then? You can tell me, I'm a police officer. I'm Lissa,' I add, with what I hope is a reassuring smile. 'Can you put your hood down, Sam? So I can see your face?'

I lower my own hood as a gesture of goodwill, and, as he does the same, I'm relieved to see the ordinary, acned face of a twentysomething with long straggly hair and a bit of stubble.

'I called you,' he says. 'I tried to call nine nine nine, like my mam says I should if I'm ever scared.'

'OK. You called nine nine nine? Why, Sam?'

'I tried to call. Tried to call. Tried to call. No answer on the phone. Then I wasn't able to get through. Then there was a lady on the phone who was cross. She didn't want to know. She didn't want to know. She didn't want to know.'

His agitation is growing. Each time he repeats a phrase he clenches and unclenches his hands on the chair back, fingers spread wide like gasping starfish, three times each.

'Know about what, Sam?'

'The lady. The lady in the car. I tried to tell her. Don't go. Don't go. Don't go.'

'What lady, Sam?'

He gestures over to his left, onwards I assume, down the road outside.

'A lady on her own, stuck in the car.'

At last! I'm relieved. That's all it is. My wandering nurse is stuck down the road somewhere. This bloke's obviously a bit 'special', a bit confused, that's all. I holster my baton in my belt and relax my posture into the friend zone.

'OK. Did you talk to her, Sam?'

'Who?'

'The lady.'

'Which one?'

'The lady stuck in the car?'

'No. She couldn't talk to me. I was in the trees at first. I was watching. I was looking for rabbits. Rabbits, rabbits, rabbits.'

'Is she OK, then? The lady? You didn't do something to her, did you, Sam?' It seems unlikely but I should ask. I get the feeling he'll answer truthfully.

'No, no, no. She's stuck in her car.'

I remember the handbag outside. 'Did you take her bag, Sam? Tell the truth now.'

'No, it was dropped by the car. I picked it up, safe. Kept it safe. I tried to call you. Nine nine nine, like my mam says. I wanted to go to her but I was scared. I was in the trees. Nine nine nine. Nine nine nine. Nine nine nine.'

'She scared you, Sam? You don't like people, I guess?'

'People don't like me. People are always cross. I stay out of their business. I don't get involved.'

I hear the echo of quotation marks around his words once more, of his following well-meaning instructions he's most likely heard many times, so I say, 'OK, all right. I'm not cross with you. Come with me. We'll go and find her, OK? The lady. She'll be all right now.'

'No she won't,' he says decidedly, as if it's a fact. 'Don't go out there. We need the police to come. You should be careful. She wasn't careful. It's not safe.'

I assume he means because of the weather so I say, 'It's just a bit of snow, Sam.'

'Not the snow. The lady. The lady on her own. She's stuck in the car. Why did she stop?'

'OK, take it easy. Tell me when this was, Sam.'

'Ages ago, ages ago, ages ago. Why didn't the police come?'

He starts to rock harder on the balls of his feet, hitting his forehead with his left hand, cold, sharp slaps, muttering, 'This is my quiet place. Quiet place. Quiet place. Where are the police?'

'OK, OK, Sam. Stop that. It's all right, *I'm* the police.'

'The real police. The police*men*.'

I want to correct him, remind him that the gender-neutral term is now police *officer*, but it isn't worth trying to explain and I'd sound like a twat. Instead I say, 'OK, I'll look after the lady, Sam. You stay here for a bit and drink your flask of tea.'

'Coffee. One sugar only because it rots your teeth.'

'Indeed it does. You have your phone on you?'

'No signal on the phone now. No one answered the phone. Then the lady was cross.'

'All right. Where do you live?'

'Top of the hill.' He gestures up behind him somewhere beyond the motel.

'OK, go home now. It's getting late. Go straight there. Your mam will be worried. Tell her you did a good thing and helped the lady.'

'I didn't though,' he says, shaking his head, hands gripping, opening, gripping. 'I didn't.'

I feel I should ask him again if he wants to come with me, but he still hasn't come out from behind the chair and he doesn't seem likely to any time soon. Instead I say, 'I'll try and send someone to get you, OK, Sam? A policeman to take you home.'

He nods, not releasing his grip on the chair as I make my way back to the foyer, back to my car, thinking that as soon as I have a signal I'll try and get someone to call his mam, or I could circle back for him once I've picked up the nurse.

The last thing I hear as I duck out under the broken door panel is him shouting after me, 'Don't go out there. It's not safe. Not safe. Not safe. Call the police.'

Then I head out into the afternoon.

The Hitchhiker – 4 p.m.

I know I've dozed off, that I'm dreaming. The damp leather of my seat under the window is too uncomfortable to sleep properly and I can still hear Shakin' Stevens on the radio, yodelling away another chorus of 'Merry Christmas Everyone'.

Despite this, despite the musty smell and the crick in my left shoulder, somehow it's no longer Rhys's flat I'm trapped in like it was earlier, it's the moment of the car crash all over again. I can even feel the singe of the flames, smell their tarriness on my tongue.

It happens the same way, always, exactly how it's formed itself in my sleep for months, from smoke and sweat and memories, mid scene, the heat of the action. Purvis is in the car and I'm already running up to it at full pelt, breath bursting, muscles screaming.

The men chasing me peel off and disappear into a side street at the sight of the car, the little shit who'd lobbed something at the windscreen is off and running too, pegging it round the corner, but there's no time to run him down and kick the shit out of him. Things have passed that stage.

I get to the car. There are flames. The door handles are too hot to touch. Purvis is trapped in his seat, the steering column twisted, his head lolling, hand dragging limply at the door handle, his sleeve on fire. The smoke is as evil as oil, a plume of black sliding up into the sky, the back of the car blood orange and flickering. The side of Purvis's face is singeing, the pink flesh curling as I watch.

The little boy's arm is still stuck on the windscreen. That small and perfect arm, a three- or four-year-old arm still follows me through my sleep and out of it, fingers outstretched. The fingernails are the worst thing, so perfect, so clean.

The boy was in the way when Purvis swerved, while I legged it out of the doorway, down the street, waving, as he was haring up to collect me. Then the windscreen exploded.

There's no sound in my head now, save for the crackle of the fire becoming a hungry roar. There's a second explosion as the back of the vehicle turns into a full-on roil of flames.

There's an old man standing on the kerb, eyes blank, a dead-eyed mutt at his feet, not afraid of the flames and noise. A strange stillness remains outside the bubble of the burning car. Birds are twittering, their trilling feels like laughter. The trees are in blossom beneath a boastful blue sky. It can't really have been like that, can it? I'm imagining that . . .

Still, I plunge around to the other side of the car, pulling at the door. The part of Purvis's head against the glass is pulped and bloody. I manage to get the door open. Smoke pours out and into my panting mouth. I put my hands into the flames to free Purvis from his seat. The black wetness seeping from his chest, his head, doesn't cool the scorch.

My fingers clamp around his broad chest. I brace my foot against the door frame and pull us free. As Purvis crushes me to the ground with his dead weight I hear an explosion. Then I close my eyes and die – or think I do – I let go of everything and just exhale.

There's no memory of the others, the ones whose hands pulled us away. It was only later, much later, when Purvis loomed up over me in the clean white bed, among the comforting ping of machines, that I realised I was still alive. For a short while I wasn't sure if I was relieved or disappointed.

Half of Purvis's face was covered in bandages, the other half looked like the old Purvis, only less cocky. The uniformed officers stationed at the door, erect, watching, were waiting to hear my story – my version.

'Lee? Lee? Wake up, you dumb fucking heroic bitch,' he'd grinned. 'You gonna sleep for ever?'

That's the closest he's ever come to saying, Thanks for saving my life, but it's close enough.

I shift now, in my lightening sleep, opening my eyes onto the cold fireplace, stretching stiffly. I've been lucky, really, to make it this far. It's the strangest feeling, as the wind roars around the pub like cold flames, knowing how Rhys is dead, how he'd died in a car crash on the B11 just one day ago, not even twenty-four hours yet, while Purvis had survived one much worse.

'Hi honey, I'm home,' I'd said to Rhys minutes before he died, after I'd called his mobile from his desk in the flat, the manuscript of my life before me, the story of fall and rise, of disgrace and redemption, one that should have changed everything but . . .

'Surprise!' I yelled into the phone after he'd picked up, pub chatter and music in the backdrop, voices and clinking cutlery.

'Lee? Is that you? Where are you, babe?'

'I'm in your flat – thought I'd just drop in and say hello.'

Silence from him then, speaking volumes as a voice, a woman's voice, asked, 'Harvey's or Cadwallader's for Friday?'

Was that Lissa in the background? Making their weekend plans? I'd wanted to make the universe laugh at that cheating, man-stealing bitch, as the background noise changed, a door was swinging open perhaps, the winter quiet of the outside afternoon reaching me, pierced by the whistle of wind over water.

'Out for drinks on the prom? Christmas party for two?' I asked, fake jollity in my voice, bright and hard.

'What? No. Business catch-up with Margaret from the Llandeilo branch. Where did you say you are, babe?'

Babe? I always hated being called that.

'I'm at home, your home, on your office phone, *babe*. Season's greetings. How's Lissa? Do say hi for me.'

Silence, then, 'Look, Lee, I'm . . . Jesus . . .'

'Beep, beep, beep!' I shouted, surprising myself.

'What?'

'Beep, beep, beep.' It had sounded nonsensical even to me, but it was an alarm sound, signalling that time had run out, that repeating my mantra and attempting my control exercises were no longer an option – sorry Pam! My patience had burned to the end of its fuse and was about to detonate.

'What's that? Why are you making that noise?' he asked.

'That noise? That noise, my love, is your thirty-second warning. That's the countdown to the sound of *this* hammer on *your* laptop, and, by the way, your manuscript is about to go up in flames, you piece of shit. Hope you made a backup.'

'Look, Lee? I can explain,' said the panicked voice on the cold seafront, but there was nothing he could say by then, not with thorns and teeth tearing through my skin, leaving me bloody.

'You already have,' I said calmly, a white hot, clear calm descending, the weapon in my hand. The choice made.

'I'm sorry. Lee, let's talk about this. Stay there. I'll come right back.'

'Say hi to your skank for me,' I said, smashing the hammer down onto the laptop keys with a satisfying swoosh, again and again. 'Merry Christmas and fuck you!'

Then I hung up, took a deep breath and set fire to the wastebasket with typed papers in it, expecting my phone to ring any minute, wondering later, all evening really, why he hadn't tried to call me back. Why hadn't he attempted to grovel and apologise, or at least explain himself? Why hadn't he come to the farm to try and find me? He must have realised that was the only other place I could go.

As soon as Mum had put a cup of tea in my hand, the old kitchen range glowing warm and slightly infernal in the gloom, I'd burst into tears properly, full on floods of them. Just like that, heaving, shaking. Mum said nothing then opened her arms stiffly, offering a solid shoulder until the sobs had wracked themselves from me.

I couldn't explain it to her, not all of it, not just like that. I thought there'd be time for that in the days to come.

How could I have known that, while I'd walked the long road home to the farm, Rhys was already haring guiltily back along the B11. He was driving instead of fretting in the pub with Lissa as I'd imagined. Perhaps she was asking, 'Why does it matter if she knows now? She'd have found out soon enough.'

Him probably replying, 'Not like this. There was no need for this. She could actually kill us, you know.'

But Rhys had got straight into his car and somehow the wheels had slipped on the packed snow as he took a corner on the dual carriageway, the car spinning out, smashing into a lorry, careering across the central reservation, sparking an inferno.

Had he had time to feel the hot lick of the flames at his back? While I was huffing up the hill? By the time I was sitting at the kitchen table drinking tea and whisky, he was already dead, by the time I'd fallen asleep on the sofa his flat had gone up in flames, too.

I only found out by accident, woken by a knock on the door hours later, to the sound of a man's voice. At first I thought it was Rhys, then I thought it was the police, come to ask me about the laptop, but it was only the voice of old Ioan Evans from two hills over, delivering a Christmas cake from his missus and extra diesel for the generator in case of a power cut.

Refusing the invitation to come in, he and Mum had exchanged a few doorstep updates before he passed on a titbit he'd just heard from his son Ewan, a fireman. He'd been called to a flat fire in the harbour that afternoon, 'the posh condo of that Rhys Tripp lad,' he said, 'the one whose father owns all the estate agents, but the terrible thing is that when the police tried to contact Tripp, his car had already been reported in an accident. That posh Audi of his was burned out on the B11 and him crisp as a piece of toast when he was cut from the wreckage.'

Listening from the sofa I remained frozen as he lamented the perils of drink driving and black ice before leaving in a flurry of season's greetings. I couldn't move, not even when Mum returned to the kitchen, her hands twisted into a tight knot.

'You heard that, I guess. You two weren't still in touch, were you? I mean, you're not together, since . . . ?'

I was barely able to nod or look at her, white-faced, tight-throated, when she said. 'But that girl, I saw them in town once or twice . . . This isn't anything to do with that, is it . . . I mean, you didn't do something . . . ?'

Her eyes were dark with fear and my own eyes must have said it all.

I don't know if she even considered I was telling the truth when I swore I hadn't meant to burn the flat down. She said she understood, but had she ever really understood anything? Why I am like I am? Why I've done what I've done? It was like the pub incident and all those other times before it – the girl who cried wolf, the girl who says, 'It's not my fault, I just snapped. He asked for it.'

On the outside at least, she displayed her usual, problem-solving resignation, but I knew from the tremor in her hands that she really wanted me to get the hell out of there, lining up the excuses; people might assume things, the wrong things, ask questions.

'With your history, well, people might . . .' she paused, choosing her words, 'perhaps it's best if . . . before your father . . . I don't need to tell him . . . I mean, no one has seen you? No one knows you're here.'

That's when I'd felt it the most, the razor edge of my patience sliding across my throat, the old rage that she hadn't even asked me what had happened. Aren't mothers supposed to protect their young, to pull you to their chests and never let go?

'You should probably leave right now,' she said, 'tonight, while the roads are still open. Did you come on the train? You can make it to the bus stop in half an hour; the ten o'clock bus is the last one. Pick up the connection down south. No one knows you were here.'

Then she pushed five grubby tenners into my hand saying, 'For Christmas. That's all I have, it's the last few months' savings.'

I was being paid off, under the gaze of the golden boy, my brother Marshall, still staring from the frame on the mantelpiece, still away in Australia but clearly the favourite one who'll get his birthright one day – the one I'll never see. So much for the homecoming . . .

Cold rage had warmed me to the bone as I trudged back out into the night, along the deserted roads, past the night-black and snow-white landscape of stark farms and solitary lanes. Swigging back the whisky I'd taken from the kitchen, I was leaving home again, empty handed, empty hearted, with the urge to feel a weapon in my hand so I could hurt the world as it had hurt me.

I was acutely conscious that I had no one else to talk to, no one to go to, and no one to call. Not even Rhys. Poor Rhys. No, not poor Rhys, shitty, lying Rhys, but . . . but what a mess, a dead loss, unless, unless I could snatch something from this twenty-four-hour disaster. Then I realised that I did know someone. At least I used to. Of course it was pretty late to call out of the blue, like the Ghost of Christmas Past, but maybe not *too* late.

But it doesn't matter now. It was never going to work here. How could I ever have thought I could be a fucking farmer or an estate agent's wife? Wherever you go you're still yourself, carrying everything with you on your back along the road. There's more than one kind of hell, that's for sure. The one I left behind and the one I'm neck deep in, in this cold, white world of home.

Wherever there are people, there is pain and jealousy and shit happening. Hell is other people, right? Didn't Sartre say that? And there's no escaping them. They're fucking here, there and everywhere.

I've made such a mess of things, but I can still make it out if I'm lucky. I want to be the hell away from here, especially this shitty pub. I can't wait any longer. I'm ready to face the storm. It's time to leave.

So I haul myself to my feet, stretch elaborately, feeling my spine click and crack while trying one last time for a phone signal. With luck I can at least call ahead. I know I might not get back in time to sign in by tomorrow morning now, but at least I'll have paved the way for an epic excuse.

I can ring Bowen the duty officer (who'll be in the pub by now anyway) and leave a non-committal message, a promise to call back. I don't have to say where I am, but I can at least let them know I'm on my way, work out the details of my excuse as I travel.

There's one bar of signal on the display if I stand on a chair, but it disappears every time I try to dial and the nurse, watching me from her seat, gives me a weary look, so I decide to make a last-ditch attempt to check the landline I spotted earlier. Even though the landlord said the phone is broken I don't believe him.

He's currently fiddling about at the back of the bar, pacing and fussing; he's obviously keen for us to leave but doesn't know how to get rid of us. If I can get him out of the room for a minute, find the main connector, I might be able to get a line up. It could just be a few loose wires.

'What did you do to your hand?' I ask, eyeing his seeping bandage, which is starting to brown and stiffen. 'It looks nasty.'

He looks down as if he's surprised to see the bloodied strip still wrapped around his palm. After a pause he says, 'The dog bit me.'

I think of the shaggy German Shepherd tied up out the back and something doesn't ring quite true. 'Your dog bit you?'

'Yeah.'

'Why?'

'He's just vicious, I guess.'

'What's his name?' I ask, suddenly uneasy.

'Er, Simon,' he offers.

'Seriously,' snorts the nurse. 'Simon the vicious killer?'

'Yeah, look . . .'

'It looks bad,' I interrupt, 'your hand. You should really get a tetanus shot after a dog bite. Dogs' mouths are filthy, you know. Do you have a fever, any headache? You can get really nasty diseases.'

He looks alarmed. 'I washed it out.'

'Yeah? But maybe she should look at it for you? She's a nurse,' I suggest, looking to my travelling companion, who's shaping a ragged thumbnail with a file pulled from her bag. That should keep the landlord occupied for a bit while I nose around for the phone jack, though she doesn't seem pleased, giving me a look.

'Didn't we see some hydrogen peroxide in your first-aid kit?' I add. 'Did you use that? You should have, shouldn't he, Becca?'

'Oh yeah, hydrogen peroxide,' she agrees with deep boredom.

'Nah, it's OK,' insists the landlord, fiddling with the sagging bandage. 'Look, I think it's time—'

'Whatever,' says the nurse, getting my drift as I raise my eyebrows, 'I'll have a look. Let's check out that first-aid box in the kitchen, right?'

I wait for them to wander off down the passageway before lifting the receiver of the phone at the back of the bar and pumping the connectors, just in case a dialling tone burrs into life, but it's dead, all right. I follow the wire from the back of the phone through a little hole cut in the panelling, picking it up by the skirting board. The cable ends in a set of frayed wires at the wall jack, as if it's been yanked out with some force. So much for that idea!

I decide to do a final check on the progress of the snow at the front door, but as I heave it open I'm hit by a blast of icy whiteness and a roar of the wind that makes me shove it shut again, cursing. That's when I think I hear it

– a phone ringing behind me, somewhere deep inside the pub. It's just a few high electronic burrs, but by the time I've registered it and bolted the door again, it's gone.

It could have been wishful thinking, could even have been an illusion formed from the shrill voice of the wind screaming up under the eaves. But still . . . if someone's got a signal, if someone can call for assistance, why not say so?

As I wander back towards the possible source of the noise, I hear it again. The nurse isn't back yet, and neither is her bag. She's taken it with her to the kitchen, so it can't be her phone ringing. Is it coming from behind the bar after all?

I pull open a couple of drawers in search of the elusive sound as the wind rises and the pub groans like a ship riding a storm at sea. There's half a life's worth of accumulated junk back here, tobacco tins full of receipts, elastic bands, papers piled high, but what catches my eye is the crumple of letters shoved behind the old till, in the gap between it and the speckling mirror.

I pull them out and smooth them off. They're from the same man, must be the old man upstairs, but they don't seem to have been sent. By the looks of it the ones addressed to Brian, our delightful host most likely, have never been put in envelopes.

'Dear Brian, I know you don't want to hear from me but I am getting very sick . . . Please call, Love Dad.'

Then there are Brian's 'replies', apparently written over several months, maybe longer. 'Dad, I know you never reply any more, but . . .'

The envelopes are shoved with them, the postmark somewhere in Scotland.

'Dad, I think you should know something, about Gary,' one says. 'I did something stupid. I lost my temper. I thought he deserved it. He just wouldn't leave it alone. Leave you alone. But I never meant for it to happen like it did . . . I just couldn't stay after that. Dad, we need to talk. I can't put it in a letter.'

It's only words on a page, but the Brian who writes these letters doesn't seem like the Brian we've been prising two-word answers out of for the last three hours.

There's something odd here.

As I put them back at the side of the till I drop one, and, stooping to pick it up, I realise there's a hatch creaking beneath my feet. Everything else is thick with dust and grime except for a set of recent-looking handprints on the handle and the wooden edge.

On a whim I lean down and pull up the old trap door, an exit/entry point I must have missed. This must be where the beer barrels would once have been taken up and down to the cellar, a steep set of wormy-looking wooden steps leading down into the clammy darkness.

I spot something else, where the darkness swallows the steps. A big duffel bag dumped carelessly, the half-open zipper spilling a couple of jauntily wrapped Christmas parcels onto the treads. I can't quite see from where I am, so I put one foot down onto the first step, testing its weight. When it holds, I take another one with my left foot, spreading my weight.

I can see some clothes scattered from the top of the bag: a big pair of white Y-fronts in a heap with a very large black T-shirt, spread like flag on the step. I catch at the edge of the T-shirt with my gloved fingertips and bring it up to my nose, the smell of washing powder's a pleasant contrast to the musty odour leaking up from below. Clean clothes, washed and ironed – clothes for a trip?

As my eyes adjust to the gloom there are obvious footmarks besides my own in the layers of dust on the steps. I lean closer, one hand clutching the edge of the hatch for support, turning over the clothes, checking the zipper pocket at the front of the bag, one ear cocked for the landlord's return. A little voice tells me it's better if he doesn't know I've found this.

In the side pocket is a wallet containing two credit cards with the name Brian Rhydderch on them; a security-type pass on a lanyard, no photo; some company logo I don't recognise, and a set of car keys.

Something unpleasant starts to tick in my chest as I carefully retrace my steps, dropping the cellar hatch behind me as quietly as I can. I stare around the old pub, feeling its judgement upon me. What is it waiting for, as it breathes alongside me? What do I need to know? What do I need to understand because its arrival is imminent, tantalising?

With a familiar cool click I'm sure there's something very wrong here. Now that I think about it, I've been sure of it for a while really, ever since the landlord opened the front door, in fact. I just couldn't gather the feeling into a single, clearly defined thought until now.

I need to talk to the old man right away, or at least try and talk to him, if he can make himself understood. I have two questions for him, and they won't wait any longer. They've been nudging in the back of my brain for hours and are now punching their way to the fore. We'd have been safer out there in the storm, I'm sure of that, but it's too late to leave now.

I need to ask the old man, Why are you afraid? And perhaps most importantly, Who is the man who says he's your son?

The Law – 4.40 p.m.

As I drive on towards Caerau, leaving the motel in my rear-view mirror, I'm not that worried about finding the missing nurse any more. She's obviously not far away, just broken down, but even though I'm expecting it, I almost drive straight past the car when it materialises at the side of the road.

Except it isn't the nurse's car – the Black Ford Focus I'm looking for. As I pull up alongside I can see right away that it's a beaten-up wreck of a Cortina, once a hideous yellow, by the looks of it, now mostly rust, which is the only thing that seems to be holding it together.

Winding down the window and leaning across the passenger seat, I can just about make out a jumble of old boxes on the back seat, and what looks like a family of weather-beaten garden gnomes hitching a ride. Something pricks in the back of my mind at the sight of them, their chipped noses and cracked hats, but it escapes me as my stomach rumbles, and I check my watch to see that time is ticking on. I need to end today's excursion and get back to the nick sharpish.

I can't be bothered to log the details of an abandoned, clearly unroadworthy vehicle right now. The nurse is my priority, but it's already further to drive back to my nick than to drive on towards Broadly outstation in the next village, where I can update Jim and tell him I'm on my way. So I settle for taking down the number plate, wind up my window, ignore the Cortina and press on closer to Halfway in the valley.

Looking for the black Ford Focus I squint through the snow and the almost total tunnel of blackness beyond, then I almost hit it. Half-canted into the road it appears through the billowing curtain of white rising and falling through the wipers, and I swerve to avoid clipping it. This time I can see straight away that it's Rebecca Nash's car.

Just to follow protocol I double-check the licence plate Carron gave me back at the nick, instantly relieved that the day isn't a complete loss after all. Now at the very least I can justify my jaunt, take the nurse home with me and take the credit for a small job well done.

Heaving my hood up, I leave the warm cocoon of my car to do a visual check, peering in through the windows, expecting to see the nurse waiting it out in the driving seat, wrapped in a travelling blanket, 'trapped in her car', like Sam said, but I'm instantly disappointed, and more than a bit annoyed, to find no sign of anyone inside. The car's empty, the bonnet cold.

Irritated, I scan the area and the grass verge, into the trees for snow-sunk footsteps, thinking surely the silly cow is nearby. Surely everyone knows that in an emergency, if your car breaks down in a desert or the outback or a snowy road in December, you should stay with your vehicle. It provides shelter and makes a much bigger and more visible target for anyone searching than a lone human being, especially from the air. But no one's really looking for her except me.

I try the door, but it's locked, so I get back into my car, cold, pissed off, and plod onwards again, reasoning that she must have headed towards Halfway for help, unless she managed to get a lift from someone passing. Either way, the old pub, right down in the hollow of the valley, is the nearest place to head for. Hadn't the nurse's boss told Carron she might have gone to check on old Mr Rhydderch for her last call today?

The Halfway has been a dump for years and I hadn't even realised the old kiddie fiddler was still alive down there, but as I drive I vaguely remember Jim saying something about Billy Fisket and The Halfway this morning, about him vandalising the pub years back when he was a teenager.

Hadn't he said something about him breaking open the beer barrels with his friends? The memory escapes me as I come to a sudden roadblock beneath a narrow tunnel of snow-weighted branches leaning in over the track ahead. Towards the end there's a fallen tree, collapsed slap-bang across the road in a tangle of ripped bark and boughs, forcing me to hit the brakes.

As soon as I get out to take a look I can see there's no sign of anyone else here and no way past in my four-by-four or on foot. I vaguely remember something on the radio about the guys from Western area closing the road at their end a few hours before, so I have a choice, once again, commit or retreat.

I can go back to the nick and sit out the last hour of afternoon in welcome warmth, buoyed by serial cups of tea and the almost true assertion that I've looked everywhere for our missing woman, or give my 'big boots' a real road test, finish what I've started and check out her last believed port of call. If I don't find her on the way, at least I'll have the benefit of saying I explored every avenue at my disposal.

It's while I'm making up my mind that I see them, as I assess the best way up and over the tree. They're lying in the snow, in the beam of my pocket torch, in the sheltered span of feet between the car and the tree fall: orange, green, red and a yard or two further along, another green. The colours are lurid as I scan the tree; a little line of Peanut M&M's. I can't mistake them for anything else, like a trail of sweeties to tempt Hansel and Gretel into the woods, glowing in their neon nuclear colours for a few minutes more before they finally disappear under the snow sifting through the branches above.

My immediate reaction is that someone is setting me up, pulling my leg. *Our heroine's sixth sense kicks in, suspecting a heinous plan afoot to tempt her into danger.* Or, more likely, to give some bored kids hiding in the trees a laugh at my expense.

Are they waiting to see if I'll bend down to pick up the sweets before pelting me with snowballs? Is that part of the joke? But it's completely dark now, apart from the snow glow, and bitingly cold. No giggles or out-of-sight shuffling betray hiding children or anyone else nearby, party to a prank. I'm sure I'm alone.

Close to the tree fall, under the M&M's, I can see a cluster of footprints, getting shallower and shallower as everything is erased by the snow like a washcloth over a whiteboard. I can see the snowfall disturbed on the flattest part of the tree trunk above me, so I hoist myself up for a better look, my old gymnastics practice standing me in good stead.

Peering down through the tangle of branches I see a few more sweeties on the other side, and also, sitting right below me, caught on a shap strip of broken bark, a plastic rectangle with a metal clip. Even from here I can see the capital letters of the name badge, stark in the disc of light from the torch, reading 'REBECCA NASH – NURSE'.

That settles it. She's probably down there, somewhere in the dark, no doubt efficiently unbothered by the spooky closeness of the woods that suddenly seem to be crying with bird calls, wild warnings and wind shrieks. Most likely she's at the pub already, briskly making tea, awaiting rescue by four-by-four, but what if she isn't all right?

I think of Sam's words back at the motel, 'Not safe, not safe.' What if she's been mugged? Or what if she's fallen on the other side of the trunk, slipped on the snow? What if, as I ponder what to do, she's lying with a broken ankle, within sight and sound of salvation, growing weaker and bluer as the night hardens?

If I've come this far and turn back now, only for her stiff corpse to be chipped free of a snowdrift by the council clearance team tomorrow morning, that'll be the end of it. I can kiss my career, already hanging by the slightest of verbal threads, goodbye.

So I decide to be a real police officer once more. *Our heroine braces herself against the elements, charging her courage by zipping up her jacket, pulling on her bobble hat and preparing herself for an odyssey into the white night woods.*

I boost myself up and over the trunk, dropping cleanly, with the grace of a cat, on the other side. Then I set off down the hill to where The Halfway waits.

The Hitchhiker – 5 p.m.

When I reach the bedroom door I pause, listening. I'm looking for the nurse, to tell her it's time to get out of here and offer her the choice to follow me, just as soon as I get the answers I need.

As I push the door open, just a sliver, I see the old man, still in bed, lying on his back. At first it looks like he's sleeping, but there's something different about him, his face slack-mouthed, his limbs rigid. I know what it is, what it means, that change, even before I step forward and see the look on the nurse's face as she stands silently by the bed.

'Poor old bugger,' she says, almost wistfully, hugging a spare pillow to her chest like a child who wants to hide behind it. 'I thought I'd check on him. Make him a bit more comfy. Found him like this.'

I step inside and move forward, instinctively feeling for a pulse in his ropey wrist. There is none. He's not cold yet, but a chill is creeping across his skin that has nothing to do with the temperature in the room, though this has happened quite recently.

'There's nothing anyone can do for him now. Rest in peace,' says the nurse, like an undertaker might say it, grave, respectful, insincere.

'Did you try CPR?' I ask.

'No point, is there? Too late.'

I can see she's right. If there'd been a time for it, it's passed. You know when a shell is empty, when it's not a person any more.

'We should probably call the landlord up,' says the nurse.

'I'm not sure we should,' I say, dropping the old man's wrist.

'Why?' She's clearly surprised and I sigh, knowing how this is going to sound, how it sounds in my own head. So I order my thoughts and point to the picture of the old man sitting on the dresser.

'I know this is going to sound nuts, but bear with me, OK? That's the old man, right? When he was younger? See that ginger-haired boy and the dark-haired woman? His boy and wife, right?'

'Looks like it. Probably. So?'

'I think, earlier on, he was trying to say "son", "my son".'

'Son? So? So what?'

'Because . . . Because I don't think the guy calling himself the landlord is that boy in the photo. I don't think he's the old man's son.'

I exercise my patience to the full as the nurse's eyes expand and she subconsciously hugs the pillow tighter to her chest. After a moment she asks, 'What? Really? Why?'

'Well, think about it. There was something off about

him right away, wasn't there? The way he answered the door? He was waiting for someone, right? Expecting someone else. Not us, for sure. He wasn't pleased to see us.'

'Maybe, but . . .'

'He doesn't know his way around a bar either. He had no idea what Laphroaig was, or what glass to put it in. I don't think he lives here.'

'Yeah, but . . .'

'And he claimed that the car outside doesn't have petrol, but how likely is that? I think it's a hire car. There was a sticker in the back window. Why would he be driving that if he lives here? And I found this ID badge with the name Brian Rhydderch on it, and these car keys, in a gym bag that was tossed in the cellar. I bet these keys are for that car.'

'Wait, what bag?' asks the nurse, confused. 'Why were you in the cellar?'

'And the dog bite,' I continue, determined to floor her with the weight of evidence before she can ask any more stupid questions. 'Would his own dog bite him? There was no dog food in those kitchen cupboards, didn't you notice that, when we were looking for food?'

'That doesn't mean—'

'There's not even a dog bowl anywhere or a lead. And that dog's not called Simon. It's a girl. I saw her collar.'

'Wait, you said there was a bag downstairs? What bag?' says the nurse, catching up.

I speak slowly, with exaggerated care, 'There are clothes in a bag, OK, chucked down the cellar stairs behind the bar. As if someone wanted to hide them quickly. I found men's clothes in there and these' – I dangle Brian's ID badge, my patience thinning and stretching tighter with each word – 'Not his dog, not his car, not his bloody father.'

'Do you think it was a good idea to go nosing around some strange guy's house?' asks the nurse, her face darkening with worry. 'I knew you fancied yourself as a detective.'

There's a slight sneer in her voice that I don't like. She seems to be wilfully missing the point, or maybe she just doesn't want to see it.

'I think we should leave, now,' I say.

'Why? What business is it of ours? Are you suggesting we take that car? We won't get it out of here tonight with the roads like they are. Why the hell would we do something as risky as that? Are you afraid of a dead old man? He's not going to hurt anyone now, is he? Don't you think we should just stop being silly buggers and wait out the night nice and quiet?'

'I wasn't fucking suggesting we steal a car!' I snap, though the thought had occurred to me. I really want to get out of this room and this pub now, while I can. I have a prickle of anticipation that things will go badly wrong if we don't leave very soon.

The old man's piss has dried in a dark patch on the bedcovers and I gesture to it. 'Listen,' trying to say it calmly and clearly, 'the landlord obviously wasn't cleaning up after the old man earlier. He was cleaning something else up, I reckon. Did you see all those used towels in the bathroom and more in the washing machine downstairs? That "rust" in the sink plughole. With hindsight I don't think it was rust.'

The nurse says nothing and the silence in the room is complete. In the middle of it I realise the TV has been turned off at some point, and the radio, too.

'Old men piss themselves all the time,' says the nurse eventually, 'and maybe he can't be arsed to do the washing. Are you one of those conspiracy theorists or something? Everything's a bloody conspiracy? The old guy was about a hundred years old. His son's a callous little shit, sad but not uncommon. Not everyone loves their dear old mum and dad.

'He might have his reasons. The old guy might be rich as Bill Gates for all we know. Maybe the son's just waiting for his inheritance, maybe the old sod is holding out on him.'

I can feel my temper rising, the tensile stretch of my cheese-wire patience almost at breaking point. I don't like this silly little bitch one bit. I'd like to smash her in her pouty, sneering face, smack some sense into her, but I check myself, as the nurse says, 'Well, love, it looks to me like his heart just gave out.'

'Really? Because you're such a great nurse? Looks to me like his face is bruised; his lips are blue. Do you know what that could mean?'

I point at the pillow the nurse is still clutching and she raises her eyebrows.

'Have you seen those sorts of injuries before? The landlord, let's assume he is that, was fluffing the pillows earlier. Nice fat pillows; little old man. Now the old guy is dead. I don't think he had another heart attack. Are you being deliberately thick or what? Don't you pay attention to the radio? Don't you know they're looking for a killer out there, not far from here?'

I want to shock this silly little girl who no doubt thinks nothing bad will ever happen to her, that she could ever find herself at the whim of unkind people like that poor old bastard has, but something clicks in her face then. She looks at me differently as she puts the pillow down and steps back from the bed. She looks like someone else. Harder. Older.

'And you're saying . . . ?' She lets her sentence trail off, the implication too much to speak.

'I don't know, but I think we should get out of here now.'

'And go where?

'Anywhere! Anywhere else.'

'Right.'

The nurse pauses for a moment, shifting her weight from one foot to the other. 'And you want to report this to the police, presumably? This half-cocked story you've concocted. The trouble is, they might just believe you, and that's a shame.'

I'm confused for a moment, but only one, before I realise the extent of my mistake, of the colossal misjudgement I've made, first back on the road, right up to this moment, in this room. It was an easy error to make, I suppose. I've been caught off guard, complacent, because this is the place I came back to in order to get away from the sort of people I've left behind.

It's a quiet, nothing-ever-happens kind of place, slow and sleepy, where people look out for each other and still leave their doors unlocked. But you should never read only the surface signs of anywhere or anyone, Purvis has taught me that if bugger all else. There's a lesson here, never assume you're the biggest, baddest thing in the woods unless you're prepared to prove it.

I see the nurse tense now; the knowledge of my knowledge has passed between us. We see each other. Our eyes lock.

I step back slightly, planting my feet solidly on the floor, on firm ground, a fighting stance. The nurse smiles, her chin comes up, but before I can react further the landlord shambles in through the door. It takes him just a second to see what's happened to the old man in the bed. Death is obvious and unkind.

His mouth falls open in a horrified 'O' as his fists clench around the hatchet in his hands. I recognise it as the one from downstairs, by the fireplace.

As soon as I see it I know it's going to happen, right here, right now.

'What are you doing?' he yells at the nurse, recovering his voice. 'Who the fuck *are* you?'

A smile plays across her lips. Unconcerned by the weapon in his hands, she looks at me as she answers.

'You know who I am. I'm the district nurse.'

'No. No you're not,' yells the landlord, 'because my mother is the bloody district nurse. You're not my mother. Why are you wearing my mother's coat? That is her coat, isn't it? I knew it, as soon as you arrived, and her purse, you have her purse. I thought maybe she'd sent you to . . .'

'Your mother's coat?' I parrot, looking from the nurse to the man and back again as she fingers the grubby collar of the shiny pink parka with the spangly Christmas badge on the pocket.

'Yeah, well . . . I needed a lift, and I needed a good coat, too. It's a bitch of a day out there and I didn't exactly have time to pack an outdoor jacket. I had a little prang you see. Your mother stopped when I stepped in front of her car, waved her down. The bitch didn't want to give me a lift though. I changed her mind.'

She pulls off the coat, though it's icily cold in the room, and puts her bag, slung across her body until now, down on the foot of the bed. I know why. She knows she might need to be able to move freely soon. I unzip my jacket.

'Your mother, eh?' says the nurse, her foot beginning to tap relentlessly on the floorboards. 'Well, that explains it. Why you're soft as shite. What a hard old bitch! She should have just let me take the car. It's only a car, right?'

The landlord's face crumples like a child. His words come out sounding like one, whining, 'What did you do to my mam?' He's still holding the hatchet, but I know you should never raise a weapon unless you intend to use it.

'Jesus, it was her fault.' The nurse sighs. 'Needs must and all that. Grow a pair, for God's sake. If I were you I'd be more worried about myself right now.'

'Where is she?' he asks.

'Not so very far away.'

'Why are you doing this?'

'Isn't that obvious? I need to get out of town, darling. Now that plan is royally fucked. What are *you* doing here, anyway? She's right, isn't she, little Miss Marple there?' She cocks her head towards me, motionless by the door. 'He's not your dad, is he? The old bugger?'

'No. I'm here with Mam. She looks after him. I've been helping out a bit lately. Keeping an eye on him.'

'Yeah, right,' I say, the wheels in my head clicking a few steps ahead. This is bad and it's going to get worse very soon. Tick tock – I'm waiting for the explosion. The landlord needs to get clear of the blast zone, but while the pair in front of me are distracted, gloating, talking and explaining, I have some time to think.

'You're looking after yourselves by the looks of it,' I continue. 'I saw the letters downstairs. Brian, right? His son? Is he coming here to find out why his dad hasn't been answering his letters? Are you cashing his social security cheques or something? Is that the scam? Is that why you lied to us?'

The landlord's eyes are trying to look everywhere except at the old man on the bed. It's a guess, but that's all the confirmation I need. His face is filling with tremulous distress. Something is missing, though it's about to click into place. I remember the old man's withered hand, flailing dumbly at me when I entered the room earlier.

'Is that his car outside? His son's? Is he already here?'

The no-longer landlord doesn't answer but his eyes flick reflexively to the bed. I glance at the quiet TV and back at the nurse. 'Tell him who you are then,' I say to her.

When the nurse doesn't answer I walk to the TV and flick the 'on' switch. A news report scrolls across the screen and the landlord's mouth drops open at the photograph there, the crawling ticker tape warning people not to approach.

'He recognised you? The old man?' I say.

The nurse sighs. 'Who knows? I think so. He saw the TV, anyway. It was on in the background earlier, you two just weren't looking. He'd been watching it all bloody day. Couldn't take a chance, could I? Him telling brain of Britain here, them calling the police.'

She shifts from one foot to the other. Almost as if she's talking to herself, muttering, 'It's a fucking mess now, isn't it? What *are* we going to do?'

'Don't call the police,' says the landlord, his eyes flickering from the nurse's face to her shifting feet. He's almost in tears, and at last I see why.

'It's more of a mess than you think,' I say, inclining my head to the bottom of the bed.

The nurse looks down and sees what I've just spotted, a hand lying an inch from her left Converse trainer. The fingers curl upwards, unmoving, attached to an arm that disappears under the bed and the draped sheets. She looks at the hand, then at me, then back to the landlord, the moment taking on a farcical slowness, her face quizzical rather than shocked.

No one screams at the sight like they might in a movie. We aren't those women, those high-pitched ditsy heroines. After a moment the nurse lifts the sheet that has fallen over the side of the bed.

'Holy shit,' is all she says when the body beneath is revealed.

Yes, that must be Brian, I think, the twisted and slumped figure, still in a feather and down jacket, shoved under the old man's bed. He must have been there a good few hours, at least since we arrived. Jesus, he must have been there all along. The old man hadn't been pointing downstairs earlier. He'd been pointing under his bed. *Jesus Christ!*

There are smears of blood on the floor under the sheet. The landlord, who isn't the landlord any more, must have been trying to wipe them up with his bowl of water. Something cool clicks in my head, enabling me to finally slip into action mode. Though it doesn't show on the surface – on the surface I feign horror like a normal person, like an anthropology student probably would, and ask, 'What happened to him?'

'Yeah,' says the nurse. 'Why is there a stiff dead guy under the bed, hun? What have you been up to? You've been fleecing this old fucker, right? You and your mam. And this is the prodigal son? Bravo! I would never have thought you had it in you.'

'My mother said she was putting the money to good use,' says the landlord, defensive now. 'What would you know about it? About anything? I can't get a job, OK? My sister had two kids but fucked off with a lorry driver two years ago, leaving us to look after them. Mam has to look after everyone, the kids and me, because I'm such "a fucking disappointment".'

'Aw, boo-hoo! Whatever keeps you sane. I don't give a shit what your problems are.'

'He was an old perv anyway, the old man,' says the landlord, a justifying whine in his voice, 'a *dirty bastard*. Everyone knows that. He was a gay, too.'

'A gay?' snarls the nurse, a nasty little smile crossing her lips. 'Yeah, cos "gay" and "perv" are the same thing, right?' She edges closer to the landlord, fists clenched, teasing her easy prey. 'So that makes me a perv, right? Because I fuck girls as well as men?'

'No, I mean. He played around with *kids*,' says the landlord, taking a step back. 'Everyone said so. That's what I meant.'

'Oh, well then, in that case he probably deserved what he got, right?' says the nurse, with the air of a cat toying with a mouse, claws out a little but not enough to kill – yet. 'I feel better now. Knowing you're not a total bigot, just an idiot. But this geezer?' She toes the limp arm of the man whose face is hidden by a thin hank of ginger hair. 'This is fucked up, my boy! You and your mother have quite a mess to clean up.'

'I didn't mean it. I didn't mean to kill him.'

'Yeah, yeah.' Instantly, the nurse is bored of the game, the mask of prettiness disappearing from her face, unravelling from her mouth upwards, quickly reaching her eyes. I see a glitter of amusement there, and something else. It cuts through the gaze of the landlord, who isn't the landlord, and makes him look away. He can't meet her eye.

'I didn't mean to. I just . . .'

'He turned up here earlier,' I offer, 'came to find out what was going on at last. You panicked because he was going to call the authorities in, right? He threatened to call Social Services? The police?'

'Yeah. He was shouting at me like a madman. I don't like it when people shout at me. We hadn't *hurt* old George or nothing. We fed him. We looked after him. But that man called my mother terrible names, then he grabbed me, went mental, so I grabbed him back and he shoved me, and then . . . and then . . . and then I hit him. He called me junkie scum, but I've been clean for a year. Then I kicked him after he fell down. He was so fat. I think he had a heart attack or something. He'd stopped breathing. Then all that blood came out of his mouth.'

'After you kicked the shit out of him? What a surprise.' The nurse grins.

I'm not surprised. I suspect a ruptured stomach ulcer

maybe, common enough in the overweight and in alcoholics. Not a nice way to go, vomiting blood, choking on it. A kick could've easily caused that.

'You called your mother from her rounds. You were waiting for her to come and sort this out,' I say. That would make sense. She was obviously the master bitch in all this, the one with the plan. Best laid plans, eh? Despite what Lil says, this is one catastrophe that presents no opportunity for anyone. This is just one to get the fuck out of and run.

'She told me she was on her way,' says the landlord. 'She said she'd come back and sort it out. She said to get the bloody dog and his car out of sight right away, but he'd tied the bloody Alsatian up outside and it wouldn't let me near it to bring it in. Then I couldn't find the car keys on him. She was taking so long I tried to hide him, the bloke, but he was so fat. I was going to try and get him down the stairs but . . .'

'Ding dong, Merry Christmas, unexpected guests!' The nurse snorts. 'Christ, was that why you were emptying the freezer? Very original, Einstein. Were you going to try and hide him with the Findus crispy pancakes?'

The misery on his face confirms her statement.

'When we turned up you had to hide him up here?' I add.

'Yeah.'

'Oh my God!' She laughs. 'Now what then? Are you going to bump us off? Is that hatchet you're holding for my benefit, or were you thinking of a little body disposal? Jesus, no wonder the old bag wasn't keen on giving me a lift. She was in a hurry to clean up your mess, retard! You know, this has been a bat-shit crazy few days. First that dumb fucker Billy and his bullshit story, then losing his shit in the middle of the fun and running out on me, now this.

'I fucking hate Wales. This is why I don't come here any more. It's full of fucking weirdoes. When I get my bloody farm I'm selling up and never coming back. Well, the party's over now, boys and girls. I'm sorry, but it's time to call it a day. The circus is leaving town.'

Lions and tigers and bears, I mutter.

'What?' snarls the nurse.

'What happened to the old man?' asks the landlord. He hasn't quite got it yet. He hasn't realised that, despite the fact that he's a young man holding a hatchet in a room with two women half his size, he's the one in the most danger.

'As I said, not exactly brain of Britain,' says the nurse to me.

'She killed him,' I say flatly, the time for a soft touch past. 'She killed that old woman up at the farm, too. Didn't you?'

'Yeah, and the old guy, too, hopefully, though I couldn't stick around to make sure. Haven't you been listening to the radio, retard boy? Don't you know there's a dangerous nutter on the loose?'

It's going to happen *now*. I see it clearly. The seconds are counting down. *Beep, beep, beep*. The silent alarm has been triggered, reinforcements are coming, but it's going to happen my way. That's for sure. The switch flicks.

There will be noise and fury. There will be damage. There will be casualties.

So here we are.

243

'Don't,' I say to the nurse. 'Whatever you think you're going to do right now, don't. You can still fuck off out of here. There's time. I don't care where you go and *he's* not going to tell anyone you were here. Take your chances, you can still get away.'

And I'm not leaving that stupid, helpless bastard with you, even if he has accidentally offed someone.

So this is it.

That bloody balding donkey understands, his red and white trimmed Santa hat at a jaunty angle, giving me that look again, as if he's thinking what I'm thinking, knows what I know – not all of us will leave this room alive.

The nurse looks at me as if I'm insane, 'Away? In this? Tonight? When I have a nice place to wait it out and a car to use tomorrow? I don't think so.'

'Then we have a problem,' I say, 'because I'm not leaving this room.'

'I know that,' says the nurse.

'Really?'

'Really.'

'You really want to do this? Be sure now. Think it through.' My claws click out, my spine straightens.

'Hmmm, well, all things considered I think I have the edge, love,' says the nurse. 'I'm a dangerous offender, after all. The telly says so – "do not approach".' Her teeth bare slightly in a parody of a smile.

'Really? And what proof have you got of that, apart from beating an old woman to death and suffocating a defenceless old man?'

'Try three years in Holloway, you interfering little cow,' she says.

'Yeah? Then try three years in Helmand, you stupid little bitch.'

The room is silent as our eyes lock.

Outside the dog howls, the sound ancient and feral, brimming with the scent of old blood. We move towards each other.

So here we go!

The Law – 4.55 p.m.

Trekking down the hill in the shrill and surging dark I'm already thinking this is a bad idea. Glad I haven't come across the nurse yet, slumped in a heap at the roadside with spurs of bone sticking out of a broken ankle, I occupy my time by rehearsing the speech I need to give to the Bryn Mill tribunal panel on 6 January at 2 p.m. sharp.

I can't possibly tell the three august elected members the truth, that when I walked into the narrow hall at Bryn Mill I was completely unprepared, that I bottled it. Lissa 'leg-it', like it or not, that was me.

It happened in a matter of seconds, after I'd spotted the rucksack sitting halfway down the passageway, on the table. I'd just stuck my hand into the top and pulled out a clutch of packets of what could only be ecstasy pills, when I realised that Big John Harvey, aka 'Slammer', was watching me from the kitchen doorway. He eyed me with surprise, but only for a second before his face relaxed into a grin.

I can see it now, the lazy way he said, 'Well hiya, Lady Copper,' placing one hand on his solid hip. 'Your mam know you're out, love? You've interrupted me making my tea and that's plain rude. Best you fuck off home, *cariad*. Unless you wanna play with the big boys?'

I must have tensed, because his smile turned into a sneer as he said, 'You deaf, love?' pulling himself up to his full height, brushing the top of the old door frame and the narrow walls of the passageway. He stank of beer and chip fat, at four o'clock in the afternoon, from two arms' length distance, and I immediately recoiled five feet. It was an involuntary reaction, but enough for a professional bully like Harvey to know how things stood between us.

His eyes followed mine down to the peeling knife in his wet hands, and he looked at the blade as if he'd just realised it was there and could be useful for skinning something other than potatoes. He made a slow show of pointing it towards me.

'Now that you've spoiled my tea I'm going to get my rucksack and go out for a bit, all right? Unless you're gonna do something about it? What you gonna do, Officer?'

The answer, of course, was nothing. Aware of nothing but the size of him, his muscular presence, his slab of a hand on the knife, my own pathetic and clichéd vulnerability, my brain had fogged over. I know there are female officers in the force who would have fronted up then, regardless of their disadvantage, the ones I see getting stuck in, sitting astride a bloke twice their size, clapping the cuffs on when it gets rowdy at the rugby club. I always thought that would be me, but it's not like the movies when it's real, it's not so easy.

So I didn't extend my baton. I didn't announce myself in a forceful manner and identify myself as an officer of the law. I didn't pull out my pepper spray and order him to put up his hands and surrender. I just stood there until he said, 'Nice girl like you shouldn't be out here all on her own. Come back later if you like and I'll give you a strip search. Bring your handcuffs.'

As he stepped towards me, chuckling, I backed away even further, letting him pick up the rucksack, zip it up with the pill packets inside and edge backwards towards the door behind him.

'It's OK, lovely. No one needs to know you was here. Our secret, right?'

I know I saw a change in the light behind him then, through the open kitchen door, somewhere outside, but as Harvey backed out through the kitchen door and across the flagstones, knife still in his hand, sniggering, I didn't yell out to warn what could only be Biggsy.

I didn't actually see him dodge out of the back door because I was too busy falling over my own feet as I ran the other way, tripping over the doorstep, wrenching my wrist as I hit the ground, like all good fleeing damsels in distress. In an instant my often-practised scenario and story had become confused. I was no longer the modern, ballsy heroine; I was the girl in need of good, old-fashioned rescue.

Harvey was already over the back doorstep when he encountered Biggsy coming up the garden path. Big old Biggsy, soft as a brush until challenged, but as tall and broad as Harvey and as naturally imposing. Harvey, startled by the unexpected mountain of uniform blocking his escape, lashed out, driving the knife straight into Biggsy's shoulder, down to the bone and muscle. I learned this later, after I'd come out from behind the shameful safety of the metal flank of the panda car out front.

It must only have been thirty seconds, but I felt as if I'd been frozen for an hour. I told the attending officers that I'd run out to alert Biggsy, not that I'd completely forgotten about him and only crept back towards the house when I heard his strangled voice yelling, 'Jesus Christ, Lloyd. Call a fucking ambulance.'

It had taken me longer than it should have to realise that Harvey was well away and my sergeant was possibly bleeding to death in the garden. By the time I reached him there was so much blood over his face and neck that it took me a second to recognise who was speaking to me. Harvey had nicked an artery. Biggsy was in intensive care for three days afterwards.

Was there a moment back then, crouched in the wet red mess trying to cradle his head on my knees, that I thought, That could have been me? That I was the tiniest bit relieved that it wasn't? I decline to answer in this case, and decline to answer on the grounds that it may be taken down in evidence and used against me. One thing I do know is that I want to be ready if there's a next time. I want to be a good police officer, the one who stands my ground.

As I head down the hill towards Halfway I run through the speech I've practised with my Police Federation rep, hoping it will be enough to get me a second chance, to show I'm made of the right stuff, that I can learn from my mistakes. That's when I think I hear a gunshot, somewhere down below in the dark. I stop for a moment, listening for any other commotion in the silence. But it doesn't bother me that much; it's probably a poacher, or maybe kids, out with an air rifle, shooting crows.

I'm almost at the pub.

The Hitchhiker – 5.05 p.m.

It takes just two more seconds for all hell to break loose. It's what I've been waiting for – waiting without waiting, but ready, as always.

The nurse pulls a hammer out of the bag she's just put down by the bed, the bag she never leaves behind. Then, from inside the parka she's hung on the bedpost, she pulls out what looks like an old revolver and levels it at me. It's a 455 Webley by the look of it, an army relic from the 1930's, standard issue once. Hardly the modern weapon of choice, but 'needs must'.

'OK, bitch, take your pick,' says my adversary, the no-longer a nurse, 'the handy hammer or my newest friend? It's all the same to me.'

'Neither, thanks,' I say as I feint forward, my hand flying up as she steps to the side. I knock the gun out of her hand in one swift move. Easy. It's always easy. Bone connects with bone but I don't mind, though the snarl that comes from the nurse who isn't a nurse any more is close to inhuman. That helps. It means I don't have to feel bad about what's likely to come next.

I don't think this woman is one who will ever look away first. I gave her the option to leave, but she didn't take it. Fair enough – that means just one thing.

I've never killed anyone, not face to face, I mean, not deliberately, in close quarters like this. But this is what I've been drilled for by the British Army's finest, and they know what they're doing. There's a wiry tornado of psychotic rage coming at me right now and this is *the* moment I become what I've been trained to be.

It's not really how it's supposed to be, I'm not supposed to want to hurt this murdering bitch, but I really do. Because of what she is, because of the cruel end of that old lady up at the farm, because of the sad and lonely end of the old man before me, because of the hurt she has caused, and will no doubt go on to cause if she's allowed to leave here. I can't allow it – she won't allow me to.

'Come on then, soldier girl, bring it on.' She grins, her hands reaching to bear hug me as she moves to raise the hammer. The mask, the performance has dropped away now. I'd known it was a performance on some level all along – that itching under my skin – what was behind the nurse's words hadn't matched what was in her eyes.

No wonder she hadn't given a shit about her so-called kid – the fat little lard boy in her wallet; the remark, 'What are you, a detective?' The sneer when she'd said, 'I guess that makes me Rebecca, Becca to you.'

It all makes sense now. Clever, though, thinking on her feet like that. I can do it too. So I do.

The nurse lunges forward with cold fury. So this

full-screw corporal, with seven years in uniform and three stalking the streets and backwaters of Afghanistan, reacts. I block and twist and throw her to the floor, a classic move, day-one basic training, while the landlord stands, stunned, the hatchet limp in his hand, his mouth a wide 'O' of horror and confusion.

There it is, the reaction I've seen a million times, the freeze of incomprehension – the disconnect – not so much in the towns any more, the bullet-pitted settlements, not after living with it all for so long. The people there are used to seeing people like me and my team, the patrols. They're used to the occasional bursts of rebel gunfire, the casual IED, even in the villages, in the quieter parts, on hearts and minds missions.

It's the freeze reaction that gets most people killed during their first few weeks of deployment. They say 'fight or flight' is an inherent human instinct, but people often forget the first instinct is usually to freeze and do nothing – you can't blame them. Apart from the ready and steady few, like me, it has to be trained out of you. The landlord has little idea what's going on and is reacting to type. I can't expect any help from him.

He wants to run but it takes him too long to decide to do it. By the time he tries, ordering his legs to move, shambling towards the open door, it's too late. He doesn't get far. Seeing his predictable flight the nurse gets to her feet, a new object of anger identified. Hurling her weight against him, at his broad back from four feet away, the hammer comes down on the back of his head.

'No you don't, dumbo! You're not going anywhere.'

It's enough to send the big man sprawling forward, off

balance, into the door frame, the hatchet flying from his grasp, skidding harmlessly into the hallway beyond. His forehead hits the wood with a thick crack that makes me wince. As the nurse falls forward, trying to right herself, the hammer slips from her grip, thudding across the floor.

Now that the gun and the hammer have been smashed from her grip, she has a penknife in her hand, pulled from her jeans pocket in a sudden snatched motion. Still, no bother, I'm ready.

But the nurse intends to finish the job she's started. As the landlord sinks to his knees she grabs the hair at the back of his head and stabs him in the side of his neck. It reminds me a little of those videos of servicemen being beheaded – the landlord is being executed, right here, right now, in front of me. His carotid artery goes at once. Pierced beneath the blade, blood spumes everywhere, under pressure.

The nurse backs off to survey her handiwork, though it's too late to avoid the blood. Somehow the landlord shuffles round and falls onto his arse, his face shocked, perplexed. He doesn't clutch at his neck. He leans back against the bed, his head lolling – I see the light go out in him. If I ever had any doubt about doing this, it's gone.

I pull out my own knife from the waistband of my trousers, the one I've kept locked in my backpack until ten minutes ago, until I found the bag in the cellar and slipped it into my belt. I'm glad I did. It's more than a fair fight now.

I head straight for my opponent, who's still panting with satisfaction at her direct hit on the landlord, blood fever high in her eyes, thrumming along her arms into her clenched fists. Before she can corner me, I skid to my knees along the wooden floor and scrabble for the gun that flung itself somewhere under the dresser after the last tackle.

My hands grasp for it amongst the dust and God knows what else that's decomposing under the chest. I don't particularly want to use the gun, but I sure as hell don't want the nurse to either. While I reach underneath I kick out behind me as I hear footfalls thud up, catching my approaching attacker square in the chest, my boot connecting satisfyingly with bone and gristle, so that the nurse staggers backwards.

For a second I'm disappointed her sternum didn't crack, I must be losing my edge, but she's off-balance, winded, doubled-up and on the back foot, just where I want her. It gives me enough time to locate the gun, straighten up and take a wide-legged stance. Two minutes of drama, now I'm in control.

'Unlucky, bitch,' spits the nurse, through the whizz of air that leaves her lungs, 'that old piece of junk doesn't work. Now what'll you do, eh?'

'Really,' I say, levelling the barrel at her. 'It's not quite like the ones we use now, but it looks in quite good nick to me. And I think the safety was on. Didn't you learn about guns in Holloway?'

'I can still rip your throat out when it misfires,' says the nurse, penknife in her hand, caked in gore. Jesus, she's an infernal sight, soaked in the landlord's blood from crown to chest, some of it's even on her teeth, which glow into a white grin amidst the horror-red stain of her face. She looks like something from hell itself, but she isn't. She's just a woman, a piece of shit of a woman who enjoys hurting people.

I can't help thinking of the face of that old man in Lashkar Gah – was it there? Second month in? I'm not sure. I only know how he'd looked when me and Purvis went into the house, guns ready, checking, searching. 'Please . . .' – one word of English. Please what? Don't hurt me? Help me?

They had nothing, that family – a few pots, a goat – but that didn't mean they weren't hiding someone or didn't have weapons under the rug. To be sure, Purvis checked outside while I stood point, scanning the scrappy garden, the outhouse, the surrounding hillocks and the dusty approach track. Then he'd patted the placid donkey chewing, untethered, by the rickety fence, put his helmet on its head and said, 'Take a photo, Lee.'

He was going through a phase then of finding it amusing, posing with props, capturing the 'local colour'. We didn't actually have a camera, of course.

'Give it a fucking rest, Purvis,' I said, hot, tired and anxious to get back to the vehicle.

'Buzz kill,' he'd shot back, a phrase he'd picked up from our American friends, slapping the donkey hard on the arse. Predictably, it brayed and bolted off into the patch of land at the side of the hut, then, *boom!* Up it went, like an exploding ketchup-red water bomb, misting blood and matted hair, chunks of fat flesh umbrella-ing into the air.

Even Purvis hadn't meant for that to happen. Too shocked to laugh, covered in donkey viscera, we were both thinking the same thing, That could have been one of us. Then the old woman started wailing, babbling in her own tongue, a clot of bloody donkey flank in her hair, running down on to her cheek – neither me nor Purvis had understood it, apart from the odd word, but the meaning was clear.

She must have known, the old bird, they all must have known, that there were mines at the edge of that field, mines meant for people like me, scouting, checking, trying to build bridges and win hearts and minds. That woman had looked not unlike this crazy bitch facing me down now, the glare in her eyes, the hate as her claw hand gripped my arm and she spat in my face.

Sometimes life has that feeling of repetition. In a way it's oddly comforting. The wheel turns, the circle closes.

We were wrong that time, the intelligence off, but I wasn't wrong the day of the car fire. When I went inside the brick house, I knew on instinct that they were hiding something, and I found the cache of IEDs, the automatic weapons, just as the occupants came home. I barely had time to get the call out – 'Come get me' – legging it to the extraction point, when that Molotov hit the four-by-four and . . .

We made it, though, and put all those weapons out of circulation, not that I think it's worth a medal, the one they've promised. It was just my job, done well on a day that turned out better than it could have. But back to the task in hand . . .

I'm still standing, waiting for the nurse to make her move, ready to defend myself. I'm a soldier not a killer. I serve my country. There are rules. The knife is in my left hand; the gun is in my right.

When she lunges I pull the trigger, suddenly tired of the standoff, tired of everything. There's a quick explosion, not very loud. It's not a very high-calibre gun. The roof of the room and the snow above muffles it. It could almost be anything, that sound, and it's almost a misfire, but it's enough to fell the no-longer-a-nurse creature, who stops short with the force of the impact, gripping the bedpost, outraged and startled.

Her bloodied hand goes up to her chest, and she falls back against the bed, staring at her wet fingers. She glares at me, confused, outraged. This is not what she expected – it's cleaner, quicker, more decisive, and she's on the wrong side of it for the first time. This is the end.

The paper-wrapped Christmas gifts on the bed, with their bright colours and curls of twine, are speckled with her blood. Some blood bubbles into her mouth. I know that at close range like this, it's already over for my opponent. I've seen enough like it in the field, but I don't need to be a medic to know the shot is fatal. I think the nurse suspects it, too. She laughs at the anti-climax of it all.

'Hah! Fuck me, it does work. Well done, soldier girl, wholly unexpected. I guess it's nice to be surprised sometimes.'

She steadies herself as best she can, half-slumped over, reaching for her bag on the foot of the bed by the baseboard. Fingers slick with blood, she manages to unzip it, clutching at the corner of a plastic carrier bag within, trying to pull it open.

'Guess it's all yours then.' She coughs. 'To the victor the spoils, right? Jesus, what a day! Time for a sit-down.'

At that moment she gives up trying to clutch at the bag and slides to the floor beside the bed. I stand still for a while, just breathing, centring myself, letting everything else fall away. Eventually I walk towards the bed to look into the bag the nurse has been guarding all day.

The moth-eaten donkey watches me from near the headboard without comment as the tarnished silver star, hanging from the roof beam, rotates slowly above. The TV flickers silently on the dresser, showing an old repeat of *Top of the Pops*; Frankie Goes to Hollywood's video for 'The Power of Love' rolls across the TV screen, three wise men riding camels.

Then I let out a bark of laughter. The universe is sharing a joke – I get it.

I stare at the gold glistening inside the open bag on the bed, at the metallic heart of the tableau, amid the three dead people. There's no frankincense or myrrh, but who needs them when there are necklaces and bracelets in this bag of storybook treasure. To the victor the spoils.

'Merry Christmas,' says Riley Finn, then she dies.

The Law – 5.15 p.m.

I'm half-frozen by the time I get to the bottom of the hill. Visibility is down to a couple of feet now and it feels like I'm inside a washing machine full of cold suds, inhaling every flake and flurry. Heroism is all very well, but sometimes it's nicer if you can perform your heroics from a warm car or cosy office.

Fortunately I'm at the front of the pub before I realise it, my vision tunnelled by my tightly tied anorak hood. I have a vague memory of calling in here once or twice as a kid, usually to use the loo because I couldn't last the extra half hour home. It had seemed wonderfully scary and ghost-story decrepit to me then, with its delightful wonky floors and ceilings, promising winding passages for hide and seek and huge, gurgling Victorian toilets with long chain flushes.

Now it just looks broken and bowed, like something out of an unpleasant road movie, the last place you'd want to call into on a winter's night alone because you know what would happen if you did.

I knock hard on the front door before I can start winding

myself up again and, with heavy authority, call out,
'Mr Rhydderch?' then, 'Mrs Nash? Anyone home?'

As the wind hushes, a temporary lull falls and the silence
is suddenly overwhelming. My slightly Gothic knock-
knock-knock puts me in mind of a legend passed down on
the Greek island of Santorini, where it's believed the
undead travel the villages at night, knocking on doors and
calling out the names of the residents. Anyone who answers
the call is said to die within three days. That's why, even to
this day apparently, the oldest women, black-clad and sun-
desiccated, never answer their doors on the first knock. It
isn't bad advice.

I try once again for luck, pounding with my fist, though
I doubt anyone is going to answer the door, no matter how
long I hammer on it. Giving up on the front entrance,
I follow the mews archway around the side. Nurse or no
nurse, I'm sure as hell not hiking back up that hill without
at least a hot cuppa inside me, though slogging through the
shin-high snow I try not to think about the crap I'll catch
from the inspector if I end up stranded here, sitting out the
night in a pub of all places while the rest of the force are
seeking our fugitive.

Imagine the nicknames I'll garner then!

Still, I can see a slant of light illuminating the snow
through the shadows out back, and there's a hire car
parked up, too. Someone has to be home, someone deaf,
perhaps. So I press my face up against the grubby, misted
windowpane, peering into the kitchen, where I'm just able
to spot a cup and plate on the table, when a wolfish howl
from behind me shreds the silence.

My head snaps around like a whip and I tense, expecting

to have to run or climb out of the way of some eager watchdog. Instead I see a shaggy German Shepherd tethered to a wormy-looking kennel, its howl turning into a clatter of barks that ricochet off the tiles and stone.

It's making far more noise than anyone inside the pub would surely be able to stand for long, and I prepare myself to face an old man with an even older shotgun, expecting thieving intruders perhaps. But no one appears to shush him, or actually, her.

She looks agitated, but calms down when I speak to her in what Jim calls my dog-whispering voice. Dogs like me, and she gives a little whine, snuffling her cold nose into my hand as I offer her a bit of biscuit from my belt pack.

'It's OK, girl,' I say, ruffling her ears. 'What are you doing out here in the cold? Where's your master, then?'

Of course she can't answer, so I try the back door, and am surprised when it clicks open on the latch. If I lived out here I'd have the whole place locked and shuttered at all times, but the old never learn; they're far too trusting. I let myself into the kitchen, shaking off the snow, puzzling at a sopping pile of food defrosting on the floor by the freezer. Apart from that, and a first-aid box open on the table, nothing seems particularly strange.

I can see a passageway and follow it through into the bar area, but there's no sign of anything untoward here either, just a cup and plate, sticky with crumbs on the table – a jacket on a chair, a bag of shopping spilling open next to it, a backpack leaning against the chair.

On the wall by the bar I spot a page from a newspaper, mounted in a frame, and smile. It's a story I was told as a child by one of the old farmers at the market, about a lion that attacked a stagecoach. Though I later learned that it had actually taken place in Exeter, not Aberystwyth, it had scared the shit out of me at the time. I'd both loved and feared the story, regularly replaying versions where I was the plucky passenger with the blunderbuss who brought the lion up short.

Nostalgia is getting me nowhere, though, I need to find someone at home or get home myself, so I leave the bar and head towards the back of the pub – *our heroine presses on, undaunted, alert to any sound . . .*

'Mr Rydderch?' I call again. 'Rebecca?' still expecting the nurse to call down from upstairs, where she's giving the old man his afternoon tea, waiting for the storm to pass.

As I start upwards I think I hear the back door creak and glance down the corridor towards the kitchen. From the gust of freezing air that ruffles the red, mildewed curtain to the old lounge I guess the wind has blown it open, so I trudge back and close it firmly this time, shushing the dog, which has begun to bark again, pulling at her chain.

This time I go straight up the stairs two at a time – *our heroine is undaunted and undeterred. She calls out loudly, announcing her presence boldly, prepared for any scene of horror, any vision of foul play among these Gothic dusty halls.* I head to the only doorway on the landing that shows a crack of light, then push the door open.

It takes a moment to process the scene that greets me, to realise that what must be old George Rhydderch is lying dead in his bed. There's no doubt he's no longer of this world; the long-rumoured paedophile and kiddie fiddler is open-mouthed and white-faced in his neatly turned-down sheets, covers tucked around his chest.

If that was all it would be simple enough to know what to do, but it isn't.

There's another body at the side of the bed, half shoved under it, a great fat man in a red anorak, with a purple splosh of blood clotted down his front. He has company. There's another big guy slumped against the bed on the right, his throat hanging open, a flap of flesh separated from the rest, blood patterned across the doorway and the floor in elaborate sprays of scarlet. And a dark-haired woman is sitting on the floor at the other end of the bed, her head hanging forward, chest bloody, hands wet with gore.

To complete the tableau, at the foot of the bed, on top of the blanket, is a bag spilling what can only be described as a shiny treasure – gold chains, bracelets, the wink of a diamond – sparking storybook colours in the low lamplight.

The whole scene is being watched by a ratty woollen donkey wearing a jaunty Christmas hat and, as it stares at me, I wait for someone to call 'cut', for the cameras to stop rolling and everyone to jump out from behind the furniture yelling, You got punked! But nothing moves in the room except me.

The tick of the clock sounds in the stillness as the smell of iron tinges the air. Earth stood hard as iron, water like a stone, I think, for no good reason, transfixed by the blood spattered and pooled around the floor and walls, by the figures frozen in time that neither move nor offer any explanation of what the hell has happened here.

It takes me more than a minute to realise that the woman slumped by the bed is the one we've been looking for all day, our fugitive Riley Finn. She's more dishevelled since the mugshot I saw earlier, but there's little doubt it's her – it's her face we've been broadcasting in our appeals for the last seven hours.

The belated booming of my heart breaks the stillness in the room as a surge of breathless nausea lurches through me and I force myself to breathe in and out a few times, pushing back the greying edges of my vision as a thousand possibilities and questions shoot through my mind.

It's only now, with our fugitive right in front of me, that I have a sudden flash of recall. I remember the 'Mrs Death' story Jim told me earlier in the nick, about Polly Lewis's death-trap yellow Cortina, the one she used to drive into town, just like the old Cortina I'd found abandoned a mile back. I remember Sergeant Matthews telling us Finn had left the farmhouse on foot, and yet . . .

And these poor buggers? Had Riley killed them all? The old man, the other two guys as well, whoever they are? Because they saw the TV appeal, maybe? Because she'd taken the old couple's car to make her getaway, tried to wait it out here and they'd realised who she was? And there's still one person missing. Where the hell is Rebecca Nash?

As I stand, struck solid with creeping panic, the TV on the chest of drawers is running the police appeal again, the ticker scrawling out along the bottom of the screen – 'Dangerous offender, do not approach'. Every detail crackles into crystal clarity as I stand in the midst of chaos. A tight Hitchcock close-up of my face would show the cogs clicking into place behind my eyes, sweat forming on my brow.

There's a penknife clutched in Riley's hand and, from

some sort of compulsion, seen many times in cop movies, I reach forward and put my fingers on her wrist, checking for a pulse. The skin on her hand is still warm, the blood wet and loose on her clothing and fingers. It hasn't started to stick or clot.

Whatever happened here, it happened very recently. The blood is steaming slightly in the cold room. Then I see an antique-looking gun close to the hand of the third dead man and think of the sound of the shot I'd heard as I'd slid down the hill a few minutes earlier. He must have shot her.

I'm not a doctor or a CSI, but it doesn't look like Finn died instantly. It seems like she dragged herself over to the bed, by the looks of the blood trail, but the end must have been pretty quick. I've missed everything by minutes.

My relief and disappointment are simultaneous and crushing as I obey the sudden urge to lift Finn's face to mine, fascinated. So this is what a psychopath looks like. So this is what death really looks like. It's disappointing actually, on both counts; it's just an ordinary face bearing a mask of absence.

As I tilt her chin upwards a breath releases and speckles my hand with blood, and just for a second, I think she's still alive, that she's going to make a classic cinematic revival, lunging forward with the knife towards my throat. Then I'll have to wrestle her to the ground and can still emerge triumphant from the struggle. For that second I almost welcome the idea.

But of course this doesn't happen. It's just the last exhalation of breath, lungs emptying as I relax the airway. Her blood speckles onto my face and lips and I recoil, falling back onto my arse in reflex, scooting backwards with my feet.

Here I stay, gripped by the inability to process it all.

I'm 3D-clarity conscious that I'm in the middle of the biggest crime scene to hit the area, *ever* – a quadruple murder to add to the murder at the farm, a manhunt ending in a bloodbath and, to top it all off, the conclusion of the forty-year unsolved Dolau gold robbery. Because it can only be that, of course, the jewellery in the bag on the bed – the booty. I quite clearly saw the dragon's head brooch, the centrepiece of the story, winking its ruby eyes at me, waiting to be claimed.

This is the story I've been waiting my whole life to be part of. This is the opportunity I've rehearsed and practised for and yet, by a trick of fate or bad timing, I've missed it. It's too late now to make a difference, too late to save anyone's life, to give pursuit, or to be the girl who gets her man.

Think of the headlines I would have made if I could have stopped some of this, tackled Finn or even just raised the alarm and given chase. They'd have been telling stories about me for ever then, the right kind of stories instead of the one about Biggsy and Bryn Mill and how Lissa legged it from danger. Instead I'm just a bumbling bit-part player again, stumbling on the aftermath by chance, running to the big boys for help.

That's when I spot the hammer on the floor next to my hand, its sticky handle towards me, smeared with blood, almost an invitation to take it. Maybe it's the shock, a dislocation from reality occurring, but slowly it begins to dawn on me that all the elements of my narrative are right here, I just have to rearrange them. If I can string them into the right order, add a few finishing touches, I'll have the best possible version of this story, one that will make me into a brave person, a good police officer – a heroine.

Though it's certainly too late for the dead littering the room, and too late for the Lewises on the hill, it doesn't have to be too late for me. I can still emerge as a warrior, one who's acted on clever hunches and instinct today, the maverick cop who followed a breadcrumb trail of clues to track down her quarry and vanquish her. If I'm careful I can build myself a house of bricks that no one can huff and puff their way through.

The silence is intense and surprisingly soothing as I turn the idea over in my head, testing it for weak links. With my plan formulated I get to my feet, open the frequency on my radio, glad to see there are two bars of signal up here under the roof. Then I make my voice high and gasping and give my location twice, briefly, through the crackle of static. I repeat the phrase, 'Officer needs assistance,' then cut the call handler off before I have to answer any of her questions.

Taking a deep breath, I put my hand on the handle of the gun and my finger on the trigger. Then I lean down, line myself up, take Finn's limp hands in my own and push them onto the front of my coat so they leave bloody smears.

After that there's just one thing left to do. I sit down again, take a huge breath and pick up the hammer. I'm thinking of Inspector Willis's story, of Tom Dooley and the night in the Cardiff pub, the one Finn was never charged in. I think of what Sue Bell said about the old lady's fingers. I place my left hand on the floorboards, knowing that many offenders have a modus operandi, a weapon of choice.

Counting down from three, I screw up my eyes and bring the hammer down on my spread fingers. As I tense every sinew in my body, pain shoots through me, the sound, like cracking nuts, almost worse than the nauseating throb that follows. Then I take three deep breaths, raise the hammer and hit myself across the brow.

I'm attempting a glancing blow to the temple, something that will look good with minimum damage, adding weight to the story I'll tell when my back-up arrives, but I swing a little too hard and rock backwards, smacking the back of my head on the floorboards. Then I black out.

The Armed Robber – 5.15 p.m.

Osion Lewis, lying in his hospital bed, has so far been the silent partner in the day's drama but now, late in the afternoon, he's gathering his strength. The widower of eight hours, with seven stitches in his head, two different types of painkillers in his bloodstream and unknown quantities of grief in his heart, is ready to start talking.

He's glad to tell it now, his story, ready to confess. He asked to see the big, tired policeman personally because he needs to tell it in one go, get it all out, then rinse his mouth out, wash away the taste and never speak of it again.

Inspector Morris looks a little impatient, obviously having a great many things to do today, such as catching the evil bitch who killed Pol, but he has to tell it to the top brass and it has to be taped, even though he's not under arrest or caution or anything. This is his choice, his testimony.

Osion starts his story, as the officer sits, pen and pad in hand, feigning patience. He explains how it all began a lifetime ago, in the long, hot summer that he and Polly started courting. Back then a gentleman walked a girl home from chapel if he wanted to know her better, and it took him every Sunday for a month to pluck up the courage to ask her to a dance.

Her father hadn't approved, not when the town's assistant banker was already making advances, while he himself was penniless. Russell Bradach, whose father ran the regional branch of Black Mountain Bank in Abergavenny, had been to tea at Pol's more than once on a Saturday, sipping Tetleys and munching Welsh cakes with her parents, offering compliments, then offering Polly a little job at his jewellery store for 'a bit of money'.

Polly didn't like him; she preferred their long walks together up to the idling pool where the water played, passing the shady yew tree where they'd sit and talk quietly about poetry and politics. They'd kissed slowly. They'd made plans.

Then, one day he'd found Polly crying, after chapel, by the James family tomb. He can't tell the inspector at his bedside exactly what passed between him and his future wife. Those words are not for his generation, who don't speak of such things. Polly had used the words 'advances' and 'uninvited', so he uses them, too, and that's what will be recorded on the tape. The inspector knows what he means, though, and his eyes spark up and he begins to write on his pad.

It happened when she'd gone into the jewellery shop to see about the job, because they needed the money, with her father laid up with arthritis. Bradach had taken her into the back to 'show her the safe'. They'd never spoken of it again; she'd begged him not to because Bradach's bank owned the loan on the farm, and it would cause trouble, but a year later Pol and Osion had married and lived in the farmhouse with his father. Times were hard, though, with the farm barely breaking even, even before his father died.

Every so often Mr Lewis would see Bradach swanning about town in his father's fancy sedan, only ten years older than him, but holding court in the town hall or library, and rage would fill his heart. Bradach was always bragging about his first kid, the prodigy of his nursery school class who would no doubt fly through grammar school and Oxford or Cambridge, his feet greased by money and privilege.

Osion and Pol wanted a family. They'd been trying for a baby, but any boy or girl of theirs would have to work the farm with dirt under their fingernails and one best suit or dress to their name. So Mr Lewis hatched a plan of his own, a plan to fund a university education for his own children – it wasn't about jealousy or anger or revenge, it was about justice, an instinctive kind that transcended simple law.

He worked on the plan in secret, during the frosty milking mornings, leaning against the cow's fat flanks, telling them his ideas in a low soothing voice. They were a patient audience and it hadn't seemed wrong, just practical. Everyone knew that Bradach managed the overpriced Dolau gold for his father, which none of the locals could afford to buy.

Richer people, the sort Bradach knew and took dinner with, came up from the coast and from Brecon way, to buy their expensive wedding rings and elegant pieces reportedly containing rare Welsh gold, hewn from the Dolaucothi gold mines and fashioned in a workshop in Llandeilo.

Mr Lewis knew that Bradach had made a big sale that weekend. He'd heard him bragging to Mr Blass at the Post Office about it. The buyer would come to collect the bespoke piece, with ruby insets, on the weekend. There was jewellery in the cabinets and cash in the safe.

This is where the inspector stops him, concerned, professional, saying, 'Mr Lewis, I think maybe you should . . . Mr Lewis, I don't know if you should tell me any more right now. Maybe you need to speak to a lawyer later, when you're feeling better?'

But he'll never be feeling better, and this is the time. So he shakes his head, explaining how he'd wanted to be a meticulous soldier once. Though he'd not been able to join up for the actual war, of course, he'd got away as soon as he could afterwards, convinced there'd always be another one, another opportunity to serve his country in some way other than his father had, by tilling and planting it. That was before the training exercise that took his three toes and his hoped-for commission. He'd hung onto an old service revolver, though, that he'd won in a card game with the corporal, tucked it away in an upstairs drawer, kept it cleaned and oiled. He found it calming, tending the mechanisms.

He'd liked the structure of the Army, the feeling of purpose, the sense of a righteous cause. He'd been looking for another righteous cause for years and had known he'd probably never find another so worthy. The part of him that had never had the chance to show and prove itself clicked into action.

On that quiet Monday afternoon, when he knew Mrs Jenny Bradach would be minding the shop, right after lunch in the slow, post-meal hour of the afternoon, he'd donned his woollen balaclava. Affecting an English accent, he'd walked into the shop, imitating one of his old lieutenants and using his authoritative vowels to tell the woman to empty the trays and racks and then the safe in the back.

He only fired the gun once, into the floor; because of the sheer power of it, the thrumming coldness in his hands had made life course through his veins again. Into the bag went the chains and bracelets, in went the rings, and then, last of all, the Welsh Dragon shawl clip, a brooch as big as a saucer, gold with cut ruby eyes, sold to the Llewellyn family from Aberaeron.

When the bag was full, the Harrods bag that had once contained a wedding vase from his brother Bernie who lived in London, he'd walked out calmly, down the street into the lane behind the high street. Once under the cover of the trees at the end, he'd tossed the balaclava and gloves into the fast-flowing river at the side of the chapel, put the bag containing the jewels inside the sack of sheep feed he'd stashed in the hedge beforehand, and walked back onto the main street.

Then he went into the Post Office, sack in hand, for a little chat with postmaster Owain Blass.

Mr Blass said he'd just been down to the police station to say he thought he'd heard a gun go off, asked if he'd heard anything strange. Mr Lewis shook his head and waited with Mr Blass until they heard the sirens, then joined the alarmed throng in the street.

The plan had been to take the stuff, bit by bit, up to Bernie in London, and find a fence. There was no hurry, though; the immediate purpose had been served. Wheels were in motion. Mr Lewis knew there were rumours that Bradach had gambling debts and was borrowing against the shop, always getting bailed out by his father.

The shop was insured against theft but that wasn't necessarily a good thing, as the police questioned Bradach at length, suspecting a put-up job. In the end the insurance company refused to pay out and Bradach's rich friends and benefactors drained away in light of the scandal. He defaulted on his many debts within a year and the money waited patiently at Ridgeback Farm for their firstborn to come of age.

How was he to know that his only son Gary would be dead before his eighteenth birthday? And for such a careless reason too – a drunken stumble, a knock on the head, a spill into the cold river, drunk on home brew the farm kids were always messing around with. Gary's college education was never funded, family holidays never taken and he simply couldn't bear to use the money for Gary's funeral.

'So that's it. That's what I did,' he says, 'and I've never been sorry about it. Not till now.'

He looks at the inspector then, whose face is dark and sad, and asks, 'Do you think that's what they were looking for? Do you think they knew it was there somehow? The jewellery? Though I don't know how they could. I never told anyone, not even Pol. She wouldn't have approved. She couldn't tell them anything. Is that why she's dead?'

The inspector sighs and lies and says, 'I don't think so, Mr Lewis. I think it was just nonsense and rumour. It's not your fault.'

So Mr Lewis explains what happened between him and Riley Finn when he'd arrived home at the farm that morning, out of the taxi, up the path and into the carnage of the kitchen. He gives clear directions to the place the inspector needs to see and, sure enough, the officers that return to the farm find the grave of young Gary Lewis as his father described, out in the copse above the meadow where the huge yew bends its head to the stream.

As Mr Lewis said, the earth is newly overturned, a spade stuck in the soil that must have been hard as iron when Mr Lewis had been forced to hack into it at eight o'clock in the morning.

The earth is not removed as deeply as the actual coffin. That last grisly effort had not been necessary. Mr Lewis had been spared having to crack open the wood and stare at his son's mouldering skull because the wooden box in the carrier bag had been buried later, long after the ceremony, only three feet down.

Mr Lewis says he'd thought he was going to die up there, among the cold firs and cawing crows, against the whisper of dawn light spreading across the valley. It was OK, though, if it meant that crazy bitch would leave and Polly would be all right.

He'd told Finn what she'd wanted to know the minute he'd seen Polly on the floor. She wouldn't let him go to his wife, she'd just marched him out to the porch, thrown him the shovel that was standing by the door from his snow-clearing the day before and said, 'Come on then, you old bastard – let's do a treasure hunt.'

He'd felt every finger-stroke of the icy breeze on the back of his neck, his hands all but numb as he shovelled. The blood taste, from where she'd hit him across his mouth, was metallic and hard. The cold, the dark and the resignation reminded him of the long training marches he'd done, except this time he was scared.

'I didn't touch it,' he says, 'any of the stuff, except for that gold link chain and a gold eternity ring, the rest should still be in the bag. We needed a new stove in nineteen ninety-six, and then there was Polly's cataract op five years later. The waiting list was massive, so we went private up in Aberystwyth. Polly likes – *liked* – her crosswords. That was the only time she smiled, when she finished one. I lived for that smile.'

Then Mr Lewis begins to cry.

He's not glad he's made it through the day. He thinks the only reason he didn't join his wife in the afterlife that morning was that his gun, the one Finn threatened him with, the old revolver he'd used in the gold robbery, didn't fire when she pulled the trigger. It was sheer chance because he must've left a round in it – careless really.

'Sorry, old man,' she said. 'Thanks for your help.'

Then he'd heard the click as she pointed the barrel at him and, to his intense embarrassment, he'd passed out.

He's not sure why she didn't finish him off. Perhaps she assumed he wouldn't last long or maybe she'd taken pity on him at the last second.

Inspector Morris doubts it. He thinks it has less to do with pity than blind luck. Jacky Davies, who'd run into Billy Fisket that morning in the Oldstones lanes, had remarked in his interview that he'd been passing the top field in his tractor, brining down extra hay, just as it was getting light. He'd thought he'd seen old Osion standing alone by his son's grave, across the field beyond the boundary wall, with a shovel in his hand. He'd waved at the figure through the morning gloom but the old man had ignored him, walked off into the trees as he trundled on by.

The inspector doesn't tell Mr Lewis he was probably just lucky that Finn was interrupted before she could finish the job, while he was out cold on the ground. He doubts the old man thinks of himself as lucky today, or ever will again.

The Hitchhiker – 5.30 p.m.

It's lung-breakingly cold as I speed-march up the far side of the valley and into the night. The pub is far behind me now, everything else is ahead.

I'd stood by the old man's bed for what seemed like an age, contemplating the enormity of the catastrophe before me, wondering if I should just call the police, trust them to understand what happened, the necessity of it, the self-defence. But even as I thought about it I'd known it was impossible for them not to start asking questions, making assumptions.

There's no one left to back me up. Then there's Rhys – I can't imagine them believing my story of accidental arson; so bloody stupid.

Why complicate things further, snatch defeat from the jaws of semi-victory? There's a good chance no one will place me in Pont. I'm just glad I hadn't plucked up the drunken courage to knock on the door of Ty Podmore's cottage last night, while I was roaming the lanes on my little self-pity trip, hoping for a friend instead of heading for the bus I missed.

It was a stupid idea anyway, sentimental, to seek comfort, to look up my first and only other school friend, who might have smiled to see me, offered a shoulder to cry on. My big old bear of a Ty.

I was glad to see him getting out of his car, hugging his other half through the curtain slot of the window as I peered in. I always knew he was probably gay. Good for him, though, for making that work, especially here. I'm so glad he didn't see me, especially as he seems to be a copper now.

Looking at the haul of jewellery in the bag on the old man's bedcovers, I can't say I wasn't tempted for a second to take a little lucky dip in. Even a handful of that lot would give my bank balance a nice boost, but I was only tempted for a moment. I'm many things, but I'm not a thief.

As I stride out into the white-black dark, I'm aware of my hands aching, of the slow burn pulsing beneath my leather gloves as the blood pumps round my body. The doctor has assured me there's no permanent nerve damage. I'll have battle scars, but I wear them well, as a badge of honour and, as my commander said, there's plenty I can still do, almost anything really.

'I'd hate to lose you,' he'd said to me, just five days and a lifetime ago, stiff but smiling in his full uniform at my hospital bedside. 'I know you've been through a lot, but you're a natural. Give it a little time; don't just jump into Civvy Street because of this. There's no suggestion of any wrongdoing, on yours or Purvis's part. There's no way Purvis could have avoided that poor little kid in the road. These things happen, and they happen to the best of us.

'Think what could have happened if you hadn't searched that house, followed your instinct, almost got killed in the process. That stuff would've been used against our boys, our girls. You'll be decorated for this, you know, for the lives you've saved. Besides, what use will you be out there? You're one of us, always will be.'

I'd wondered, though, after he'd left, if I always wanted to be *that* person, the one watching and waiting? Sitting in the empty dayroom with the sky darkening into snow, I'd had a sudden visceral urge to see Mum again, to smell her Yardley and wool scent, a spur-of-the-moment thing really, the urge to return.

Technically I should have had a weekend pass from the hospital, but I've been recuperating in my own room and they're down to skeleton staff this weekend. It's hardly AWOL if you're not on the barracks.

I thought it would be a chance to visit Rhys, too, surprise him, kiss him, maybe lie naked with him in his clean, large bed, feel skin on skin again, in a quiet little village where no one tries to kill you. So much for that! Sentimental, like I said.

I get it now. Nowhere's safe. I understand and, as if in acknowledgement, the moon flies into view for a few seconds – a sign, an omen. Somewhere high above me, above the snowstorm, I think I hear the universe snickering. At least now I can laugh back, grinning as I extend my middle finger and flip it the bird.

I'm glad I never took my gloves off, not the whole time I was in that godforsaken pub, or the nurse imposter's car. I wonder what happened to the real nurse? I couldn't hang around to find out, but I don't fancy her chances.

At least I know there are no fingerprints to speak of my presence and I've covered my tracks. I returned my knife, unused, to my back pocket, put the gun into the landlord's hand and squeezed his fingers on it before dropping in on the floor next to him. I give the police a simple indicator that there's no need to look for anyone else.

The nurse's head was slumped forward on her chest and I didn't disturb her. She's not going to be making a sudden return to life and deathbed confessions and revelations about a rogue soldier. Unlike the movies there's no chance of a last-minute resurrection.

I'm the final remaining ghost, invisible, perhaps imagined, no sign of me in that room's story.

It was almost a different ending, though, when I heard that thumping on the front door and a voice calling from the front hall, 'Hello? Mr Rhydderch? Mrs Nash? Anyone there? Are you home? It's the police.'

Luckily, whoever it was didn't see me. I had just enough time to unbolt the back door for them and then hide. While I was tucked in the dining room alcove, behind the curtain, she took the invitation of the unlocked door, walked straight past me and up the stairs. Then I was out the back door in a flash. The bloody dog almost gave it away, but I was safely round the corner by then.

The only thing linking me to The Halfway now is Brian Rhydderch's car keys, which I forgot to put back in his pocket. After a second's thought I throw them into the undergrowth at the side of the road, pulling up my collar and hood, picking up my pace.

For a moment I think something else is wrong, that something is missing, then I realise it's simply that, for the first time in a long time, the voices in my head are silent. For the moment my patience is pruned, nothing pricks or scratches. There's no need for music or mantra, either, to still my mind. It's made up and therefore quiet.

It's strange, but as I walk, what seemed like bad luck at first, to be dropped in the middle of all this, caught in a snowstorm, in a shit-storm, takes on a different perspective. As Lilli-Anne says, 'There's no such thing as bad luck, or good luck Eleri, you daft bint, the universe puts you in exactly the place you need to be when it's time. It's not always easy to see why, but that's the pattern of life, and we'd be crazy to try and understand it. If we could we'd see the face of God and shrink in fear.'

Lil only calls me Eleri when she's sermonising, when she wants to sound impressive, but maybe she's right. Perhaps I was brought here to stop that Finn bitch in her tracks, to save the life of the dumb little policewoman who announced herself for all to hear like a prize idiot. She would surely have been Finn's next victim if she'd encountered the mad bastard and her knife.

If I hadn't come along, who might have lived and who might have died? Either way Lilli-Anne was right, something can happen, even at the last moment to make you realise where you belong. It's not here. I never have to come back here again, and that thought keeps me warm against the snowstorm, against all storms still raging, inside and out.

It's good to be moving now. Hopefully I can still make the late train and be back at the hospital before anyone's the wiser. As I reach the top of the ridge the snow lifts, and over to the west the land emerges from the sky of clouds like a great basking whale. The chilly moon slips into view again, and in the distance I can see a blessed link of lights, sliding along through the black woodland that slopes to the edge of the silver sea. The trains are still running.

I take a deep breath of the liquid air then exhale, breathing out until my lungs are empty, wonderfully, invigoratingly empty. As the last inch of muscle finally gives I spit out the cluster of spikes that have been sticking for years, making room for an in-breath of pure ice-cold oxygen. It hits my head, making me dizzy, but it's all right.

I know now that everywhere is a war zone, every village, every house, every relationship, every heart. I might as well be where I know what the dangers are, where I'm suitably armed.

I'm through the darkest days now, surely, past the tipping point, the solstice almost ended – from here on out it gets just a little lighter every day, edging towards spring. So I head downhill to the sea, whistling as I go, the last song I heard on the radio before I left the pub, 'It was only a winter's tale . . .'

I'm halfway home already.

The Law – 23 December 2007, 4 p.m.

By the time I come round in the hospital, by the time I'm officially well enough to talk, twenty-four hours have passed since I called for assistance and it's already dark again. I'd woken up half a dozen times throughout the night they brought me in, aching and alert but playing groggy for as long as possible while I was bandaged, X-rayed, injected and tucked up in a private room on a well-packed ward.

I spent those long hours pretending to doze, to be confused by the strong painkillers they'd pumped into me, which wasn't hard as until dawn my hand felt as if it was being squeezed in a vice of fire and someone was banging a gong inside my head.

Yet all that time I was listening, quietly, carefully, behind closed eyelids to what was being said, first by the parade of officers who came and went around me in the night hours, whispering, muttering, sharing bits and bobs of the story I'd missed, then to the nurses gossiping outside when they thought I was asleep.

Inspector Morris and DS Matthews came in once, before midnight, and tried to ask me a few questions, but were promptly shooed away by a shushing, tutting doctor. I'm to be handled with kid gloves it seems, the brave survivor, a delicate injured flower who took on a heartless monster and triumphed.

Everyone has to treat me gently, with a certain reverence, even bluff old Inspector Morris, unless he wants to look like a heartless twat, which suits me, I still need a little time to line all this up.

By first thing this morning I'd known it was safe to tell my new and improved version of events at Halfway, the one I'd engineered, because the scene in the pub has already told most of it for me, exactly as I wanted it to.

There are a few loose ends, but not as many as I'd feared. The first officers responding to my call for assistance were so horrified and keen to come to my aid that they'd helpfully cross-contaminated most of the bodies in the first five minutes – I heard Inspector Morris say so to Matthews, around midnight, I think, whispering by the door.

Sue Bell and the other pathologists assigned to the case (it's too much work for just one doctor) apparently differ a bit when it comes to the time of the death, but I'm not that worried. It was so cold in the pub it'll be hard to pinpoint a time through loss of body heat and so on, and in the end it won't matter.

They'll do their job, the boss and the sarge, but in many ways this story is just too good to query, and the force has come out of it quite well already. I heard Paul, the press officer, telling Morris so this morning.

The murders were all down to Riley Finn, not a known

offender in our part of the world, so we can't be held responsible for not seeing it coming. In theory at least, it had taken us less than eight hours to track her down and put a stop to her terror spree while hopelessly under-manned and hampered by an exceptional snowstorm.

By the time the inspector came back to take my first account after breakfast I was ready, though I've kept things vague for now. I don't want to be too specific too soon and talk myself into a corner. He looked at me in an odd way when I gave my explanation, when I described how the hairs on the back of my neck had tingled as I approached the inn, my police instincts telling me something was amiss, then steeling myself to ascend the stairs, baton drawn, hearing a panicked cry for help; seeing the man bleeding, dying; seeing Finn with the gun in her hand; the wrestling match between us, the hammer coming down on my fingers, my firing the gun at Finn to stop her.

I could see there was a lot he wanted to ask, but he had to make do with what he had when I feigned dizziness, putting my hand to my head, causing the nurse to stop the interview. There'll be time for details later.

He explained a few things to me, though, that the big guy in the anorak, under the bed, was George Rhydderch's estranged son Brian, apparently back from Scotland. He was suffering from prostate cancer, inoperable as they discovered when they called his long-term, on-off lady friend Deirdre on the mobile phone they found in his pocket. The guy with the neck wound was apparently Rebecca Nash's son Simon.

The inspector wouldn't commit to anything but they're working on the hypothesis that Brian came home unexpectedly and there was a confrontation with Simon. He was cagey about the circumstances, about why Simon was even at the pub, but told me they'd found Becca Nash, who was the old man's nurse and home help, while I was still unconscious.

The late shift eventually got round to checking her car, spotted at the roadside, and was damn lucky they did because she was trapped in the boot, cold, miserable and drifting in and out of consciousness from a whack to the head and because she's diabetic and had missed her insulin. Morris left it at that, but he'll be back soon and I'll be ready.

Now it's teatime. I'm dying for a cuppa and am glad to see a properly friendly face when a knackered-looking Jim appears in the doorway, dark rings around his eyes and thick stubble on his jaw. He waves a bag of grapes at me as he grins. 'Hey, slugger. Safe to come in?' There's a tear in his eye, too, soft old bugger, and for a moment I'm touched.

'You OK, love?' he asks, sitting beside my bed, taking my hand. 'Just saw your mum downstairs getting a tea so I thought I'd sneak in under the radar. You're not supposed to have visitors yet, except family, but bugger it, what are they going to do, fire me? Jesus, you've had a rough night. You look like hell.'

Turns out he's just off a crippling double shift on the cordon and is a mine of information. He knows all about Sam Shotton, my strange motel friend, who came in to be interviewed first thing this morning. It seems Sam followed my instructions, went straight home to his mam after I'd left him and she'd promptly phoned the police. He really had been trying to call us all morning. Poor sod must've thought I was the cavalry arriving and been very disappointed.

Sam, predictably, has learning difficulties, but he's reliably confirmed Rebecca Nash's account as far as he can; that he'd seen her and Finn arguing by Mrs Nash's stopped car, seen a struggle and Finn pulling Mrs Nash out and hitting her, then pushing her into the boot before he'd run away.

Later I'll tell my colleagues how I started to put it all together after speaking to Sam, of my inspired hunch forming piece by piece. How it was the sight of the gnomes in the back of the rusted Cortina I came across soon after leaving the motel that set my police alarm bells tinkling. That their chipped hats and missing noses made me think of Mrs Lewis, aka Mrs Death, driving into town, once upon a time, in a beat-up old yellow Cortina.

I'll add that Detective Sergeant Matthews had said that Riley Finn had fled the Lewises' farmhouse on foot, but reasoned that perhaps, in his traumatised state, the old man might not have realised Finn had taken their old Cortina, such a distinctive old wreck, as a getaway car?

Then I'll explain how, on finding Rebecca Nash's handbag, I suspected – synapses sparking, connections being made – there was a link between the two, that she'd got into serious trouble. I couldn't just leave without her then, could I, after finding her car abandoned? Knowing our fugitive might be out in the woods?

Of course I'll remind them there was no radio service in the blackspot and no time to drive back to the nick for back-up. Jim had told me that Billy broke into The Halfway, years back. If he'd mentioned it to Finn she might have thought it would be a good place to hole up, just down the hill from where I'd found the missing nurse's ID badge in

289

the snow. What choice did I have but to press on and try to come to her aid, time being of the essence?

Speaking of Billy Fisket, Jim rolls his eyes when he tells me it was Billy's father Fred who was to blame for the idea there was a treasure hidden at Ridgeback Farm. Apparently Fred Fisket had told his son he'd been a school friend of Gary Lewis and that Gary had liked to brag about the 'treasure' his father had brought back from 'the war' (precise war unspecified because it was obviously a fiction).

Gary liked to trot out the story of how his father kept a bag of loot hidden in the house, concealed in a green velvet pouch, embroidered with gold lettering, insisting his dad looked at it in the dead of night when he was spying from the landing. Gary would never actually tell Fred where the treasure was kept, the secret location of the final X that marked the spot.

'Seems weird that that lying little shit Gary was actually telling the truth,' muses Jim, running his hand over his hair, suddenly looking much older than his sixty years. 'All these years later, this is what comes of it. Osion Lewis too, I mean, who'd have thought it . . . that gentle old guy, the Dolau robber . . . The world's a strange place, love. Strange how the past comes back to haunt us, how it won't stay buried, just pokes its fingers up now and again to trip us all up.

'I guess there's a lesson in there somewhere, though right now I'm too knackered to decide what it is. Guess what, though, on the bright side, I'm getting a dog for Christmas!'

'What?' I say, wrong-footed and surprised, knowing how his wife feels about what she calls slobbery fur bags. 'Audrey doesn't like dogs.'

'Yeah, well. I worked on her heartstrings, now I'm soon to retire. We're going to keep that Alsatian of Brian Rhydderch's, nice old girl. She'll love the farm to run around on. Brian Rhydderch's girlfriend, this Deirdre woman, told Morris she'd never been able to handle the dog on her own, got an old mother to look after, lives with her and what not. That's why Rhydderch brought the old girl with him in case he'd needed to stay a few weeks to sort out his father's affairs.

'She wants the dog to be rehomed and, well, I just couldn't bear the thought of that when they brought her into the nick kennels all forlorn-looking. Not fair, is it? An animal's for life and all that.'

Soft old git, I think, glad there's one happy ending today at least, though I'm not really listening as he chatters away about buying a dog bed and chew toys and a nice pig's trotter. I've got too much on my mind. I pay even less attention when he starts telling me what a busy forty-eight hours it's been on top of our multiple murders. A bus full of people trapped out at Pandy, 'by the roundabout for nine hours, almost resorted to eating each other' and dozens of minor road bumps.

I only really snap back to attention when he mentions one 'poor bastard gone up in a fireball on the B11'.

'Who was it, then, the code blue?' I ask.

'Bloke called Rhys Tripp, according to the car registration,' says Jim. 'But, according to the Trumptons, they'll have to identify him properly from his teeth.'

'What?' I manage to ask. 'When? I mean, how?'

'Yeah, RTC, night before last, before all this kicked off,' says Jim through a mouthful of seedless grapes. 'What a mess.'

As my brain processes the news I realise we hadn't checked the overnights yesterday morning because it was all happening too fast. That means that by the time I set out with the hope of meeting Rhys yesterday he was already dead. Jim doesn't know this has any personal significance for me, of course. Rhys is just another name on the overnight list. I'd never told anyone I was dating him, I hadn't seen the point.

He had nice teeth, is my first thought. Then, No wonder he never answered his phone.

'Yeah, weird thing is, his flat went up in flames, too,' continues Jim, yawning theatrically. 'Looks like the seat of the fire was a cheap wastepaper bin that melted and set the carpet alight. The top Trumpton thinks a stray cigarette might have started it, could have been smouldering since that morning. Pretty bloody careless, mind – the poor buggers in the flat below will have to spend Christmas in a B & B because of the water damage.'

It's possible, I suppose. Rhys was always smoking stinky roll-ups when he worked. They helped him think, he said. I think he just liked the idea of sitting at his desk writing, pretending to be Truman Capote with a Scotch in his hand. I read a couple of pages of an awful potboiler he was working on once, pretty grim stuff, a melodrama, I think, about a soldier. Not the sort of story I'd tell – not the sort I'm going to tell from now on, the one that will change everything. It's already begun to.

Mum actually said she was proud of me this morning; she was almost tender when she ran her fingertips over my impressive bandages and bruises, her eyes starting to glisten. The day gets even better when the greying head of the Chief Constable appears in the doorway, in full uniform, hat under his arm, flanked by Alison the beaming press officer.

Jim almost chokes on his grapes and pops to his feet muttering, 'Boss' as Mr Ferris edges in through the door with the words, 'Little surprise visit. Can't stay, just wanted to say how proud we are of you, young lady. You're a credit to the force.'

'Absolutely,' says Alison, ringing phone in one hand, notepad in the other. 'Do you want to give me a line or two for the reporters before we start? The network are out there, too,' she adds, checking her watch, prickling with anxiety.

I realise they're on their way to a press conference right now.

'Indeed, you're quite the heroine, PC Lloyd, very brave. How's the arm?' asks the CC.

I sort of jiggle it a bit in answer and wish I hadn't, trying not to look at my black and blue sausage fingers. The doctor has said they'll heal well and that the hammer-inflicted head wound won't leave a scar.

'Not too much slacking now,' says the boss. 'We want you back on duty as soon as possible.' And he grins to show he's exercising his senior-officer humour. 'I'll be recommending you for a medal for this, you know. Very brave, the sort of officer that makes us all proud.'

Then a sudden rush of acid panic boils up into my throat and it's all I can do to croak, 'Thank you, sir,' because this is it now. This is me, the face of the future, the poster girl for Pont. This is who I am. It's already finalised, in print, as Alison waves a copy of this morning's *Western News* at me, bearing the headline, 'Dangerous Fugitive Felled by Halfway Heroine'.

As they grin and sidle away I realise it's too late to worry about how I'm going to sustain this fiction. I have no choice. I have to live the lie and play the hell out of the role I've created. I can't ask myself ever again how I did this so easily, something so insane, so risky. I can't ask if, twenty-four hours ago, when I raised the hammer over my hand, I was in some sort of shock, or make excuses for myself, because what does it matter?

In those minutes after I entered the room I suppose I *was* outside myself, watching someone who looked like me, moving, acting; but I also know it was one of the only times in my life that the storytelling voice in my head was totally silent. I can't pretend I didn't know what I was doing.

Lying here through the slow, soft hours of the ward-lit night, I've had time to think and I've put it down to a matter of survival. Not in the way it was for the others who didn't make it out alive, but for my own survival beyond Pont, one that means options instead of dying a little more every day in a tiny town with a small life, disgraced, doors closed to me.

Survival is always raw and ugly, and I told you before that maverick cops often have to break a few rules and work in the grey area to make their names. So do villains, of course, but I won't think about that.

No one has said anything about it yet, but I know there won't be any formal investigatory hearing or inquiry concerning Bryn Mill after the Christmas break. What would be the point? In the light of what's happened it'll all go away, any questions about whether or not I'd followed procedure are moot. No one doubts the grit or guts of the Halfway Heroine.

It'll serve its purpose, what I've done, provide me with a springboard to shoot me towards a better career; up, over, out. There's just one thing that worries me, one detail I can't rewrite and narrate into a suitable ending, something I can't control – the possibility that there was someone else at the pub yesterday.

It's only a thought, like a tiny splinter under my thumbnail that I can't pick out, but Sam Shotton apparently told the inspector he saw another woman on the road yesterday morning, close to Rebecca Nash's car. He says he tried to warn her but that she walked away towards Halfway, carrying a huge rucksack.

It occurred to me this morning, as the painkillers were wearing off, that I saw a rucksack, didn't I? In the bar, by the chair? Military-looking, olive green. No one's mentioned it, so maybe I was wrong. If there was someone there, surely they'd have come forward by now and exposed my lie? Unless . . . unless . . . they've got something to hide, too, or perhaps something to gain by waiting. I don't like the idea of a loose end, someone who's biding their time, with their own story to tell . . .

But in the meantime I'm going to get out of this hospital, soon, this town, this life, into that elegant office with a view of the London skyline. OK, maybe it's a few years down the line yet, but why not think big? Why not imagine that great mahogany desk, the pips on my collar and a handsome junior officer to bring me a Lilt and Snickers as I ready myself for a meeting with the commissioner.

It's a nice thought, a cinematic thought, and I can do it all now. I can say, I told you so, to my mum and dad, to Inspector Morris and to anyone else who doubts me ever again, for the rest of my life.

As I lie in my hospital bed I smile as I think of what's to come; of the praise and congratulations heading my way, of the respect and admiration I'll receive at last, of everything I will be and all the possibilities that await me.

Then I start to cry. Because it will never leave me now, will it? The truth, of what I am, this cluster of something sharp and spiky stuck in my throat I'll never be able to cough up. I'll learn to live with it, smile on through, because there'll be compensations, of course. But I'll tell you one thing, if on a winter's night a traveller comes calling, if there's a knock on my door in the dark, I won't answer.

I already know what's waiting outside.

Acknowledgements

I would like to thank everyone who has supported me in bringing *Halfway* to life, especially my agent Peter Buckman at the Ampersand Agency for his brutal honesty, unwavering enthusiasm and excellent advice.

I'd also like to thank Krystyna Green and her team at Little, Brown for their continued faith in my dark and twisted little stories.